MW00639914

THE
TRIGGER
EFFECT

THE TRIGGER EFFECT

a novel by

JEREMY LOGAN

in collaboration with **BRENDA SEVCIK**

Deeds Publishing | Atlanta

Published by Deeds Publishing in Athens, GA
www.deedspublishing.com

Printed in The United States of America

Cover design and text layout by Mark Babcock

Library of Congress Cataloging-in-Publications data is available upon request.

ISBN 978-1-947309-02-9

Books are available in quantity for promotional or premium use. For information, email info@deedspublishing.com.

First Edition, 2017

10 9 8 7 6 5 4 3 2 1

TABLE OF CONTENTS

CAST OF CHARACTERS

In Order of Appearance or Mention

Edgar Brown	Delivery Truck Driver
Officer Damien Burris	Thomas Glen Police Dept.
Lieutenant Reed Pascoe	Thomas Glen Police Dept.
Detective Denise Smith	Thomas Glen Police Dept.
Blair Jefferson Rogers	Victim
Sarah Jane Thompson	Victim
Robert EvansMedical	Examiner
Gaylord TuckerForensics	Officer
Mrs. Rene Thompson	Mother of girl victim
Mr. Douglas Thompson	Father of girl victim
Vincent James Thompson	Step brother of Sarah
Mr. David Rogers	Blair's father
Mrs. Victoria Rogers	Blair's mother
Detective Gary Branch	Thomas Glen Police Dept.
Detective Miles Judson	Thomas Glen Police Dept.
Chief Clifton Meadows	Thomas Glen Police Dept.
Mayor Madeline Coleman	City of Thomas Glen
Carl Meeker	First suspect
Ramona Beamon	County profiler

Lily Evans	Sarah's best friend
Donnie Marks	Blair's best friend
Virgil Hempstead	Homeless witness
Cathleen Pascoe	Reed's wife
Zach Smith	Denise's husband
Jameson McGladrey	Sarah's secret boyfriend
Elizabeth Worthy	Policewoman
Dr. Phillip Edwards	Sarah babysat for them
Peter d'Arnaud	Milton Detective
Brad Lindgren	Sarah's biological father
Pastor Dan	The Rogers family pastor
Harry Richardson	TV News reporter
Jack Arnold	Rapist
Laura Holmes	District Attorney
KennethBenson	Assistant Prosecutor
Lou and Ike	Old West Trading Gun Shop
Arthur Benator	Attorney representing Vincent Thompson
Timothy Peters	Suspect who escaped in Louisiana
Dr. Rubin	Psychiatrist
Bennett Frazier	State Attorney General
Arthur Benator	Defense Attorney
Dominic Minelli	Judge

ACKNOWLEDGEMENTS

SPECIAL THANKS TO MY CO-AUTHOR, BRENDA SEVCIK, FIRST for her willingness to embark on this journey of collaboration. Thanks also for her patience and dedication as we discovered how to make the co-author relationship work for the benefit of the project.

I wanted to explore the impacts of tragedy and loss by adding a female author's perspective. Although Ms. Sevcik is just beginning her writing career, I was impressed by her compassion and empathy in her early works, qualities that have always been difficult for me to express.

To my editor, Ann Fisher, whose talent for knowing what to throw away and what to expand is uncanny. To my publisher, who encourages and supports me, and to their cover designer, who has a talent for cover design that captures my imagination.

PROLOGUE

THE INSPIRATION FOR THIS STORY ARRIVED VIA A NEWS RE-
port while driving in my car. Two seventeen-year-olds, a boy and
a girl, were found early Monday morning shot to death execution
style, behind a local grocery store. It was August 3, 2016, the first
day of their school year.

I knew where that grocery was. It was in an upscale, suburban
part of town. These kids were going to be high school seniors. Their
parents were affluent, if not wealthy. They were honor students with
no police records or pimples. They were good looking and popular.
Drugs were not involved.

I said to myself, probably the same thing half the town was
thinking, *what could these teenagers have possibly done that warranted a bullet in the back of the head?* Instantly, my imagination went
into overdrive, conjuring up all kinds of scenarios — none of which
made any sense. Before the day was over, I had written an outline
for a plot that became the storyline for this novel.

I urge you to keep in mind that the only thing in this story that's
not made up is the death of the teenagers. Everything else is invent-
ed, a creation of my imagination. Do not attribute anything you
read in the following pages to what is real. The killer, the motives,

the descriptions of the characters and their activities in this novel are untrue, and not meant to reflect on the real events, characters and their motives involved in the actual, real life, investigation that began on that fateful morning.

In an effort to prevent anyone from thinking that any of this story is true, I moved the crime scene to another state. This is all being said because I don't want to bring any more grief and sadness to the family and friends of the victims. In real life, I was horrified by the actual events, feeling deep empathy for the real-life victims and their families.

The making of this novel is not an attempt to profit from their loss. It is merely a testament to the reality that horribly bad things can happen to good, law abiding people.

1. NOT IN MY BACKYARD

EARLY SUMMER MORNINGS IN TEXAS ARE USUALLY GLORIOUS.
The humidity is low, and the blooming oleanders, Russian olives,
and small China roses, provide color and the sweet smell of the sea-
son. The bedroom community of Thomas Glen, offers luxury country clubs, expansive golf courses, equestrian venues and a quaint city
center. Everything is new, fresh, expensive, spotless and perfect.

Elegant brick homes smugly reign over well-manicured lawns.
At the back edge of summer, the sun is burning off the slight humidity of the previous evening. The wealthy inhabitants remained
in their climate controlled mini-mansions, turning down their ther-
mostat at the first moment of discomfort.

With the estate-type residences, came the young, upwardly mobile. Twenty-five percent of the households have professional de-
grees. The median family income is beyond three hundred thousand
dollars a year. The landscaping industry calls it *The Garden of Eden*.

This is not the old Texas. This cosmopolitan melting pot was
created by the allure of Dallas, a city bred to be a competitor to New
York and L.A. Thomas Glen was the newest, priciest community of
all the new towns that Dallas has spawned.

No matter what everyone was doing in the metropolitan confines of Dallas that Monday morning, it was placed in suspension. If the television, car radio, or news app was on, you paid attention. Forget about getting the kids ready for school, driving the car to work, or preparing for a morning jog. For that moment, this tragedy hit home…deep in the gut.

So together, metro Dallas imagined that it had to be a mistake. This was the kind of community that should have been immune to this sort of incident. Not here. Maybe somewhere else, but not here.

Like so many things, appearances can be deceiving. The truth of the matter is…there are undercurrents that threaten to erupt into chaos at the slightest disappointment, triggering a cascade, or perhaps an avalanche, of distress and agony.

***

It was about seven in the morning when the bakery delivery truck arrived behind the supermarket in the new strip mall. Sunlight entered the alley-like delivery area, piercing the ground like daggers slicing through the tree limbs and leaves. The slanting rays of light blinded Edgar, the truck's driver, as he walked to the rear of the vehicle to open the delivery door. Edgar felt a charge in the air, a negative energy, as if enemy combatants were about to jump out of hiding. He shook it off as superstitious. It was decades since he fought for his country in the South China Sea.

Then something caught his eye. It was next to the big green dumpster. Two eyes near ground level were staring at him. It could have been any kind of animal, or perhaps a stuffed toy. Edgar walked toward the dumpster until he could see it. And then, he wished he hadn't.

Edgar was a large man, over six feet and had his share of second helpings. Not too many things scared him, but this did. He turned away and blinked, trying to erase the image from his mind. He gathered himself and pulled out his cellphone from his pants pocket, fumbling nervously and almost dropping it. He dialed 911, and leaned against the cab of the truck to steady himself.

What became of the breeze that tickled Edgar's mustache? Where did the birds go, serenading one another? Only silence, the quiet of dread blocked his ears.

When the police arrived, Edgar was sitting in his truck behind the wheel. He was staring into the daylight as if in a trance. Edgar was a black man in his sixties, and a Vietnam combat veteran. He'd seen a lot of horrifying things, presuming that nightmare of his life was over.

The store's delivery doors were open now, and the store manager and a few other employees were milling around. They had all taken a stroll toward the dumpster, and they stopped and retreated after seeing what Edgar found.

Officer Damien Burris approached Edgar and asked him, "Sir, what's your name?"

The truck driver didn't acknowledge the presence of the policeman, so he opened the truck door and poked him, and asked again. "Sir, what's your name?"

"Edgar, Edgar Brown," He wished he could retreat into the earlier, more innocent morning.

"Mr. Brown, would you mind getting out of the truck so we can go over what you found?"

5

Edgar hesitated, then relented. He couldn't stop glancing at the two policemen standing over the bodies of the teenage boy and girl, dumped and abandoned, like old clothes. More police arrived. Some were placing crime scene tape in a circular pattern around Edgar's truck, the dumpster and the two bodies. Ten minutes passed when Burris gave way to Lieutenant Reed Pascoe, Dallas County Sherriff's Office. Pascoe reminded Edgar of movie detectives, circa 1940, standing about six feet tall, fair skinned, slender, with steel blue eyes that captured everything. Even in this heat, the lieutenant wore a felt Fedora hat.

After questioning Edgar, who was trying hard to wrap his head around his discovery, Lieutenant Pascoe started in with the store manager. Several unmarked cars arrived with more men in suits. At least two people were taking photographs, and a few others, wearing blue nitrile latex gloves, were placing markers on the ground. The medical examiner, who had just arrived, was picking at the clothes of the victims, and talking into a recorder.

As Pascoe was walking around the crime scene he spotted his partner, Detective Smith. The pair made eye contact and acknowledged one another, each focused on the evidence around them. The Pascoe-Smith team were renowned around the Dallas metro area. They were the first to be called with difficult homicide cases; but usually they were located away from the safe haven of Thomas Glen. The fact that this was in their own backyard was unique. These crimes simply didn't happen here. At least not until today.

Together they approached the dead bodies. From what Pascoe could make out, two kids, perhaps high school age, were deposited next to the dumpster. Both blond, and with apparent gunshot wounds in the back of their heads. A trail of blood smears, originating about ten feet from where they lay, gave Pascoe the impression that they were killed somewhere else and driven there for disposal.

"It looks like the killer dragged their bodies here, probably from a vehicle," offered Pascoe.

Pascoe and Smith were examining the wallet that the ME removed from a pants pocket of the boy. He also showed him a decorative ring with several keys attached. Pascoe put on his latex gloves, and with tweezers he pulled out the driver's license and vehicle registration for a blue, Toyota Corolla.

"I want as many officers as you can spare searching the parking lot for a blue Toyota, tag BFD-6374," Pascoe announced loudly. Then he focused on his partner. "Smith, got any more crime scene tape?"

"One step ahead of you, sir." Denise Smith was walking with purpose toward a pair of officers, one of whom had a roll of yellow film tape that read, 'Crime Scene, Do Not Cross', dangling from his right hand. She was a petite woman by physical standards, but with her competent, no-nonsense demeanor, her co-workers saw a larger figure: a trust-worthy, capable officer who always got it right.

Denise's looks fooled everyone. If you removed her from her personality, she wasn't a pretty woman. Her intelligence radiated from her, accentuated by a halo of thick brunette hair she wore simply. On a hot day like today, it was pulled up in a twist, and off her neck.

Pascoe was quick to recognize her assets. As he saw his partner walk toward the officers with the police tape, he was reminded that Denise was the best "man" for the job.

Pascoe took a moment to observe his surroundings. At the far right end of the parking lot, he could look behind the supermarket and see the dumpsters. On the left was the back of the market. On the right was a steep grassy embankment with shrubs covering the apex of the slope. Between the two, asphalt that dead-ended into a dense stand of pines — one way in and isolated from any potential witnesses who weren't behind the store. The dumpsters sat at the base of slope.

He bent over to shade the sunlight so he could read the name on the driver's license — Blair Rogers — Caucasian, seventeen years old, 191 Spyglass Circle. There was forty-one dollars in the wallet and a picture of Blair and the dead girl, now lying on top of him, next to the dumpster. The boy was placed face down on the pavement, his head turned upward with open, empty eyes. His hair, once sandy blond, was stained with dried blood that ran down his long, freckled neck.

The girl was dumped atop the boy, facedown. Her hair was also covered in dried blood, eyes closed, with her arms haphazard, but her hair was neatly pulled away from her face as if her killer needed one last look at her face before he departed the scene. She looked so innocent to him. Pascoe's first impression was bewilderment — *what could go so terribly wrong that someone felt their execution was the answer?*

Pascoe, holding the picture of the girl in his hand, turned it over. On the back of the picture it read, *My Sweet Sarah*, which was just below what appeared to be in different handwriting that read, *Always and Forever.* He looked again at the dead couple. "Damn," he whispered.

Detective Smith appeared from behind. "Pascoe," she nodded toward the south. "Car's on site. Towards the front of the parking lot, parallel to Highway 75."

Without saying a word, Pascoe followed her to the front of the store parking area, stopping to look inside the Toyota's door that was opened by the police. There was blood everywhere. He stopped and looked at his partner. She said nothing, turning her gaze to the car parked next to the Toyota.

"Has this BMW been here the whole time?" he asked.

"Appears so," she affirmed. "There's a lady's purse on the passenger seat." Smith stopped to complete a text message. "Running the tags now. I've already requested forensics to come in and dust so we can confirm this is the female victim's vehicle."

Pascoe walked over to the BMW and looked inside the window on the passenger side of the car. "Get a photographer over here immediately," he barked. Denise nodded and headed toward the dumpster. He had noticed the 'S' monogram on the side of the purse, suspecting it stood for Sarah.

Soon the photographer and Denise arrived. She looked at Pascoe, "You thinking what I'm thinking?" she asked.

Pascoe nodded. "The BMW is the girl's car. It looks like a new model, maybe a year old." Pascoe hesitated, looking at Denise. "These kids must have rendezvoused here."

Pascoe thought to himself as he looked back toward the dumpster, *what a great place for kids to park for a little romance.* A few moments later, the photographer and the forensics officer walked up to him. "Sir. Vehicle ready for your inspection."

Putting on a fresh pair of gloves, Pascoe lifted the purse with a rod and carried it over to a place away from the cars and set it on the pavement. Using his tweezers, he pulled out a wallet. Inside was the driver's license of Sarah Jane Thompson. He looked up at Denise, "It's the girl's," he said, shaking his head.

He had two kids about their age. He took a deep breath. "Put the purse back in the BMW. I want both cars inspected for prints, fibers, the works." He turned to the policemen standing beside the cars. "All kids have cell phones, where are theirs? I want the area between the cars and the bodies searched for footprints and tread marks. That means the entire area from the cars to the dumpster is now a crime scene." The lieutenant paused and scanned the parking lot.

"EVIDENCE," Pascoe shouted. "We need to find something, anything, and don't let anyone inside the tape until it's all collected." Still enraged he added, "And I'd like an estimated time of death, goddamn it!"

Pasco led Smith around a new imaginary perimeter, away from the path between the cars, the store, and the dumpster. Officers and detectives were taking statements of the store employees and the delivery truck driver. The ME and the forensics expert were examining the bodies, and when the ME noticed Pascoe, he approached.

"One bullet each in the back of the head—execution style. No weapon found, and they were dumped here after they were shot. My unofficial time of death, eleven pm."

"Jesus," Detective Smith shook her head.

"These kids don't look like the type," Pascoe said, "you know, lousy backgrounds, but here they are, killed by a professional, and why?"

Neither said it, but Pascoe felt they both knew. This case would not slide under the media radar. Whatever law enforcement did would be scrutinized. But for Pascoe there was more to it. He thought to himself, *not only would the community live in fear until the killer was caught, but **Jesus Christ!** What a goddamned waste.*

As so often happened, his partner said what he was thinking. It was in a whisper, only decipherable by Pascoe, "She was a beautiful girl, and he was a good-looking boy. This is going to be a high-profile case; bigger than anything we've ever had."

"Thanks for cheering me up," Pascoe said. "I suppose it's time to contact the parents."

Denise tore off a sheet of paper from her notepad and gave it to him. He called the home of Sarah Thompson first. A woman answered the phone, identifying herself as Rene Thompson. She had already called the local police in the Thomas Glen Sherriff's Department and came in early Monday morning to file a Missing Person's Report. She was in tears before he could explain his reason for calling.

"Can I talk to Sarah?" she asked frantically.

"I'd like to come by if that's alright with you," Pascoe said.

Between tears and hysterics, she agreed. Next, he called the home phone of Blair Rogers. The boy's father, David, answered the phone. He made an appointment with him for later. His home was a half mile from the Thompson residence. Pascoe and Smith drove to the Thompson home in silence, each distracted by the endless number of possibilities running through their minds.

2. THE WORST POSSIBLE NEWS

THE THOMPSON HOME WAS LESS THAN A MILE FROM THE crime scene, in a gated golf course community. The house was a large, tan brick traditional, with a curved driveway, professionally manicured lawn, with a pool in the back. When Pascoe and Smith arrived in their unmarked car they sat in the driveway for a minute to compose themselves.

They have everything money can buy, and it won't even matter," Pascoe said.

"Bet this house is worth over a million dollars," Denise said with a sigh.

"Money won't make any difference in a few minutes," Pascoe remarked.

Together, they got out of their police cruiser and headed to the front door.

Both Sarah's parents answered the door, appearing anxious. Pascoe had been a homicide lieutenant for sixteen years and made the same kind of visit dozens of times. He hated this part of the job, and it never got easier.

The Thompsons, trying to maintain an air of control, ushered the detectives into the well-appointed living room where the four of them sat down. "We filed a missing person's report," Mrs. Thompson said.

Pascoe politely nodded, clearing his throat. "I'm afraid we have some horrible news. Your daughter Sarah, along with her friend Blair Rogers, were found dead this morning in the back of Gold's Supermarket."

Mrs. Thompson shrieked and began crying immediately. Her husband gasped as if he was drowning.

Pascoe pulled Sarah's father aside, and they walked out of the living room to what appeared to be Mr. Thompson's home office, leaving Mrs. Thompson and Smith in the living room.

Detective Smith, after Mrs. Thompson calmed down a bit, began asking questions. "Any brothers or sisters?"

"An older brother, Vincent. He's at work."

"No other siblings?" asked Denise.

"No, just Sarah and Vincent."

"Where does Vincent work?"

Mrs. Thompson swallowed, closing her eyes, working hard to concentrate and form a sentence. "He works at Zenon Technical Group, an IT firm on Alamo Pass Road."

"And how old is Vincent?" Denise spoke gently.

"How old? Umm. Twenty-one. He's twenty-one." Mrs. Thompson let out a gasp. "He loves Sarah so! He's going to be crushed!" She put her head in her hands. Denise put her arm around the woman, as her entire body rocked.

"Mrs. Thompson, we didn't find a cell phone," Denise continued softly. "Did Sarah have one, and if so, what was the number?"

"Yes, of course. Her number is …." She went blank, then reached for her phone on the end table, and showed Detective Smith the contact entry on her phone. Mrs. Thompson stared at her phone and burst into another wave of gut-wrenching sobs.

Denise wrote it down and texted it to the crime lab. She was hoping her partner, in the next room, was faring better with Mr. Thompson, but her experienced guess was he would be equally inconsolable.

In Mr. Thompson's office, Detective Pascoe saw a father struggling with grief, unable to cope with his loss.

"It's apparent you have a loving family," Pascoe said as he examined the family photos on the credenza. Mr. Thompson wasn't answering. He sat on the edge of his leather arm chair, head in his hands. Pascoe calmly pulled up the rolling desk chair and sat next to him and sighed. Tears were running down the father's distraught, red face.

"She was everything to me—a gift. Sarah was the light of my life. Oh, God, I can't believe she's gone." He paused for a moment

"We tried to call her," Thompson said, his voice breaking. "No answer. Damn technology, our locator apps were on the blink." He composed himself with a deep breath.

"What about the boy, Blair Rogers?" Pascoe asked.

"Blair was a good kid," he said, as tears ran down his cheeks. "Sarah knew him since middle school. We know his parents; they go to our church. They've been dating for about six months."

Pascoe sifted through his mental notes, searching for the next question to ask when Doug Thompson asked, "When can I see her?"

Pascoe fumbled for an answer. "Of course, let me call the medical examiner to see if he's completed his examination."

Pascoe's walked to the foyer to call the ME. "The girl's parents want to visit. Are you ready?" Pascoe asked the ME.

"Need to finish gathering and recording the evidence," he replied.

"These folks need something I can't give them. Maybe seeing her will help. Jesus Christ, I need to see her call record." Pascoe paused. "Punch me through to the tech lab, will ya?"

The police technical lab had the recent history of Sarah's cell phone. While he was getting the report, Smith walked up to him in the foyer with Mrs. Thompson. Pascoe ended the call. "Your husband said he wants to go to the morgue and see Sarah. Is that what you want to do?" Pascoe looked at Mrs. Thompson for a reaction.

She looked at her husband. Doug Thompson nodded and she said, "Yes, yes I do."

"We want to go with you," Detective Smith said. "But we need to give the ME some time. Can we get back with you later in the day to go to the morgue?"

"Yes, but I want to see her today," Doug Thompson demanded.

"Of course," Smith said. "We'll call you as soon as we hear. It should only be a few hours. By the way, I never asked either of you if you knew if someone was bothering Sarah or if she was worried about anyone threatening her in any way."

The Thompsons looked at each other as if neither knew of anything, and then Rene Thompson said, "Anything like that should be in her diary."

"Sarah kept a diary?" Denise asked somewhat surprised.

"Oh yes, Detective. She never went anywhere without it."

"We didn't see it at the crime scene," Pascoe said, "I'll make sure the investigators look for it at impound. Would you mind looking for it in your home? It could be quite valuable in finding a motive or her killer."

The Thompsons nodded.

"I'd like to stay longer," Pascoe said to Mrs. Thompson, "but we have an appointment with the parents of the Rogers boy. We'll see you later."

The stunned parents, clinging to each other, nodded in agreement and walked the detectives to the front door. The wounded pair lingered at the entryway, watching as the detectives drove away.

***

On the way to the home of Blair Rogers, Pascoe read several text messages on his phone while Denise Smith drove.

"The girl's phone had no activity after 10:55. The GPS on it indicated it moved into the range of two other cell towers, but she didn't initiate a call. She got a call just before eleven, but it wasn't answered. However, there were several unanswered calls up to then."

"That sounds like it was either turned off or destroyed, but that answers the other question I had. The killer took their phones, but not their credit cards. The motive was not robbery, but something else. Probably one or both of the victims knew the killer. Does this make sense to you? Add in the fact that the perp carried the phones with him, driving around town."

"How do we know the perp drove around with the phones?" Denise asked.

"Her phone pinged several towers before it went silent." Pascoe replied. "Something had to be on the phones that connected the perp to the kids. And the father said something about their locator apps weren't working—we need to follow up on that. But, assuming the perp has the phones, what was the purpose of that?"

"What about a drug connection?" Denise asked,

"We'll have to see the toxicology report, but the message I got from the medical examiner before the bodies were moved said there were no signs of the use of drugs, no grass, no needle marks, and no pills or other drug paraphernalia anywhere."

Denise furrowed her brow. "I didn't get the sense these kids were into drugs."

For the next several moments they drove in complete silence as they approached the Rogers home. It was bigger and more lavish than the Thompsons. As their Ford Crown Victoria entered the driveway, Denise whispered to Pascoe, "More high cotton. But it'll mean nothing in a few moments. Damn. Two in one day."

Again, they delayed in the car for a moment, composing their thoughts, trying to reset themselves as they had to deliver the horrific news again. Finally, Denise broke the silence, "Same play? I take the mother and you the father?"

Pascoe didn't want to be distracted by his partner's questions. He usually had a hunch about the motive for a murder after the first interviews and the preliminary medical examiner's report, but, so far no clue. That bothered him.

"Yeah, sure," he idly replied.

David Rogers greeted them with a look of dread on his face. Pascoe showed his badge and said, "Lieutenant Reed Pascoe and Detective Denise Smith, Thomas Glen Police. May we come in," Pascoe asked calmly.

"What's happened to Blair?" Rogers demanded.

Reed remained stoic, looking first to Mr. Rogers, then, noticing Victoria Rogers standing in the foyer, before he spoke.

Denise couldn't ignore the similarities between the Rogers and the Thompsons. Both couples were in their forties. The mothers quite attractive, and both fathers were handsome and looked very professional. Their homes, professionally decorated, were not mansions, but probably worth close to a million each.

"May we sit down and talk?" Pascoe asked.

They were led into a huge den where Lieutenant Pascoe delivered the tragic news of their son's death. He recanted the events he thought were most relevant. They had the same horrified reaction as the Thompsons, but there was a difference. David Rogers was mad and wanted to know the details.

"Who killed my boy?" Rogers demanded after he collected himself.

"We don't have any leads yet," Pascoe said. "We didn't find a cell phone. If he had one, can you tell me its number?"

"Why Blair ever started up with that Thompson girl, I'll never know." Rogers shook his head angrily as he dug out his phone from his pants pocket. He said showing them his phone screen.

Denise Smith texted it to the crime lab while Pascoe put it in his notes. Mr. Rogers kept talking. He was genuinely upset, but acted like he wanted revenge.

Denise, paying close attention to the mother, sensed that the best way to get an authentic response from Mrs. Rogers was to remove her from her overbearing husband. "May I have a glass of water?"

Victoria Rogers led Denise to the kitchen. "When was the last time you talked to Blair?"

Mrs. Rogers resumed weeping, dried her eyes and paused before answering. "Probably between eight and nine last night," giving the detective a bottle of water from the "Sub-Zero" refrigerator unit. "He said he was going to meet Sarah to get school supplies, then go out for ice cream and he'd be home by eleven. I tried to call him later, but my call went straight to voicemail."

Mrs. Rogers leaned against the kitchen island, breaking into tears. With compassion, Denise remained silent, giving her time to gain emotional control. "We called a few more times, but he never answered," she said. "About 11:30 Sarah's mother called. That's when we really started to worry. Sarah's parent's calls were also going to voicemail."

In the other room, Pascoe waited for the women to be out of ear shot to query David Rogers. Pascoe assumed Rogers would understand his line of questioning, as he was an attorney by profession.

"Did you know your son and Miss Thompson were together last night?

"Yes. After Blair's lacrosse practice they were going to pick up last minute school supplies."

"Did any of this strike you as unusual or odd?"

"I thought it was kind of late, especially since school was starting in the morning. But I didn't say anything to anybody...wouldn't do any good." Rogers was staring into space, quietly mouthing words. "Mrs. Thompson talked with my wife last night. I'm sure it was past eleven."

"Did Mrs. Thompson say where she thought they might be?" Pascoe asked.

"No. She didn't know any more than we did," he answered. "She said she was hoping they might be here."

"Had Blair mentioned any confrontations with anyone recently?"

"No, nothing like that. Blair was a great kid. He was a peacemaker, not a troublemaker. He stayed away from trouble."

"How about Sarah? What was she like?" Pascoe asked.

"She was popular. Ran in a different crowd. I was surprised when they started dating."

"Why so?"

"Let's just say she had a reputation...of being demonstrably affectionate with her previous boyfriends. Blair wasn't like that. He was a modest, private soul," he said as his voice trailed off.

In the kitchen, Denise wasn't getting any better information about motives for the killings. Mrs. Rogers was a homemaker with two other children younger than Blair; a boy in middle school and a girl a year behind him in fifth grade. She had a hard time talking about Blair and Sarah, often breaking into tears.

***

After gathering as much information as they could, Pascoe and Smith left, promising to call later in the day with an update.

"So, Lieutenant," Smith started in as she sat behind the wheel of their squad car. "Do you have any clue?"

Pascoe paused, shaking his head. "Doesn't add up," Pascoe said staring at his phone. "None of it. Not a damn bit."

Denise started the engine and drove out of the circular driveway. The red roses were in full bloom, the white crepe myrtles had flowers the size of soccer balls, the clouds moving slowly in a pale blue sky. If one hadn't heard the news mention *the teen killings*, it would have been a flawless day.

***

As Pascoe and Smith headed back to the Thomas Glen police complex, they called the Thompsons, arranging to meet them at the morgue an hour later to view Sarah. As one might imagine, the morgue in the Thomas Glen Justice Complex was not large. On this day there were only two recently departed crime victims, Sarah and Blair. They met Sarah's parents in the main office, and during the walk from the police station to the morgue, the Thompsons were silent.

Denise couldn't help noticing the faces of Sarah's parents, drawn tight and colorless. Sarah's father seemed more anxious and agitated, swaying back and forth on his feet, nervously twitching his hands. Sarah's mother appeared to be barely breathing. Denise deduced of the two, Rene Thompson was the strong one, capable of holding her despair behind closed doors. Denise knew the look. Rene was building an emotional firewall in an attempt to hold the family together.

"Please, we want you to take your time. Deputy Smith and I will be here with you if you need anything." Pascoe said, his tone genuinely compassionate.

Once inside the room where the victims were stored, Rene didn't budge from the door, staring at the table on wheels where a sheet covered the body of her daughter. Rene covered her face with her open hand, tears flowing, but no audible sound could be heard. Denise walked over to her side to make herself available for Rene to grasp if she needed to steady herself.

Doug Thompson hovered close to the table, waiting in anticipation of Sarah's unveiling. The morgue attendant slowly pulled the white linen shroud from above Sarah's head very gently. He tugged at it until her head and entire neck were revealed. Doug stood over Sarah, tears welling up in his eyes. Slowly his right hand reached for her face, gently combing away some strands of hair that were stretched over her eyes. He put his hand on her bare shoulder, feeling her cold skin. His body started to quake in silent sobs as he slowly bent over and kissed her forehead, letting his tears rain down on her.

Rene Thompson watched her husband, as if waiting her turn. When he composed himself, Rene took a deep breath and slowly stepped to the opposite side of Sarah, and took her daughter's hand in hers, gently stroking it as she might have done countless times in the past. Doug Thompson stood back and watched his wife.

Rene assured her daughter in a whisper, "I'm so sorry baby. It's not fair. You had an amazing life ahead of you. There were so many plans. But how many times did you tell me that plans were meant to be broken? God, this feels so unreal.... But here you are.... Dad, Vincent, and I will miss you terribly, but don't worry about us, we'll find a way...." Her voice trailed off.

Holding onto her daughter's hand, Rene appeared weary. She turned her gaze to her husband.

Lieutenant Pascoe stoically watched, his lips pursed, eyes wide open, He had witnessed such scenes several times over his police

JEREMY LOGAN & BRENDA SEVCIK

career, but his duty and empathy as a father kept him from running out the door to avoid sharing this pain. He thought he had built a wall of protection from the emotional part of his job, but there was something so poignant about this one. Perhaps it was the angelic face of this victim or the gentleness of the parent's affection toward their departed daughter.

A moment later, Pascoe stood behind Doug Thompson and placed his hands on the father's shoulders. "Are you ready?" he asked quietly. Doug Thompson slowly shook his head and his feet remained planted near his daughter. When he was finally ready, Doug Thompson reached for his wife's hand, and she grasped it. They looked at each other, said a final goodbye to Sarah, and turned around to leave. It was the beginning of helping each other grieve.

3. COLLATERAL DAMAGE

DAVID AARON ROGERS KNEW HE SHOULD BE WITH HIS WIFE after the police officers left. Normal expectations would have them together comforting each other. Instead he went straight to his den and shut the door. He needed to order the chaos that had entered his world. For several minutes he just sat, stunned.

Although he had abandoned Judaism when he married, he needed a compass to make some sense of Blair's death. He opened the bottom left drawer of his desk and looked down at what he saw, glaring at him. He tried to resist. Finally, David reached in, pulling out one of the items, a big volume of Hebrew prayers.

Dusting off his father's Siddur, David opened the old book and found the blessing for the dead. He stared at it, unable to utter the words.

It had been three years since his father had passed away. He had mourned that loss, understanding it followed the expected cycle of life. In honor of his father, not due to his belief in God, David said the Mourner's Kaddish, the prayer for the departed, every day for a year, following Jewish tradition. This ritual linked him to his father, giving some comfort. But this unexpected death—murder—of his son made no sense to him.

Gazing at the prayer for the dead, David was frozen. He couldn't say it—not for Blair. Saying it would make his death real. He did not want to believe his first-born son was gone and not coming back.

By no means was David a religious man. He was brought up in a conservative Jewish home, attended Hebrew school, learned to read the language of his ancestors, and studied the history of his people. He had many questions, and despite scrutinizing the Midrash, writings by Jewish scholars interpreting biblical text, he never reached any satisfactory conclusion why his faith remained disinterested. He decided not to decide, simply shelving any authentic faith.

When he fell in love and got married, his wife, Vickie, a devout Baptist, simply assumed they would worship together. Because he adored her and could see it was important to her, he never protested. Although he was uncommitted to God, he was committed to his wife, and found himself in a Christian Church, attending services regularly on Sundays with his family. He had to admit, he enjoyed the time they all had together, away from school, sports, and friends; it was peaceful. But he never reconciled his faith, or shared his doubts with Vickie.

Busy with his career and his family, God remained on the shelf, in the back of a proverbial closet. Now he needed someone to explain to him so he could understand. He began interrogating God.

"Where are you, so I can ask you?" he cried aloud. *"Explain to me what happened to Blair. The scriptures say you spoke to Abraham. Why can't you talk to me, so I can understand?"*

David had to have answers. Could they be in the symbols of his past? He looked at the Jewish prayer book. Alongside it, in his desk drawer, was also his father's prayer shawl, his kippah, and shofar.

His father had been proud of the shofar, a beautiful ram's horn, purchased on a trip to Israel. Its use signaled rededication to his God. Why he kept them close to him in his desk and not in a box in the attic, was perhaps a sign that his old faith was more a part of him than he realized.

Urging the feelings of complete faith from his childhood to resurface, David reached down and gently retrieved his father's holy articles. With measured care, he put the blue and white prayer shawl over his shoulders, and the matching felt kippah on his head.

As hard as he tried, David could not even feel the slightest breath from God, which would allow him to live in a world with light. Even with the tallit and kippah, God remained silent with no illumination.

Soon the darkness changed hands with a horrible vision. With his eyes closed, he saw his son, Blair, behind the supermarket, a bullet in his head, his body drained of blood, lying near a dumpster. He thought to himself, how *much did Blair suffer? What did he do to deserve this?*

Tears filled his eyes. He slumped in the oversized chair in his study. There was nowhere he could find solace. He wanted to lash out; his rage bubbling. Raising his fist, he brought it down on the padded arm of the chair with great might. He recalled scripture that had troubled him when he was young, but found purpose in it now. "A life for a life, an eye for an eye, a tooth for a tooth, a hand for a hand, a foot for a foot, a burn for a burn, a wound for a wound, bruise for a bruise."

"A life for a life..." David Rogers wanted to find the sonofabitch who robbed him of Blair and suck the life out of the evildoer, slowly and painfully. Was it not sanctioned in his bible? Was it not the law given to him by the God of his youth?

Vickie's God would say something different. Vickie's God would say forgive seventy times seventy. Jesus Christ! David knew with his bare hands he could rip out the eyes of the bastard, but it would be a cold day in hell before he could offer forgiveness.

"A life for a life," David repeated a third time, still grasping his old prayer book, he turned to the page that held the petition, adjusted his tallit and kippah and read:

Yitgadal v'yitkadash sh'mey rabbah...

As he read the Hebrew, the years of attending Hebrew school and Sabbath services kicked in, and he found himself reciting the prayer in Hebrew by memory, appearing as every other devout congregant in the synagogue—standing straight, legs together, his eyes closed facing upward, and bowing at the appropriate moments. After finishing the prayer in Hebrew, he read the English translation:

May God's great name be exalted and hallowed throughout the world, as is God's wish, May God's sovereignty be established, in your lifetime and in your days of the House of Israel....
May the One who brings harmony on high, bring harmony to us and to all Israel, and to all who dwell on earth. And let us say: Amen.

"A life for a life," David repeated a third time. Revenge had taken complete possession of his thoughts. As if he had traveled back to ancient times, he devoted himself to avenge his son's murder.

"If I have to slay the assassin that robbed Blair of his life, I will do so. And I don't mind, not for one second, if it means I'll rot in prison. Justice must be served."

With the kippah on his head, the tallit on his shoulders, he looked up and said, "Abraham, Moses and David all lived by your justice, oh Lord. By those same laws, I will find my son's murderer and by the words given to me in the holy book of Torah. Amen."

With care and respect, he placed the Siddur on the far right corner of his desk, removed his prayer shawl and kippah, and neatly arranged them in the back of his desk drawer. And without blowing into the shofar, he set it next to the kippah, resisting the urge to slam the drawer shut. "A life for a life—from my lips to God's ears."

***

Blair's mother also needed her alone time. She was relieved when her husband went into his study and closed the door.

Vickie got on her knees and prayed to God. She asked him to wake her up from this terrible nightmare. She began her conversation with God: *We tried hard to be good parents. Why did this have to happen to Blair? God, you call us each by name. Why did you have to call us to this? Oh, God, please, tell me this isn't true. Please tell me they were wrong.*

She collapsed on the floor and cried tears of grief only a mother could cry.

4. I AM A PARADOX

This is it. The wandering in the darkness is over. The pain has vanished and so have the fears. That book is closed and forgotten. I am reborn, and I clearly see the future. All the wondering, calculating, preparing and planning are coming together like a perfectly composed opera. We have the orchestra pit, with the various musicians, the beautifully tuned instruments, and our main opera singers: the mezzo-soprano, who is such a lovely prima donna, and the tenor who will absorb his diva's high notes.

No rehearsal is even necessary; this orchestration is so precise, so perfect. As the maestro, I am omniscient and see it all: from the opening aria, starting with a slow-moving cavatina, which crescendo's up to a climatic cabaletta, or second part of the aria. The main part of the event, the musical score, is so dramatic and moving, all breath will be suspended. Tears will be shed. This shall be no black comedy. Yes, it will be dark, as it should be, filled with the sadness of betrayal and deceit.

Pianissimo, pianissimo, pianissimo. I have been quiet for very long. I will stay hidden and silent. I will remain backstage. So brilliant my direction, with such an unexpected plot and resolution, all will be dumbfounded.

I am renewed, fresh and flourishing. I have supremacy over my dominion. My mind expands with every breath I breathe. I feel the strength growing inside me.

I am the Maestro. May the show begin.

5. WHAT DO WE HAVE

THE MORGUE VISIT WITH SARAH'S PARENTS, SO TENDER AND sad, provided the Pascoe-Smith team additional inspiration to find her murderer. After Pascoe called ahead to gather the investigation team for a meeting, Detective Smith asked him for his gut impression.

"I'd give it to you, but I don't have one yet," he snapped. "Sorry, you know how I hate this shit. I don't like being so clueless…"

Denise nodded. "That makes two of us."

It was past lunchtime when they got back to the precinct. Another officer had ordered a delivery from their favorite takeout place, a Cuban restaurant just a few blocks away. It was a somber meeting, with no surprises. Pascoe was becoming irritated by the lack of leads. He was hoping the murder weapon would turn up, or better yet, a motive.

About two in the afternoon, Chief Meadows came in and announced they would hold a press conference at four o'clock. The Chief was a hulk of a man, standing well over six feet. At forty-six, his balding head of gray hair made him appear sixty-ish. He'd been through two failed marriages, and was known to drink himself to sleep every now and then. When he did, he'd arrive in the morning at the precinct with a reddish complexion, hungover, but sober. His troops respected him, rarely complaining.

"Listen up, if we've got nothing to go on, that's our message. The media has been on this story since noon, but we've put them off until now. You know the routine, but don't think this is going to be like any of the recent crime investigations you've seen. The FBI and Representative Cummings will be coming in at three. I'm taking them by myself. It's too early for them to get close to this. Our investigation is going to need a real team effort. I'm going to leave you alone until you tell me you're ready for the press."

Meadows walked out, sucking most of the air in the squad room with him as he left. After an awkward pause, Pascoe said, "Let's focus on the evidence. What do we have on the bodies?"

Robert Evans, the Medical Examiner, stood up and gave his report, "I've placed the time of death at 0015 hours or a quarter past midnight." He walked over to a bulletin board and pointed at the photos at the upper left-hand corner. "The bullet was a nine millimeter, and two shell casings were found on the floor in the backseat area of the Toyota. The only items of significance were the fibers found in the skulls and the hair found on the upholstery of the vehicle. It's consistent with what you would find if the shooter used a pillow to muffle the sounds of the shots. No such pillow was found anywhere."

"Have we seen anything like this recently?" Pascoe asked.

"Negative. I checked our database for the last ten years. It's my opinion that this was a premeditated act carried out with precision. Based upon the angle and trajectory of the bullets, the shots occurred in rapid fire sequence. I believe the two victims were shot from a gun fired by a person in the back seat."

"Jesus," Detective Smith commented.

"Ballistics," Pascoe shouted.

"Nothing much more than what the ME said," reported a man in the back that Pascoe recognized from past investigations in the county. "It's a nine-millimeter weapon with commonly sold ammunition in the retail marketplace. Until we trace the stamp on the shell casings or we find the weapon, that's all that can be said."

"On the scene interviews," Pascoe demanded.

Detective Gary Branch, sitting in front row opened his ring binder and cleared his throat. Branch was the youngest of the Thomas Glen detectives, recently promoted. He was married, and his wife was carrying their first child. Gary was the only African-American in the squad. He was a solid investigator, but not flashy.

"This is a 24/7, 365 market. Deliveries can occur around the clock. The back doors were closed between the last one and the one delivery this morning. Brown, the bakery truck driver, called the delivery supervisor when he arrived on Monday morning at approximately 0700 hours. That's when Brown observed the bodies and called 911. Between the two deliveries, none of the employees on the scene said they had been behind the store at any time."

"At the time when the last cell phone of the victims was operating, the store traffic was minimal and the employees were in mid-shift. That means the parking lot was almost empty, and the employees were busy restocking the shelves. Nobody noticed the victim's cars. None of the employees remember seeing any of the victims in the store. In other words, we've got no witnesses and nothing we didn't see for ourselves."

"All right," Pascoe said quietly, "What do we know about the scene?"

Detective Miles Judson stood up from his seat in the front row. "We have a partial video of the parking lot and delivery area."

Judson was the hotshot in the squad. He was handsome, bright, and a rising star. He also had enough ego to fuel the entire squad. He walked up to the large flat panel TV in the corner of the room, and with a remote control in one hand and a pointer in the other he powered it up and faced the screen.

"As you can see," he started, "the monitor is divided into six equal segments, with the respective camera scenes from the outside at the top of the screen and views inside the store at the bottom. The footage inside the store didn't reveal anything associated with the crime, so we won't bother with that footage

"The three outside views, are in order from left to right. Camera one was located on a pole about ninety feet from the main entrance facing the front doors. Camera two was located above the main entrance and viewed the nearby parking spaces to the East. Camera three was located on the building to the west of the doors and viewed the nearby parking space on the West side of the lot.

"At 2208 hours Sunday, the BMW arrives and parks. It's at the extreme right of the screen for camera two. A moment later we see the illumination of another vehicle's headlights to its right, but that car is out of view of all cameras. The female victim gets out, and her shadow from the back lights of the lot show her walking toward the vehicle to her right and then out of view. We may assume from the slight jiggling of the illuminated area of the second vehicle's headlights that she got in it just prior to the driver cutting off the headlights.

"Fourteen minutes later we see the shadow of a third person approaching the Toyota out of view and on foot from the rear. The

36

shadow indicates this person is probably wearing a hoodie. That person gets inside the Toyota, and nothing happens for nine and a half minutes. The Toyota leaves the parking lot at 2231 hours and doesn't return until 0011 hours Monday morning; almost two hours later. The headlights go off immediately, and then we see the shadow of the person wearing the hoodie, leaving the driver's side of the vehicle a few seconds after that.

"Based on the ME's time of death at 0015 hours, and video number three, we can assume that the perpetrator shot and killed the couple soon after returning to the supermarket. It appears he killed them in the Toyota when he was parked near the dumpster. After removing the bodies, he drove the Toyota back to the space next to the BMW and left the scene. Camera two views the scene in front of the doors and captures only the first six parking spaces on the screen. The BMW and the Toyota are out of view, being that they are seventeen spaces away from the front of the supermarket. Looking at camera one, we see that the store blocks the view of the dumpster. However, at 23:56 hours Sunday night, we see the Toyota drive behind the store from the East side. It parks out of view and doesn't move until 00:10 hours, fourteen minutes later. We can assume it takes the perp that amount of time to kill the victims and move their bodies from the vehicle to the place we found them, next to the dumpster. Next, he drives the car back to the space next to the BMW and leaves on foot."

Pascoe paused for a moment and then asked Judson, "Is that everything in your report?" Judson nods. "We appear to have a single perpetrator. What else can we surmise or assume?"

Denise Smith responded, "Our perp appears to know something about the range of the security cameras."

"Anyone else?"

"Where did they go for almost two hours?" Judson asked,

"Good question," Pascoe commented. "We know the victim's cell phones were disabled soon after the perp entered the Toyota for the first time. What else can we surmise?"

A patrolwoman said, "He's tech savvy. Not only did he know about the range of the security camera, he knew their cell phones might tell us where he took them for almost two hours."

"What else?" Pascoe asked.

Smith said, "This guy is a pre-meditating sonofabitch who knew them, killing them in a well-planned manner with precision. He either followed them to the market or knew they would end up there near the time they arrived."

"Or he contacted them and this was a designated meeting place," Pascoe suggested followed by a moment of silence.

Detective Branch asked, "Why not leave the victims in the Toyota next to the dumpster?"

"The killer was telling us he was discarding them. They were now a part of his past, and worthless trash," Detective Ramona Beamon said, sitting in the front row.

Pascoe added, "Detective Beamon should know. She's the County's profiler, and in case you haven't come across her previously, she's rarely wrong. Now, what do we know about the grounds at the crime scene?"

"Okay," Branch said, "but why did he get back in the Toyota and return it to its original parking space? He could have left it there and walked away. It doesn't make much sense."

"Good point," Pascoe remarked.

A patrolman from the second row stood up. "Six of us, along

with two photographers searched all the paved areas within the taped perimeter, some with regular light and some with ultra-violet light, which as you know, detects blood. We found nothing of relevance. We're still processing the prints from inside the vehicles. The pillow that the ME suggested was used to muffle the gunshots must have been removed from the Toyota when the perp left the scene for the last time."

"I'd guess the pillow and the murder weapon are stashed somewhere together," Denise added. "But why didn't he take the shell casings with him? If he was careful about fingerprints, the pillow, and not being seen by the security cameras, it seems odd that he'd leave the shell casings for us to investigate."

Nobody wanted to speculate on that oddity.

"What about background on the kids and their friends and classmates?" Pascoe asked.

Detective Branch said, "I've got that. I visited the school with two officers. We talked to three kids that the principal of Thomas Glen High School brought to us. A school policeman was in the room to observe. Both victims were honor students. They were involved in several activities each, including band, honor clubs and sports. The girl was a cheerleader once and last spring both were on prom court. They were well-liked, and the boy especially, was a favorite of the principal. Neither had disciplinary issues. We have two all-American kids without any blemishes on the records or their faces."

Pascoe and Smith spent the next half hour relating their interviews with the parents. Detective Smith finally instructed, "We need to see all the arrest records of crimes within a half mile of the supermarket in the past year, and I want that cross-referenced with students from Thomas Glen High School. Also, the parents of both the kids attended Mount Bethel Baptist Church. We need someone to interview the pastor."

Pascoe announced his assignments and the records officer, Elizabeth Worthy, recorded them in the duty book.

"Let's get this all done by the end of the day," Pascoe announced as he turned and left the room, Smith right behind him.

"Are you heading for the Chief's office?" Denise asked.

"Roger that. Damn. He won't be happy about our lack of progress."

The FBI and the state representative had come and gone. Chief Meadows waved them to enter.

"What can you tell me? Anything with meat on it?"

"The best piece of information we have is what's on the store's security cameras, and they don't show the perp, the killing or anything that might identify him or her."

"Are you telling me we have no theory of the case?" Meadows was getting agitated.

"We have one, but it's as vague as it gets," Pascoe responded. "We believe the perp knew the victims. He - or she - is very calculating, precise, and cool as a cucumber. I'm going to assume at this point the perp's a male. I think he's either a pro or a psychopath, and I've got my money on the latter. I'm guessing he reads a lot of crime novels or watches a lot of crime dramas on TV. He's knowledgeable about evidence, security cameras, and is tech savvy, probably a geek who had a score to settle."

Meadows nodded. "Okay then. Detective Smith, what's your take?"

"I agree with Pascoe, although I'm not willing to name the perp as a male yet. I'm all in with that being our theory of the case."

Meadows looked at his watch and saw the gathering of reporters on his video of the press room. "It's show-time. Let's meet the press."

6. FIRST BREAK

AT THE PRESS CONFERENCE, THE THOMAS GLEN MAYOR, Madeline Coleman, read a statement to kick it off. "Police Chief Clifton Meadows is spearheading the investigation of this heinous crime. It deserves our highest priority until we bring the culprit or culprits to justice. Chief Meadows will now lead this briefing."

Chief Meadows cleared his throat, "Our community has lost two precious, bright, young adults. Sarah Jane Thompson and Blair Jefferson Rogers, seniors at Thomas Glen High School. Both were found Monday morning, shot to death, behind the Gold's Supermarket. Leading the investigation team is Lieutenant Reed Pascoe. He will provide a statement, and we both will take only a few questions. Lieutenant Pascoe?"

"We are not providing the cause of death or the condition of the victims. We are still processing evidence, and we expect to provide a more complete report in twenty-four hours. We are also withholding any leads at this time, because…. I'm sorry to report, we have neither any suspects nor a motive."

"I ask that you give the parents time to deal with this. They're consumed with grief, as you would be if you lost one of your own children. Detective Denise Smith and I will head the investigation under the supervision of Chief Meadows, and we ask that you direct your questions to either one of us. Also, I urge the public, if you have any information on the case, please call the Dallas County Sherriff's office at 972-555-6078."

The press reacted with their usual outburst of questions as Meadows walked Pascoe and Smith away from the media spotlight. The Chief gave a few sound bites for the press before he reached the sanctuary of his office where he huddled with the mayor, Pascoe and Smith. They sat there is silence for a moment before the mayor said, "The press will be demanding something from us soon. I'd like to have progress reports to give them before they start showing up every time we walk out of our office."

"We all know what that's like," said Meadows, "We'll try to avoid that." He looked at Pascoe with his familiar "grumpy old man" stare that suggested it was up to Pascoe and Smith to save them from that distress.

***

On the drive back to the station after making his rounds, Detective Miles Judson called Pascoe with the first promise of a break. The cell phone owned by Blair Rogers was on and providing a GPS signal. "We're on our way to the station," Pascoe said. "Smith and I will meet you there."

Judson in his vehicle, and two patrolmen in their squad car, led the way out of the station parking lot, followed by Pascoe and Smith, heading to a residence in the Alamo Pass Community north of Thomas Glen. The neighborhood was originally a hunting and fishing area of small cottages and trailer homes with boats parked in the driveways and pickup trucks of all vintages parked on the front lawns.

The officers and Judson parked on the street, and one accompanied Judson to the front door while a patrolman circled around to the rear of the house. Pascoe and Smith, already there, blocked the driveway, and stepped out of their unmarked police car.

A twenty-something white, male with stringy, long, brown hair answered the door. As he let them in, Judson waved to Pascoe and Smith to come along. Inside the home, the kid identified himself as Carl Meeker.

"What's this all about?" Meeker asked. "I haven't done anything."

"Where have been today?" Judson inquired.

"Here and there."

"How about we start with the last couple of hours," Judson said.

"My cousin and I were at the mall. He dropped me home about an hour ago," Meeker responded.

"What's your cousin's name?" Judson asked.

"Lennie, Lennie Duggar…. Come on now, tell me what you think I've done."

"We're looking for a cell phone? Have you gotten one recently?" Judson asked.

"As a matter of fact, I found one at the mall today," Meeker admitted. "Don't tell me that the police are so bored that they're sending three cops to track down lost cell phones."

Meeker shook his bowed head in silence. Smith poked Pascoe in the side and pointed to Meeker's hands. They were twitching nervously.

45

"Come on, Carl," Judson said, "Where did you get it?"

Carl stammered, "You-you-you're not going to believe me. You-you never have."

"What do you mean, Carl? We've never seen you before today," Judson continued.

"Okay, but once…you've got to believe me. I heard it. It was making a sound like Lennie's phone. I thought it was his, but he was in the bathroom. I looked around. I was on a bench, and there was nothing next to me but my backpack. I looked everywhere. Then it chimed again. I looked in my backpack, and there it was. I thought it was Lennie's. But when I asked him, he pulled his out of his pocket. I swear, I have no idea how it got there. You've got to believe me."

"Show us the phone, Carl," Judson said.

"It's still in my backpack—over there on the chair."

Carl pointed to a black North Face backpack on a kitchen chair. Detective Smith walked over to it, put on a pair of latex gloves from her purse, and lifted it out of the backpack.

Judson took a notepad out of his jacket pocket and opened it. Then he dialed a number on his cell phone. The phone in Smith's hand rang. "It's the boy's."

Pascoe and Smith exchanged glances, remaining silent, allowing Judson, who was doing quite well handling Meeker, to finish up with him.

"Carl, I'm afraid you'll have to come down to the station with us," Judson said.

"What? Why? What do you think I did?" Meeker said, pleading like a child.

Judson said, "This phone belonged to a high school boy found murdered last night."

"What?" Meeker pleaded more than asked. "No way. I told you the truth. Hey, you're not talking about the two kids just on the news?"

"I'm afraid so,"

"Wait, wait. It couldn't be me. I was over at Lennie's. He'll vouch for me, and his mom was there."

"Look, Carl, you appear to be a kid at the wrong place at the wrong time," Pascoe said. "We've got to check out your story. I'll tell you what. If everything checks out, you'll be home later tonight. Now, could you show us where you were at the mall when you found the phone?"

"Can I call my mom before we go? She's at work."

"Yeah, sure," Pascoe replied.

"Can I use my cell phone?"

"Sure," Pascoe said as he looked at his partner.

While Carl Meeker called his mother, Denise whispered in Pascoe's ear, "Perfect, his cell phone should tell us where he was last night."

***

Carl rode with Pascoe and Smith to the mall, and he talked all the way. "You're going to find this out, so I'll tell you now," he said, "I've been in trouble before, but nothing like you're talking about. I've got a petty theft arrest from when I was twelve for stealing a hunting knife and a DUI last year. That's why I don't have a car. My mom's real strict. She won't let me drive until I earn enough to pay her back for the legal costs, back rent and car insurance. I work at the German Auto Repair shop next to the strip mall on Hwy. 141."

"How do you get to work without a car?" Denise asked.

"Lennie takes me. He works at the auto glass shop attached to it."

Pascoe and Smith were rapidly getting to the point where they believed Carl.

***

At the mall, Carl led them to an intersection adjacent to the mall's food court. He walked directly to a concrete bench.

"I was sitting here, just watching people and playing a video game on my phone," Carl said. "And my backpack was next to me on this side. I don't remember if anyone sat next to it—lots of people were passing by. Lennie came out of the bathroom over there, and I told you the rest."

Pascoe looked at Judson and Smith and announced, "That's all I need to know. Okay, Carl, we'll go down to the station and get your written statement. After we do that and look at your phone, you'll be free to go."

***

At the stationhouse, Judson checked out Carl's arrest record, He

48

had some traffic tickets, but nothing other than the DUI and petty theft he mentioned. Carl's finger prints were already in his file. They processed his cell phone while he sat in an interrogation room.

The Thomas Glen Justice Center was barely five years old. It was some architect's vision intentionally designed to avoid the appearance of a municipal building. It was modern with curves and high ceilings. It should have been called a complex, because it was difficult to figure out where everything was. Somehow, though, there was plenty of room for everyone, including the police, the courts, the jail, morgue and offices for elected officials.

The Technical Services Department was located on the basement floor with the morgue, the records and evidence rooms. Most of the employees in Tech Services were recent grads from local schools who were known as the geek squad. They reveled in their reputation, but they were also very capable.

A bit later, Denise walked into Pascoe's office. "Carl's cell phone backs up his story. We checked to see if his fingerprints were at the scene. Nada. I've ordered a copy of the mall's tapes from their security camera. Judson is going to fetch it now."

"He's probably a slacker, but not a coldblooded killer," Pascoe responded. "See if a patrolman is free to take him home."

Denise returned a few minutes later and said, "They're going over the Rogers' phone at tech services. As you suggested, I cut Meeker loose. Judson drove him home." She paused, "So, what's your theory on the boy's phone?"

"My best guess right now—the killer cleaned the phone and drove to the mall looking for a patsy. He saw Carl, the open backpack, and voila, we're distracted while he's up to something else."

"Yeah, that's pretty much how I see it. I wonder where Sarah's phone is. I think I'm getting a better picture of what we're looking at. Our perp is connected to Sarah, not Blair. His taking Blair's phone was to throw us off, delay us. The reason he didn't leave Sarah's phone in Carl's backpack is because of what might be on it, or for reasons we can't fathom right now."

Reed smiled, and Denise looked at him, silently acknowledging they were on the same wave length.

***

Somewhere in a dark, secret and secluded place, the killer is talking out loud.

I laugh.

They're off the trail, and the cell phone in the backpack play. It's all working like a charm. Even the police can be manipulated. "Just like Ike", my buddy on the web, was so right. Today, they are my puppets, and I'm the puppet-master.

It was all so very easy. As if the moon and the starts were following my command, everything fell into place.

Justice.

This is so much fun. It only makes me thirsty for more. Yeah. Why can't I do it again? Something totally unrelated this time. Perfect! And this time, I'll have more time to plan it down to the minutest detail.

Now, who will it be this time?

7. T MINUS TWENTY-TWO HOURS

THERE'S A SAYING IN LAW ENFORCEMENT, *IF AN ARREST IS not made in the first forty-eight hours of a murder investigation, the odds of solving the crime are cut in half.* As of 0800 hours Tuesday morning, twenty-six hours had passed from the time the police came upon the dead bodies of Sarah and Blair, and they still had no solid leads. Nobody was talking about the dwindling hours, but everyone could feel the urgency to latch on to something, anything.

The Thomas Glen station squad room was filled with anxiety, and a cloud hung over the investigation. Lieutenant Pascoe knew he had little to go on except hunches and even Smith's intuition was hazy. From what she shared with Pascoe, she sensed the killer was cocksure he was going to get away with the crime. This morning, the room was occupied by more than the usual homicide investigation staff. Chief Meadows was there, along with a member of the Texas Bureau of Public Safety, Agent Jim Franks. Everyone had a pastry and their morning beverage of choice, but black coffee dominated the mugs.

The first item on the agenda was a presentation from County profiler, Ramona Beamon. She was an ambitious and eye-catching redhead, who had designs on an FBI position. Her specialty was serial or mass murderers. "This is what we know about our kill-er—statistics of similar crimes tell us, there is over a ninety-percent likelihood that the killer is male. Since the victims are teenagers, he is young, perhaps no more than five years their senior."

She paused, consulted her notes and rattled off a series of com-mon traits psychopaths share. "He has an above-average IQ, and he's studied murder investigations or they are his favorite TV pro-grams and movies. He is single, maybe living alone or somewhat in isolation. In all likelihood he is very meticulous in dress and how he lives. His residence will be spotless and very organized. He is an introvert, shy and self-conscious, but he also operates with an air of confidence. The victims are not complete strangers to him. In all likelihood, he has stalked them for a while and planned their execution in advance. As far as the motive, there might be personal reasons for the killings; revenge, betrayal, loss of affection or aliena-tion that are private or secret to him. And they don't have to be real reasons, but imagined ones."

"He plans on getting away with this crime. He probably knows he's well ahead of us, but he isn't infallible. He's left us with some clues at the crime scene, and inconsistencies how he's dealt with the victim's phones. He could also be a psychopath, a killer without re-morse, but I'm reserving that opinion until we have more evidence. I wish you luck."

Pascoe stood up and continued. "I'm dividing up the homicide squad into three parts. Judson and his deputy will focus on the tech-nical aspects of the investigation and local criminals whose record indicates they might be capable of this double homicide. Detective Branch and his deputy will head a search of witnesses who may have seen the perp in the commission of the crime. For instance, our perp seems to have been knowledgeable about the extent of the view the security cameras at the supermarket could show. That means he had to have been in their offices prior to the crime and observed the security monitors."

"This guy could have more killings on his agenda. We need to question each detail and run down every lead. And finally, I want you all to keep in the back of your mind what Specialist Beamon told you today.

"Detective Smith and I will continue to interview the family, friends, and persons of interest. We're still withholding details of the crime scene. That means nobody in this room may discuss the investigation with anyone outside this room without prior authorization. That's all I have to say. We'll need your best to catch this bastard."

The meeting broke up, and Chief Meadows caught Pascoe on the way out of the squad room. "If you've got a minute, Mayor Coleman is in my office waiting to talk to the three of us."

"Sure, Chief," Pascoe said and Denise nodded. The three of them walked down the hall in silence, expecting they were about to receive the pep talk she was famous for. Mayor Coleman was a veteran politician from the corporate world who made the switch to public service about the same time Thomas Glen was incorporated as a city.

"Hello, Reed," Mayor Coleman said as she greeted Pascoe, "And it's Detective Denise Smith, is that right?"

"Yes, Mayor," Denise made direct eye contact as she shook the mayor's hand. "I'm pleased that the two of you are leading this investigation," Coleman said with conviction. "It's going to be a pressure cooker, and you're suited to deal with it. The media is all over us. We've got a press briefing set for eleven this morning, and the demand for a seat in the room is twice what we can fit. Be prepared to give the latest on the evidence at the scene without giving away too much information. The killer will probably be watching. It would be wise to find a place for Detective Smith to say something about how important it is for us to provide closure for the families, and again ask if the public has information to contact our office." She paused, thinking before she finished. "It's chauvinistic and po-litical drivel to do it this way, but I'm confident we'll be thankful in the end."

After the mayor left, the three police veterans sat in silence for a moment. Chief Meadows was about to say something but Pascoe interrupted. "We know, Chief. You wish us your best, and you want us to bring back the killer with a confession."

The Chief smirked and Pascoe and Smith headed out the door to their interview with Lily Evans, Sarah's best friend.

***

They arrived at Thomas Glen High School about an hour before lunchtime. The high school was in its fifth year, but had an enroll-ment of over two thousand students, an indication of how fast the community was growing. Because of the affluence of its citizens, it was attracting a lot of the best teachers and administrators in the metropolitan area.

The principal escorted the detectives and the school's security of-ficer to a private room adjacent to his office where Lily Evans stood alone, next to a table in the center of the room. She was a statuesque blonde, and seventeen, like Sarah. She was clutching a tissue in one hand, nervously squeezing it.

Denise gave her the usual preamble she used for sensitive interviews. "Lily, I'm Detective Denise Smith, and this is my partner, Lieutenant Pascoe. We're working on bringing justice to Blair and Sarah." Lily was shaking as she found a chair; trying to keep everything together. Denise used her soft, compassionate voice. "This is a difficult time, isn't it?"

Lily swallowed. "I can't believe I won't see Sarah again."

"I'm so sorry, Lily. Sarah and Blair did not deserve this." Denise stopped to assess how composed Lily was. "Lily, take a few deep breaths. I know this is very difficult." Lily breathed deeply, looking up at the ceiling. Denise could see the tears forming in the girl's eyes.

"Lily, you were close friends with Sarah. Right?"

"Uh huh," she replied. "We shared everything with each other."

"Those kinds of friends are hard to find." Denise spoke from the heart. "You probably know more about Sarah than anyone else. Can I ask you some questions that may help us?"

"Of course." She had to stop again to compose herself. "I want to help, if I can."

"Thank you, Lily," Denise said. "Her mother said Sarah kept a diary. Have you ever seen her write in it?"

"Many times. Sarah always had it with her. I think she was on her fifth or sixth book." Lily smiled. "I teased her that she was writing a reality show for Netflix." Denise smiled back at Lily.

"Where did she usually keep it? We didn't see one in her purse, her car or at home."

"Are you sure? If it wasn't in her purse, someone took it. I saw her after church Sunday afternoon. We went to her house for lunch. She wrote in it then."

"Do you have any idea what she was writing about?"

"I'm not sure. She didn't say, and I never looked at what she wrote. She was very protective of it. But if I had to guess, it was about her mother arguing with Vincent. We could hear them upstairs. He was locked in his room and she wanted to talk to him. She gave up and came downstairs. Her mother looked annoyed when she spotted us in the kitchen."

"Do you know what they were arguing about?"

"No, but I got the feeling Sarah did, and wasn't happy about it."

"In what way?" Detective Smith asked.

"Sarah has always been Vincent's protector. She didn't like people pressuring him. She looked worried. The look on her face was like she was thinking that she was going to have to intervene again on his behalf. A lot of home stuff was worrying her all summer. She wouldn't say, but I could tell."

"Any guess what his mom was pressuring him about?"

"Not really. I hardly ever see him, and Sarah rarely talked about him. A couple of times lately I overheard her talking to him on the phone. He's got issues, and Sarah mentioned after one call that she didn't have the time to deal with him like she used to. She spent most of her time with school and Blair. She and Blair were in love. They were the perfect couple. I was happy for her. In the past, Sarah had some really awful boyfriends."

Lieutenant Pascoe's phone was vibrating in his pocket, signaling a call. He tried to ignore it because he wanted to observe the complete interview with Lily. He gave in, grabbed his phone and looked at the caller ID—it was Chief Meadows. He excused himself from the interview and walked out of the room and into the school hallway.

"What's up, chief?"

"You two need to get here about fifteen minutes earlier than you anticipated. The Rogers father has some influential contacts with the FBI. They're coming to the briefing, and they want to talk to you and Detective Smith before you take the stage. Mr. Rogers appears like he's about to come undone. He's been calling for you and Smith, wanting an update and accusing us of withholding facts. He mouthed off to Patrolman Worthy using very salty language, and she was visibly upset about the call."

"Perfect," Reed retorted. "Consider us warned."

Pascoe was unaware of it, but a small crowd of curious students gathered around him during his phone conversation with the chief. It surprised him, but he smiled and silently returned to the interview. From Lily's body language, it was clear Detective Smith had earned her complete trust and confidence. The girl appeared more relaxed and in control, allowing Denise to better retrieve those small, important morsels which could help solve the case.

"Did Sarah have any enemies, or old flames– or anyone who was jealous of her?" Smith asked Lily.

"I don't think so. She was so sensitive about that kind of thing. She broke up with Jason Birch after the New Year, but it was more about him cheating on her. He goes to a different high school. About the only thing that bothered her that I can think of was the teasing she got from her friends in band. It's no secret that she's the teacher's pet, so to speak. He didn't use her name when he talked to her—he called her 'Sunshine'.

"What did Sarah think about that?"

"She just laughed. Sarah was used to that kind of attention. She didn't let it get to her head."

"How about Blair's friends? Any ill feelings toward Sarah — or him, for that matter?"

"I don't know of anything. Blair was a great guy, everyone liked him. I think Sarah was the first girl he fell for. He got teased a little because he was shy with girls before Sarah came along."

"Do you know why they were at the market late Sunday night?"

"Nothing other than the usual fooling around. I talked to her about eight. She said she was going to meet Blair and they were going to get some stuff for school, then have ice cream. My guess is that all the ice cream shops were closed and they ended up at the supermarket to get some."

"Why did they meet so late?"

"I think she said he had lacrosse practice until seven."

"Isn't that unusual for a Sunday?"

"Lacrosse is a club sport, run by boosters — not the school. They always seem to have odd times for practice. It's about scheduling the field I guess."

"Before we go, Lily, is there anything we haven't covered that might help us find out who did this?"

"I don't think so. I hope you find out soon. Besides missing Sarah and Blair, we're all scared."

***

Pascoe and Smith left Lily and talked to three of her friends from her church, who also happened to be members of the school band. One of them recalled that Sarah kept a diary, but that's all she knew. Two of the girls saw her in church Sunday morning. They said they chatted with her afterward, and that she seemed normal and not preoccupied or worried.

When Detective Smith asked about the band director, they rolled their eyes. One said, "That was kind of a running joke. Last year some of the band members weren't happy about who got to be first chair in the flute section, and there was a lot of bad blood. Mr. Cummings totally ignored them. Sarah talked to him and the kids, and figured something out, and it seemed as if they were all real tight and happy after that. Mr. Cummings said Sarah was a ray of sunshine, and that's why he started calling her that. Just about everyone thought it was lame and teased her. But it was all in good fun. She didn't care."

"What did Sarah do to make the flute section so happy?"

"She got the first four chairs to agree to rotate every month so they all spent time in the first chair," she said. "Sarah was probably a better flute player than all of them, and she didn't like to hear them squabble. I think they listened to her because she didn't play in the marching band. She was a cheerleader instead. Besides, she was always finding ways to soothe hard feelings among her friends."

Pascoe and Smith looked at each other, both realizing that Sarah's negotiating skills should have been an asset if an argument or disagreement was what led to her death. Among all the other oddities this was minor, but with everything they learned about Sarah and Blair, they were building a mountain of characteristics that didn't add up to the tragic outcome.

Denise took out her cell phone and dialed. Pascoe looked a little puzzled until he overheard the conversation.

"Mrs. Thompson, this is Detective Denise Smith. I'm sorry to bother you, but I was wondering if you were able to find Sarah's diaries. Uh huh. Okay. No, don't you worry. We'll figure something out. Thanks so much."

When she hung up Pascoe asked, "What did she say?"

"She wasn't able to find them. She asked if the police would be coming there to do a search. She seemed pretty worried her house would be trashed by the police. I think we need to make an appointment with her for a friendly search, you know, where she gets to watch so see that her home is treated with respect and everything is put back in good order."

"Call Miles to make it happen. Those diaries are looming more important with everyone we interview."

8. THE MEDIA GAME

PASCOE AND SMITH WANTED TO MOVE ON TO BLAIR'S friends next, but they had to get to City Hall for the scheduled press briefing. "How did the rest of interview go with Lily?" Pascoe asked.

"You didn't miss anything," Denise answered.

On the way to the station they discussed Lily and Sarah's band friends. "It's just like everything else we've been seeing," Denise said as she was driving. "We're looking at two normal kids with normal lives. Sarah tries to be a caretaker, star negotiator, and somewhere it got the two of them killed. I'll talk to the band director, but I've got a feeling that he's a dead end."

"Careful, Den. Don't go into an interview with a pre-conceived notion. You may miss something." Pascoe continued, "What did you think about Lily?"

"She appeared very helpful. And like I said before, Sarah's missing diary is big. Could tell us who might have had a beef with her."

"What I found the most interesting, was the fact there were several diaries. That's an item we don't want anyone else to know about except us. We need some time to talk about that later."

City Hall was on the opposite side of the block from the police station. Pascoe and Smith checked in at the station first. Chief Meadows saw them arrive and followed Pascoe into his office.

"What?" Pascoe said, annoyed.

"Tell me something while you're getting ready. You know, give me a little heads up on what you know."

"That's the problem. I don't know shit. But thanks to Judson, I see the vehicle inspection reports here on my desk. Can you leave me alone for five minutes so I can catch up with what I need to know? After all, you don't want me to look like an idiot on camera, do you?"

"Okay, I get it," Meadows replied and then mumbled something unintelligible as he headed out of Pascoe office, but then stopped and turned back to him. "If you don't have anything, you can't tell them that. You can say you can't share any information at this time. And that this is an ongoing investigation, and you do not want to compromise any leads."

The Chief meant well, but Pascoe had heard it all before. The grumpy old man wasn't happy. Neither was Pascoe. He could feel the level of frustration rising inside him, messing with his ability to focus. He shut his door and read Judson's reports.

Denise was conferring with the other detectives on their efforts. She was given a list of four potential ex-cons in the vicinity with a record worth bringing them in for questioning. Judson also left her with a report on what was found on Blair's phone, which was normal stuff a seventeen-year-old might have. He also mentioned that there were still no leads on what happened to Sarah's phone, which remained missing. Detective Branch, who was waiting for her to see him, updated her on his canvas of the supermarket employees, and their customers who made purchases with credit cards during the time the crime was taking place.

"We've got some vague potentials we need to run down," said Branch. "One is a past employee they say was creepy, two customers that remembered seeing a young couple on the frozen foods aisle, but no one recollected the two cars parked in the far corner of the lot. I also talked to the drug store manager next door to the supermarket to see if they went in there or if their security cameras reached their cars. Nothing. Hell, if they went in the store to buy ice cream, where's the damn wrappers?"

Pascoe appeared at Denise's desk, looking at Branch. "Hey Gary, how's it going?"

"Not great. Denise has my report."

"Hey, do me a favor, Gary, and see if the boys in impound found a diary in the girl's car or purse."

"Sure. Anything else?"

"That'll do it," Pascoe said.

Branch walked away and Pascoe whispered, "Are we ready?"

"I've got what there is, but it's nothing worth reporting. How about you?"

"Bupkis," Pascoe retorted. "Is there anything you saw worth digging into?"

"Judson left me the mall's security tape of the scenes with Carl Meeker in it. I ran it a couple of times. The camera views with him sitting on the bench are blocked by shoppers walking between him and the camera. I couldn't find a clear view of anyone near his backpack, but it does have him showing the phone to someone, and it looks a lot like what he told us. Maybe if we zero in on a suspect, we can see if he matches any of the shoppers that walked past Meeker."

"The only other things are two messages from Police Officer Worthy. I asked her to arrange interviews with the Thompsons and their son Vincent. She left me a note saying Mrs. Thompson sounded like she was unraveling, and that Vincent keeps avoiding her. It sounds like both families aren't coping well."

Pascoe didn't respond. Instead he silently led Denise toward Chief Meadows' office where an FBI agent was awaiting them. The FBI agent wasn't happy about being there. It was meant to placate David Rogers, Blair's father, who was raising hell with anyone that would answer his phone calls. A Texas Bureau of Public Safety agent came in, introduced himself, and sat with them. He had no contributions, and when they stood up he joined them as they walked toward City Hall.

Pascoe said to Denise, "I forgot to tell you. Judson left me the details on the inspection of the kids' vehicles. They couldn't find anything we didn't expect. The shell casings remain the only thing to go on. He's got requests out to all the local arms and ammo dealers looking for sales that match the shell casings found in the back seat. There were plenty of prints, but nothing on record. We're going to have to print everyone who remotely resembles a suspect. Oh, and most of all, no diary."

Mayor Coleman caught them before they walked in. "Detective Pascoe, did you find anything I need to know about?"

Pascoe walked closer to her and responded, "I'm sorry, Mayor. So far it's a dry well. I'll try my best to calm the community. We need to catch this monster, before he strikes again."

***

The mayor and the Chief of Police made similar opening remarks as they did the day before, but much more brief. The gathered press corps appeared restless, anxious and biting at the bit to hear the latest. Concerned members from the community had genuine looks of fear on their faces, and the tension in the room reflected it. Pascoe ran down the evidence: the cars, the shell casings, the cell phones, the security cameras, the dead-end lead on Blair's phone that was planted on an unrelated, innocent party and the status of the interviews.

After the expected first two questions from local television news stations, David Rogers, Blair's father, stood up.

"Tell us you have a lead on who killed my son!" he shouted, looking like a chained pit bull who wanted to pounce on Pascoe. "You have to have some progress. It's been two days! What aren't you telling us?"

Pascoe appeared calm and controlled. "I promise you, Mr. Rogers, we're being as forthright with you and the press as we can."

"You have to have more information than you're telling us—you have to!"

You could see the veins popping out of his forehead. Rogers' wife had a hold of the sleeve of his suit, as if trying to restrain her husband.

"I know you don't want us to compromise this case," Pascoe replied, the look on his face revealed that he was losing his patience. "Believe me, we all want to find who killed your son and his friend. If everyone lets us do our job, we'll bring the murderer to justice."

Without warning—in a total rage, Rogers leaped for Pascoe. Two patrolman who were monitoring the situation intervened, each grabbing Rogers, wrestling him back toward his seat. "May the goddamned murderer rot in hell! Justice needs to be done!" Rogers screamed.

As he was yelling, the officers took Rogers back to the office to calm him down. Pascoe looked at the Mayor, and then The Chief. No one seemed willing to take his place at the podium.

It became quite a scene as the community began shouting above the commotion. The crowd looked more like an angry mob, searching for someone to lynch. Several patrolmen entered the hall and formed a human barrier between the stage and the rest of the attendees. Pascoe stepped back from the microphone and let the crowd calm down. When they did, he approached the mic again.

"Look everyone, we're as disappointed as you are that nothing concrete has been identified. Everyone that can help is on the case. FBI and the Texas Bureau of Public Safety have lent us their expertise and resources, and we're optimistic that something will break soon. I wish there was more to tell, but there isn't, and as soon as something worth reporting emerges, we'll issue a press release."

Following the mayor's signal, Detective Smith walked up to the microphone. "Ladies and gentlemen, we all wish closure on this case, but let us keep our thoughts and prayers on the families of these innocent young victims. As you can see, this is a very difficult time for them." She paused and the room quieted down. Denise continued looking straight into the TV camera, "And again, we're asking the public to please contact the Dallas County Sherriff's office at 972-555-6078 if it has any information on these crimes. Thank you."

With those final remarks Pascoe and Smith stepped away and left for the backstage hallway. The quiet decorum Denise had earned while she spoke to the crowd was soon gone. The crowd began growing loud again, apparently disappointed with the lack of information. It appeared that the Mayor and the Chief were going to give final remarks, but they quickly changed their minds and joined Pascoe and Smith, anxious to get out of Dodge.

Pascoe said to Meadows, "Detective Smith and I have interviews we need to get to."

Without waiting for the Chief's response, they left City Hall. Denise took the wheel, as usual, but she laid a little rubber as she sped away from the police station. Pascoe, still tense from the briefing, was holding tightly onto the armrest as Denise weaved her way around traffic at a speed that would earn a regular citizen a ticket.

After finding some open road, they both took a couple of deep breaths and tried to relax a bit. Denise said, "Our first interview is with Donnie Marks, Blair's best friend. We've got forty-five minutes—just enough time for a fast lunch. If it's okay with you, let's just take the drive-through window at the burger place. I think we both needed some comfort food?"

As they ate their lunch in their vehicle, Denise a salad, and Pascoe a double cheeseburger, Denise said, "You should have seen David Rogers spring from his chair. If Officer Raymond hadn't caught him as he tripped on the cables taped to the floor, he would have been in your lap."

"I didn't see that, but I could see the looks on the faces of the press in the front row. I sensed something happened behind me. That's when I turned and saw Rogers being restrained."

"I think it's going to be uglier than we imagined," Denise stated. "The entire town is demanding answers. They're used to getting what they want. If not, they're going to run us out of town on a rail."

"Pascoe nodded as he chomped on his big burger 'with everything on it.'

They finished in silence as they pondered what it might be like if they couldn't find a prime suspect quickly, working long hours and having little time for their own families. Denise thought of her own children, more precious to her than ever before, safe and sound at home, and hopefully unaware of the crime they were working.

***

Pascoe scored the highest on all his exams and procedures at the police academy, and he was the first of his class to reach the rank of lieutenant. There would be a chief of police promotion for him in the not too distant future; so long as he didn't screw up. Everyone who knew him expected it. So was he now wondering if he was losing his nose for finding the bad guys. Quietly, he analyzed what the profiler said. This guy wasn't your ordinary crook or killer. He was smart—maybe real smart. He had heard about killers who like to toy with police, proud of their ability to stay ahead of any investigation, laying traps and dead ends along the way just to amuse themselves. That would be the worst scenario of all. It would take much more time to find him, and even longer to find enough evidence to convict him.

***

Harry Richardson, a reporter employed by the local NBC affiliate, had sat in the front row of the press seats. He had stopped taking notes after David Rogers went ballistic. Instead, he studied the faces of Chief Meadows and Lieutenant Pascoe. He'd never seen them look so lost, and he'd been covering the Dallas County beat for several years.

What Richardson saw now was opportunity. He sensed there was more than a murder mystery here. He could feel it. Emotion was as high as he'd ever seen from this citizen base. He knew he had to have the inside track. Harry had one very solid contact inside the Thomas Glen precinct; Liz Worthy, a policewoman whose desk jockey duties included the role of records specialist. Harry helped her get her brother out of an illegal real estate deal that could have bankrupted him, so she was in his debt.

After the press conference, Harry contacted Liz at the station-house. "Liz, I'd like to do a story on the teenage killings from the human-interest angle." He knew she had a soft spot for that kind of piece, and he figured it would elicit the most cooperative response. He was right. She gave him some copies of the reports on the initial interviews and crime scene observations. Had she any idea how valuable that information was, she would have asked for more in return.

Harry was confident that there were many aspects of this crime that had appeal for network coverage—the image of the victims, their families, their affluence, the impressions of a wholesome upbringing that dripped from the accounts of the investigators; and of course, the lack of evidence or clues. His experience told him this investigation was going to continue for quite a while, and that the community, maybe even the nation, would remain hungry for any news of developments.

Harry's strategy was to approach Lieutenant Pascoe. Harry expected him to delegate press approaches to a detective whose roll would be to put him off. So, the first item on Harry's agenda was to interview the parties in the police reports, and find some nugget of information he could use as trade bait.

Swapping information was the gold standard in investigative reporting. Typically, a news reporter cannot gain the confidence of the police investigator without providing valuable information in return. This is what Harry was best at, identifying an item on the clue list that might have been low on the priority list, but high on value if it led to something.

The one obvious unresolved item with that potential were the shell casings. Harry reported on a murder investigation two years ago where finding the store where the ammunition was purchased helped law enforcement identify the perpetrator. In that case, one of the witnesses was a consultant who knew how to trace munitions. Harry saved the man's name in what he called his 'resources' address book. The man was Edwin Wiese.

Harry sent him pictures of the shell casings. An email came back a few hours later, *Old West Trading*, in Arlington.

Harry immediately drove to the store and questioned Ike, the owner operator.

"Most of our purchases are from gun enthusiasts and beginners," Ike said, "The pros and experienced hunters buy in bulk from the discount houses."

"Do you remember any purchases from young adults?"

"Hell, I don't know. Wait a second." Ike dialed a number on his cell phone and said, 'Lou, come out front for a moment." A few moments later, a bald-headed man in his sixties, emerged from a door behind the counter. "Lou, this reporter is looking for a man who might have purchased ammunition from us in June. Didn't we just respond to the police on a similar inquiry?"

"That's right, a day ago. I told him about a twenty-something guy who was very squirrely. He wore a baseball cap and paid in cash."

"Why do you say he was squirrely?"

"I didn't think about it when I spoke to Detective Branch. It came to me after we hung up. It looked like to me that he always kept his face away from the security cameras. This guy must have been inside the shop before, and he wanted to make sure he couldn't be identified from the video."

"Can you describe him?"

"Not really. With the cap on, he looked like any other kid. The only thing that I remember about him was his wallet. It was like what you buy in an Indian souvenir store, the kind with the dark, leather stitching on the outside seams, like the way a moccasin is made. He paid in cash."

"Do you still have the surveillance video?" Harry asked.

"I doubt it," Lou replied. "We keep it for sixty days, and then it's recycled. I can let you see what we have. The police said they wanted to see it too, but I haven't had a chance to look through all the cartridges. You'll have to wait a while."

Harry looked at his watch. He felt he could sit an hour or so. "If you don't mind Lou, I'll wait here while you look for it." Harry opened his wallet, took out a bill, and placed it on the counter. Harry's payment for the trouble wasn't persuasive, but Ike had to complete the same search for the police, so he rationalized Lou wasn't going out of his way to help the reporter.

Lou grimaced. He didn't like searching records, but the cash helped. Lou also had a heart. Harry kept bringing up the two murdered teens and how their families were coping. A half hour later, Ike emerged from the storage room with the disc. Lou inserted it into his laptop, and the three of them watched it. Sure enough, the buyer's face was always out of view, and it looked deliberate to Harry, as if he knew where the camera was and he didn't want the image of his face to be recorded. Nevertheless, Harry knew he had something to trade.

***

The next day Harry came by the police station and talked to Lieutenant Pascoe. He spotted the lieutenant in the hallway behind the front desk. He whistled. Pasco looked his way and spotted Harry. Harry gave him a hand signal that he often used to ask to be let in. Pascoe nodded and approached the lobby door and opened it.

"Hey Harry, what do you need?"

"I'm doing a story on the murdered teenagers, and I'd like two minutes with you."

"We're not giving individual scoops yet. It's too early on this one."

"Aw, come on. I just need two minutes with someone...anyone."

"I tell you what, you know Chief Meadows, right?"

"Sure," Harry said.

"If he says it's okay, we'll give you two minutes."

Harry got to see the Chief after waiting about ten minutes, telling him he had something to trade. Harry eventually got a meeting with Detective Denise Smith, whose reputation preceded her. He quickly discovered that dealing with her would be more of a challenge than it was with the other detectives.

Denise's office was in the bullpen area of station. Harry didn't want to negotiate the trade where anyone walking by could overhear, so Denise took him into an interview room where she could record the conversation.

"I want to make this very clear," she said as they sat down across from each other at the interview table. "Thomas Glen is not giving you or your news station any kind of exclusivity with this case. Do you understand?"

Harry nodded.

"The Chief said you have information that is valuable to the murders, and our quid pro quo is that we share the information we have that directly relates to the value of your information. Is that correct."

Harry was taken aback by the brusque manner in which she delivered the rules. "Now…what do you think you have that we don't?"

"I was thinking about doing a human-interest piece on how this crime has impacted the community when I ran across some information."

Harry stopped right there, expecting Detective Smith to say something that he could play off of to weasel some news-worthy nuggets. Denise didn't bite. Instead she merely raised her eyebrows in a way that suggested he elaborate. "I get the impression that this killer, whoever he might be, is not a random guy, but someone who took steps to plan it and avoid detection."

"What gave you that impression?" Denise asked.

"No finger prints, no video observation, no weapon," Harry replied.

"Where did you get the impression we don't have such evidence?"

Harry was taken aback by how incredulous her question was. "Detective, I was at the press conference. I heard what everyone said. Don't you think I took notes?"

"I'd like to see them...because we said nothing of the kind. All we said was, nothing we had pointed to a prime suspect, which was true and still is."

"You're trying to play games with me, aren't you?" Harry was miffed by what he perceived as a stubborn attitude to avoid cooperation.

"No, sir. I don't play games. What game are you playing?" Denise folded her arms across her chest.

Harry shook his head. He was getting angry, realizing he was fighting a losing battle with her. Denise, on the other hand, thought his approach was condescending and amateurish. She wasn't about to play her cards without seeing his first.

"So, you have the prints of the killer, video identifying him, as well as other evidence you haven't provided the press?" Harry demanded.

"We have an ongoing investigation. I won't share any details which might jeopardize it. Do you get it now?"

Denise would never allow anyone to underestimate her, and if she felt a condescending tone from anyone, male or female, she shut them down quickly. She never apologized for what she termed a competitive trait, not a combative one. How else would an admitted tomboy, sports enthusiast, and soldier act in what many perceived as a *man's* job? She'd rather be called a bitch by patronizing males with egos too large for their brains than change how she performed her job.

Denise tried her best to appear sympathetic to Harry's failure to compete with her. "May I call you Harry?" she asked as she walked around the room.

"Harry's just fine," he replied. His eyes followed Denise as she slowly walked around the table.

"Now," Denise said with a little tilt of her head that exuded sincerity, "may we get down to the business of communicating about what's on the table?"

Harry realized he was going to have to fib to get his way. "The other day I happened to be at a gun shop I regularly frequent. I was talking with the owner about the two kids murdered, and he mentioned that the ammunition came from his store. I believe you know this, but I know that your killer is a meticulous plotter and a detail freak."

That got Denise's attention. Neither she nor Pascoe recorded anything in their reports about hunches or personal assessments.

"Look, Harry, if you got this from the gun shop owner, so can I," Denise said.

"Not so fast, Detective Smith," he argued. "You wouldn't have known to go back to him if I wasn't here, right now."

Denise knew, in all fairness, he was right.

"Okay, Harry, I'll play ball," Denise said. "I'll tell you how I've been looking at it, if you tell me what you've got. But before we go any further, you've got to give your word that none of what I say will ever be attributed as something you heard from me or the Dallas County Police."

"That's always how I work, and yes, you have my word," Harry said.

Denise nodded and Harry told her about the surveillance video and his conversation with Lou. She, in turn, told him about her suspicions that the killer knew the victims, that he was aware of surveillance cameras, and had planned it in advance. Harry suspected much of what she told him, but he didn't know that the police also considered him conscious of surveillance cameras.

"Now if you can find me a motive, you can play on our team." Denise said and winked.

9. GRIEF

DONNIE MARKS WAS AWAITING THE POLICE'S ARRIVAL IN THE teacher break room where they met with Lily. Donnie was a senior, but a year younger than Blair because he skipped a grade. They'd been friends since preschool. He was expected to be the class valedictorian, and already was headed for Rice University.

He was impressive and articulate as he spoke, but clearly grieving the loss of his best friend. "Blair was hoping to join me at Rice next year. We were all confident that between lacrosse, his excellent grades and all his extra-circulars he would land there. He applied for early action and expected to find out before the holidays

"I can't believe he's gone. We've been tight forever. Blair was special, not full of himself, you know? Things like this are not supposed to happen. Why Blair?"

Donnie turned his head away, and wiped his eyes. "I don't get it. There wasn't anybody even jealous of Blair. Last spring, he was voted class president. No one even ran against him."

Pascoe asked, "Has anything been bothering him lately?"

"If there was, I'd have known it. This summer we spent a month together in Europe on a school sponsored tour. We got back three weeks ago. It was the most time we've had together since he started dating Sarah. That cut into the amount of time we hung around together, but don't get me wrong, I thought the world of her. She was good for him, and he adored her. Since I've been dating Sherrie Hubbard, we would often all hang together. God, they were so much in love. Really, they were two of the nicest people I knew. It just doesn't make any sense."

The rest of the interview turned up nothing, except it was clear that Donnie was the last friend or family member to see Blair before he died. "I was at lacrosse practice with him. I'm not nearly as good as he was, but we've been teammates for ages. I knew he was heading to pick up Sarah."

"Did he tell you where they were going to meet up?"

"No. He just said he was seeing her later."

"Was there anything unusual about that?"

"Not really."

"Why do you think they were at the market so late?"

"That was one of the places they parked. You know…made out."

"Anything else you might know?"

"I wish I did. I haven't stopped thinking about it. Trust me, there's nothing that makes sense."

***

Vincent Thompson was at home resting before going to work in a few hours. He was lying flat on his back on his bed grieving his sister. He had a spikey, red stress ball his psychiatrist had given him months ago, and he was tossing it up in the air with his right hand, catching it with his left. He had lots of practice and to his surprise, was actually getting good at it.

He was still trying to process Sarah's death. At first, he thought it would be just like when playing a video game and dying. All that had to be done was to click the 'play again' icon and instantly another, new fresh life would be granted, allowing for another chance to make it to the next level.

He had always adored Sarah, coveted her, and a deep, dark dread was beginning to wrap around him from the inside out. He could feel his stomach clench, his heart skip a beat, and his skin crawl. Clicking on the 'play again' button would not bring her back.

10. DETAILS

DETECTIVE BRANCH, IN HIS ROLE AS PART OF THE HOMICIDE squad, was assigned to perform the tedious parts of the investigation. In that capacity, he tried to confirm everything Carl Meeker said in his statement. That meant visiting with his cousin, Lennie Duggar and Lennie's mom, who Carl said was his companion late Sunday evening. Before he left to find Lennie at work at the auto glass shop, he checked Duggar's record. He found a rap sheet that included two assaults on women, which were later dropped, a burglary, and a theft by taking arrest. He served nine months in the state's correctional system for the burglary, but that was his only prison time.

When he got to his jobsite, Lennie was agitated. "My boss doesn't know I have a record. You can't just show up like this," he told Branch.

"I called in advance. I spoke to Ron. He said you were at lunch. Didn't he give you the message?"

"You talked to Ron. Jeesh, he's my boss. I'm screwed," Lennie said. "So now that you're here, what do you want?"

"I need to know what you were doing Sunday night."

"Sunday…that's two days ago. Let's see…oh, yeah…I was home alone. What's this all about?" Lennie asked.

"The two high schoolers shot behind the grocery store."

"Oh, yeah. No, I wasn't alone. Carl was there with me. I almost forgot," Lennie said nervously. "We were watching TV."

"Anybody else there?"

"Don't think so. Wait, that's not right. My mom was there, but she was strung out."

"What's your mother's name, and where does she live?"

"Her name is Louise. Louise Duggar. And I live with her. 523 Burnt Sienna Drive."

"Where's your mom now?" Branch asked.

"Why do you need to know?" Lennie responded.

"It's all part of the same investigation. We need to verify everyone's story."

"Oooh, don't bother my mom. She won't remember a thing. Really, leave her alone."

Branch wrapped it up with Lennie and headed in search of Duggar's mother. She lived in a neighborhood not much different than Meeker's. An old Ford Torino, mostly a mass of rust, was sitting in a carport to the right of a mobile home that looked like it hadn't been mobile in decades. After no one answered the door of the circa 1960's factory built house, he walked around to the back. A woman, perhaps in her fifties, was sitting in a lounge chair on the deck, smoking a cigarette with her eyes closed. Branch walked up to her and introduced himself.

"Are you Louise Duggar?" Branch asked.

Without opening her eyes, she answered, "That's me. What did Lennie do this time?"

"Nothing, I'm here to find out what you were doing Sunday evening…let's say, ten-thirty."

"You ain't needing my alibi for nothin'. I'm not stupid. Just tell me what you need. I've stopped lying for all my useless family," Louise replied.

"It's about Carl Meeker. Was he here Sunday evening?"

"Really. My sister's boy has finally crossed over. Oh well, Sunday night was pretty much the same as every Sunday. That's the best night on TV. I was home, but I don't remember any visitors. I'm pretty sure Lennie was here most of the night. We fought over who got to watch TV on the flat screen. He wanted to watch a Cowboys pre-season game. I didn't. I won. He watched it off-and-on in his room on the little portable. If Carl was there, it wasn't for long, and I didn't see him."

"What show did you watch?" Branch asked.

"That series about the college kid arrested for murdering this girl he picked up in his father's cab. Check it out. You'll see I ain't lying." Her voice was low and scratchy from years of too many cigarettes.

That was all Branch needed. He wrote up his report, highlighting that Carl Meeker's alibi didn't stand the test of verification. What nailed it for him was Louise. He watched the same show she did.

Louise never opened her eyes during the entire conversation. Detective Branch wondered if she was blind or under the influence of a drug. She coughed, and then he saw it. In the pocket of her house coat was a prescription bottle of OxyContin.

On the way back to the stationhouse, the contrast didn't escape Branch. An hour ago he was driving through a community where it seemed everyone was wealthy, had the best of everything and all the advantages. A half hour away, he saw the flipside. He thought

JEREMY LOGAN & BRENDA SEVCIK

to himself, "Did Carl, Lennie and Louise ever have an opportunity to live the life of the Thompson's or the Roger's? Or were the cards stacked against them? Did they understand that there was always another way, or were they covered in so much social muck that it blinded them to alternative choices?"

He knew bad things like murder can reach anyone, regardless of social status, luck or hard work. He wondered what changes might take place in the homes of the grieving parents. Could they begin to head down a path of destruction to where they might be self-medicating to forget the hurt of losing a beloved child? What was this woman's back story? What happened in her life to damage her? With his introspection, Branch decided he could not judge Louise Duggar.

Branch, remaining objective, entered the report in the computer version of the case file, and placed a photocopy of the report in Pascoe's inbox.

Detective Gary Branch was also given the task of making interview appointments with the extended family members of the Thompson and Rogers households. Getting an appointment with Sarah's brother, Vincent, was growing troublesome. He worked the four to twelve PM late-night shift at a security software company on Highway 75. That meant he was most likely available from nine AM to three PM. But he kept coming up with excuses why he was unavailable.

***

Following the interview with Donnie Marks, Smith and Pascoe talked with the school principal, Blair's lacrosse coach, two teachers and the band director. Nothing they said stood out as interesting. When those interviews were over, they headed for the stationhouse, knowing more, but empty-handed. Pascoe and Smith were disappointed they had learned nothing worth getting excited about. Denise said, "We're making progress by narrowing down the list of potentials."

Pascoe gave her a "yeah, sure," look. "Y'know, with good kids, they usually make close friends with equally good kids. Like attracts like, I guess."

"They have their own form of radar," Pascoe absent mindedly responded. He was deep in thought. Ironically his own radar felt nonexistent. It was looking more and more to him that they were hunting a sociopath, who painstakingly, selected random targets. Among many, one thing was particularly bothersome today. *Rarely do killers of this nature refine their craft to this extent with their first victims. The problem with that,* he thought, *was that there were no unsolved crimes in the national database that resembled this homicide.*

***

Lieutenant Pascoe and Detective Smith were exhausted and frustrated, but they had a squad meeting they hoped might provide some leads. After Detective Smith gave a report on the recent interviews she and Pascoe completed, Detective Judson did the same. His targets were the persons on the list of locals with an arrest record that might suggest they could commit such a crime.

"I've got a couple of potentials," Judson said. "I'm in the process of confirming their alibis. But here's the most promising thing I found. One of the ex-cons I talked to, they call him Lone Star, put me on to a homeless guy that regularly scours the dumpsters in this neighborhood. He does his scavenging in the evening, after all the employees leave so he doesn't get hassled. I plan on finding him before morning."

"Now that's the story of a cop looking to be promoted," Pascoe said.

11. I AM IN CHARGE

THE KILLER, OBSERVING AND SURVEYING THE COMING AND going of the police, is quite entertained by their lack of progress.

Ants. Little ants. I have toppled an ant hill. The mindless creatures are running around among the spoiled granules of their former home, with the queen ant destroyed. They are clueless. They have no idea. This is more enjoyable than I ever dreamed.

I can follow their every move…they write it all down…and they're so prompt at keeping records. It's as if I'm in their head. I know what they know. Do you like puzzles? I am a puzzle inside of an enigma, inside of a conundrum. Nothing about me makes sense. That's why I'm valuable.

What I used to hate, I now love. I used to hate being underestimated. Now I love it. Nobody considers me. I see them, but they don't see me.

Being invisible used to grate me. It was a knife in my gut; being ignored and side-stepped. Now my invisibility cloak is serving me well. No one even glances. They think I am nobody.

And I am happy to remain so.

12. BREAKTHROUGH

IT WAS SIX-THIRTY TUESDAY NIGHT WHEN MILES JUDSON BE-
gan to look for Virgil Hempstead, aka The Verge. He was the homeless man his snitch, Lone Star, told him about. According to his
source, The Verge usually started his rounds after dark, closest to
his favorite domicile, the All Saints Shelter on Oro Valley Road.
Not only was it a meal and a warm bed, he usually received his
medication there. One treatment lasted two months or more and
controlled his symptoms of schizophrenia.

The Verge's episodes of clarity were such that he could cohabit
with strangers without incident. At such a time, he set up his meds
with All Saints. Although the shelter was not licensed to dispense
meds, this was an exception in the regulations to benefit those with
The Verge's special needs. The shelter representative would refill the
prescription with his doctor, and dole them out.

He had two distinct patterns based upon his preference for re-
ceiving medication: One was to wait until the urges became intol-
erable, and then go back to the shelter for another dose. The other
times, when he felt he needed a diversion and some excitement in
his life, when the voices came, he hung out behind the six-story

office building next to the strip mall. There was a dumpster behind it that held cardboard, paper and broken office equipment.

The Verge liked it there. Usually no food waste was collected in it that would create odors or attract rodents, making it more bearable. Sometimes the janitor and security guard would help him get what he needed out of the dumpster to make a bed for himself. His favorite spot was behind it and near the brick perimeter wall. In a way, the Verge served as a hidden early warning device if something back there wasn't right. Virgil didn't tolerate gangs, drug dealers or other unsavory characters.

Judson was lucky, The Verge was still at the shelter, noshing on three-day old bread and chocolate milk. This homeless man didn't look so homeless. He was clean-shaven and recently bathed. According to Rich Stewart, the volunteer male nurse at All Saints, The Verge was in the middle of one of his medicated periods. Stewart said, "Virgil is one of our longest standing patron-residents. He goes off the meds so he can have periods of sensory gratification and emotional exploration. On the meds, he appears perfectly normal, but that's when he lives in a dulled existence of little emotional stimulation."

Judson explained to Stewart what he wanted, and he agreed to introduce him to Virgil, who was talking to another resident, Too Slow Sam.

"Excuse me Virgil, I want you to meet Detective Miles Judson. He's a friend of ours."

Virgil extended his hand and Judson shook it. "Hey Virgil, how's it going?" Miles said.

"Not bad. I bet you want to talk about Sunday night," Virgil said.

"How'd you know?" Asked Judson.

"I've been waiting for you. That's why," Virgil answered.

"Is that right? Why so?"

"I heard the shots, and I got a quick peek at what he looked like."

"No kidding," said Judson.

"No kidding."

"Would you mind taking a ride with me?" I'd like for you to take me through your night leading up to the gunshots."

"Okay, but you got to buy me dinner afterwards," Virgil demanded.

"Sure. It's a deal," Judson said.

In the car and on the way to Virgil's first stop, which was the supermarket, where he borrowed his shopping carts, Judson asked, "Why is it that you're not like most of the homeless people I see?"

"Because we're not all the same. Take me for example—I have a college degree. I also have a job that I work two days a week. And, I have a cell phone, a mini, which is usually turned off. I hide it in my clothes. My problem is I've got schizophrenia. It's genetic, you know. Well anyway, I'm medicated right now. I can think normal, but I can't feel much—nothing excites me."

The two men talked in Judson's idling car with the air conditioning on. Judson was listening with interest to everything Verge was saying. "I'd been on my meds for several days. I knew what I saw and heard was real. That Sunday night I took one of the shopping carts here and headed for the dumpsters behind the strip mall. I got empty ink cartridges, a defective electric lawn trimmer, a dead car battery, a busted step stool and electrical wire. I take them for their scrap value, gives me some extra money. I go as far as the auto repair shop to scavenge, turn around and head back doing the same thing on the other side of the street.

Judson drove to the repair shop adjacent to the supermarket and parked where Virgil said he was rummaging before he heard the shots.

"I heard someone drive up and park. I don't like anyone watching me, so I ducked behind the repair shop's dumpster. I waited a minute or so, hoping they would get out and go in the store or leave. I peeked out and saw the car drive to the parking lot at the rear of the store. I couldn't see anything back there. The shots scared me, and I ducked behind the dumpster again. I should have run away, but I guess I had to know what happened. I could hear the car doors opening and closing, and someone talking, but not like conversation, like a man talking to himself. A few minutes later, I saw the same car drive back to the parking space it came from. A guy wearing a hoodie got out and headed in my direction.

"I thought he was coming for me, but then he started to run toward the side street. That's when the wind caught his hood. He pulled it back on, but I saw his face for an instant. He looked right in my direction. He scared the hell out of me."

"What scared you?"

"His face, man. He looked like Satan."

"What do you mean?"

"His hair was short, and a pointed brow…just like Satan." Virgil shuddered as if he could see him again.

"Do you mean his hair was in a…." Judson paused in thought. "A widow's peak?"

"Yeah, that's it," Virgil said. "A widow's peak. He scared me. For a moment, I thought I was in hell. Man, he scared the shit out of me...That's why I didn't say anything. You know, he might have come after me next."

"Virgil, would you mind riding with me to the stationhouse? We've got a sketch artist. I'd like for you to help him draw the face of the man that looked like Satan."

"It'll cost you."

"How much?" Judson asked.

"I don't want my name mentioned in any of your reports. I won't be a witness, and I want money for a shave and a haircut at the barbershop."

"It's a deal."

***

At the police station Judson was completing his written reports while The Verge was working with the sketch artist. As a courtesy, he called Pascoe to give him a heads-up on Virgil.

"I might have something, or it may be nothing," Judson said. "The tip we got about the homeless guy—he says he was in the store parking lot and heard the two gunshots. The time of day is right and his story appears to be genuine, but the description of the assailant is a little sketchy. I'm looking right now at the artist rendering of his face. He looks just like Satan from the drawings in my Bible. Oh, and I forgot to mention, our witness suffers from schizophrenia."

Pascoe didn't know what to make of Judson's news. Before he went home, he read the written report that Judson prepared. He came across mental health-related crimes in the past, and found a psychiatrist that was helpful in understanding the issues. On the way home, he called the doctor on his speaker phone. The doctor advised him that The Verge could be quite credible, and that he had treated high functioning patients with schizophrenia. The lieutenant sensed they had their first solid lead.

***

Denise Smith couldn't go home right after the squad meeting. She needed to complete her reports and enter them in the records. She was drained, and Zach and the kids were delaying dinner for her. On the way home, she called her mom. It was her habit to call her during her drive home to share the events of the day. Denise and her mother had their issues over the years, but they put all the arguments behind them when her father died two years ago. Now they were comrades. Her mother worked as a nurse in the Vet Center in Dallas.

When Denise hung up, she thought about her own children who often amazed her with their compassionate, thoughtful, well-balanced souls. Knowing she could give herself little credit, she often wondered where they came from. She had given birth to them, so biologically she knew, but they were so wise and loving—in short, so unlike her. All she could do was to be thankful.

Of course, her husband, Zachary, was a large component in the equation, but they still were better than the sum of their parts. Especially her part. She imagined all parents had similar thoughts.

Her parents were also preoccupied with their careers. Once she and her brothers all reached middle school, they hardly gave them much thought at all. Denise was certain her brothers did more parenting, looking out for each other while mom and dad were busy with things that didn't make much sense to her.

Growing up Denise promised herself she would never be a parent. First of all, from the example she had seen, she didn't think she had the patience to raise children. Secondly, she acknowledged her own drive and how a career was her calling. Denise wouldn't call herself naturally maternal. She liked children enough, but didn't trust herself to give them the attention she wanted as a child. That was the issue in her mind. She wanted more time with her parents than they could spare, and she didn't want her children in the same boat.

Meeting Zachary, of course, changed everything.

***

Wednesday morning brought some hope and humor to the homicide squad in the Thomas Glen station. The first order of business was Judson's report from the night before. They had a bona fide witness, but one who had issues. They all got a chuckle out of the sketch artist's rendering of the perp — a cartoonish depiction of Satan. Denise wasn't laughing. She stared at the sketch, wondering if it was a delusion or a facsimile, marred by the witness's paranoia.

After covering the latest interview transcripts, Pascoe handed out assignments. He and Denise had a ten o'clock appointment with the Thompsons. Among other things, they wanted to find out more about Sarah's missing diaries and Vincent's whereabouts on Sunday. The two detectives got in their unmarked Crown Vic, with Denise at the wheel.

When they first paired together as an investigation team, they fought over who should drive. They were both control freaks. Pascoe eventually gave in after several complaints from Denise about his inability to multitask effectively. Between the police radio chatter and her interest in discussing everything, there were plenty of distractions. After a few assignments with her at the wheel, it became obvious she was better at it than he was.

13. UNCOVERING STONES

WHEN THEY ARRIVED, DENISE PULLED INTO THE DRIVEWAY. Placing the car into park, she paused. Pascoe recognized this was her way of getting into character. She became hyper-focused, assembling the known facts and organizing her thoughts.

They both knew that Mr. and Mrs. Thompson were taking days off leading up to Sarah's funeral on Friday, spending time at home. After a few moments, Denise opened her car door with a renewed sense of purpose and Pascoe followed.

The Thompsons were still distraught, but trying hard to compose themselves. Mrs. Thompson invited them into the living room where they sat on the couch with the detectives sitting in high-backed, elegantly upholstered chairs.

"We saw the press conference yesterday," Rene said fidgeting. "It feels as if the entire metro area is watching us."

Denise looked at Pasco, who was looking at her, sitting stoically, his signal he wanted her to respond. "We're doing everything we can," she answered. "To be honest, there have been few leads, nothing to get excited about. And that's why we're here today. We're trying to find any small detail that might provide a hint that the murderer had previous contact with them."

Mr. Thompson blinked, and swallowed. Denise continued.

"Some of our questions will seem like we're prying or trying to find blame, but trust me, that's not what we're after. We're looking for any information that may link us to important clues. Are you okay with that?"

Rene and Doug Thompson nodded. Denise spoke in the gentlest voice she had. "Lily and you both said that Sarah kept her diary with her, and that she kept it in her purse or backpack. Is that right?"

"That's right," Rene said. "It's been her habit for years." Doug took his wife's hand in his. "Your policemen were here early this morning looking for them. They were very considerate. We looked everywhere. I can't imagine where they could be."

"They weren't at the crime scene and they're not here. What do you think might have happened to them?" Denise asked.

"I've been wondering the same thing. I expected to find them here—somewhere. We even looked in the basement and attic for the old ones. I so wanted to have her thoughts...so I could feel as if she's still here."

Rene began sobbing and Doug tried to console his wife. He wrapped his arm around her shoulder. "Where did they go?" Rene paused, then suddenly stood up. "Who would even want them?"

"Where did you last see the old diaries?"

"In her closet...on the shelf above her clothes. I saw them within the last two weeks. She was showing me her new cheerleader uniform."

"Do you know of anyone else who might have known where she kept them?"

"Honey, did you know?" she asked Doug.

"I didn't go into her room unless to talk, and she never talked to me about her diaries. I don't know if I ever thought about it." He looked at his wife. "Would Vincent know anything?"

"I really don't see him being very interested in that sort of thing. I think Sarah told him everything." Mrs. Thompson pushed that idea out quickly and easily.

"Okay, let's move on to everyone's timeline, and as you mentioned him, let's start with Sarah's brother," Denise said. "We haven't been able to talk to him yet. Do you recall seeing him leave the house that night?"

Doug responded, "Vincent left right after Sarah. He said something about work and left in a hurry."

Pascoe asked, "Did he tell you anything about it?"

"Not really," Doug answered. "How about you, Rene?" he asked.

"No, but that wasn't unusual. He almost never shared details with us. Only Sarah. You may have noticed if you talked to Vincent that he's a little different. We adopted him soon after I had a miscarriage. He's been tested for Asperger's Syndrome and counseled for ADHD, and in his case, it might be little of both, but none of the tests were conclusive one way or the other."

"I see," Pascoe commented.

"The main thing is that he's always been socially awkward. He's very sensitive about it. The only person that gave him comfort was Sarah. When he got frustrated, she could calm him down. He was seeing a psychiatrist. But he stopped a few months ago. Sarah and I were working on his returning to therapy."

Rene began to weep again. Denise paused once more, giving her time to compose herself.

"Sarah was gifted that way, and Vincent adored her. He protect-

JEREMY LOGAN & BRENDA SEVCIK

ed her, and she protected him. In case you're wondering, a couple of years after adopting Vincent I got pregnant. I carried her full term. Vincent was already having issues we didn't understand. But when Sarah was born, he seemed to get better. He took an immediate interest in her. It was like her being around soothed him. And what was surprising, she seemed to notice his attention to her like no one else."

"To be honest, we stopped worrying so much about Vincent," Rene continued. "Sarah was always there to iron out his problems."

"It sounds like they had a special relationship."

"They really did," Rene said.

Denise absorbed Rene's yearning look—how the mother longed to return to the past. "What a blessing for both of them," Denise said, then continued. "Can I get back to my earlier question; did either of you see Vincent come home Sunday night?"

"I think it was close to midnight when he came home, but I'm not sure. Doug and I were both up, trying to locate Sarah," Rene answered. "We began to panic when we couldn't reach her. We were on the phone with her friends and their parents. We even spoke to Blair's parents. Vincent really wasn't on our radar."

"One final question," Pascoe said. "Do you remember what he was wearing when he left the house?"

Doug looked at Rene, who shook her head. "I don't remember," he said. "Why would that be important?"

"Don't know," Denise replied, "but you never know. It's merely one of the many routine questions on our list. If either of you recall it later, please let me know so I can complete my report."

"Ok, we'll think about it," Doug said. Then he looked at Denise, "so you really have no leads?"

"None," Denise responded. "That's why it's so important we know every small detail which might help the investigation."

Doug looked at Rene with a pleading look. She shook her head.

"Rene, this may be important," he said. "Officers, shortly before you arrived my wife and I argued about this matter. It's been an issue in our marriage for a long time. I have no idea if this may help, but it might be of interest. I'm not Sarah's biological father."

"Doug, I'm not sure this really matters," Rene's tone indicated a last-ditch effort to quiet her husband, but she sensed her actions were fruitless.

"Rene has never told me who the father is. I just know Sarah's blood type doesn't match mine. My wife, officers, has not always been faithful to me." His voice was ridged with anger. "How do we know...maybe he had a part in this?"

"Could any of this information really matter?" Rene's voice was thin, as if she would shatter.

"It could. What can you tell us about Sarah's birth father? Did he have any contact with her?" Denise asked.

Rene looked at the detective. "I don't think so. I can't imagine that he would know about her. It was so many years ago. A client and I had too much to drink one night. I have never contacted him since. He might have known I had a child, but he couldn't have known Sarah was his. She had his same blue eyes. But I have no reason to think he has ever seen her."

"Do you remember his name?"

Rene looked at her husband. "Yes. His name is Brad Lindgren from Austin, worked at Bank of the Great Southwest. At least he did over eighteen years ago."

Doug looked as if he was ready to punch a hole in the wall, but he was desperately trying to keep his cool while the detectives were there.

Rene stared at her husband, trying to settle him down. Doug's body language remained defensive, his fists clenched, his jaw tight.

There was a pause and Pascoe seized the moment, "Did Sarah know any of this?"

"I never told her," Rene sounded tired and she sighed. She looked up at her husband, as if questioning if he said anything to Sarah.

Doug tried to control his agitation and tension "Of course I never said anything. I had been the father that raised her....I was the father she always knew. She loved me and I loved her...."

"As far as all of us are concerned, Doug, you are her father, Rene said. "There was never anyone else. Please believe that."

Pascoe and Denise were quiet. Experience told them the circumstances that the Thompsons were facing left people raw and vulnerable. They quickly completed all their interrogation and left.

The Thompsons, though, were not finished expressing their feelings. There was an uncomfortable silence as if husband and wife were complete strangers. Rene retreated to the kitchen for fear she might say something to Doug she would later regret.

Doug had no interest in allowing Rene any sanctuary or relief. He followed his wife. "Why don't we get it all out now? Just tell me who it was. Who was Sarah's biological father—this Brad Lindgren from Austin?"

"Oh, Doug...." She was drained emotionally. All she could think of was the times she wanted to have this conversation with her husband, but never had the courage. "I thought we agreed years ago to put this all behind us. We agreed we'd just enjoy the gift of Sarah we never thought we'd have."

"But we don't have Sarah any more, do we, Rene? God, I never thought I could hurt this bad."

"Does it mean that much to you to know the story?"

"The story. Yes. Just as much as I want to know who took Sarah from us," Doug was aware his voice was too loud, so he paused, and spoke more softly. "I want to know…where she started. How she began."

Rene looked straight at her husband. She was too tired to fight, so she surrendered. "Okay. I'll tell you exactly how it was. Maybe I should have told you right away, but at the time it happened, I couldn't think straight. Hell, I didn't want to think about it. I needed to survive. Plus…I didn't think anyone would believe me."

Doug remained silent as Rene shakily started to tell Doug what he demanded to know.

"It's not a nice story but we got our Sarah out of it… that's how I coped." Her voice sounded small and far away. "Remember when I worked for Taylor, Moore, and Martin? We had that big banking client in Austin?" Doug nodded. "I drove to Austin and made a presentation. The client seemed very interested. I wrapped up, and all the fellow bankers left the room — all except the vice-president. He drilled me on details. I thought he just wanted to see how confident I was.

"He insisted the two of us go out to dinner and discuss it further so he could get a better idea of how the deals would work.

"We met at the restaurant in the hotel lobby. The meal was outstanding. And he knew his wine. He ordered a bottle of red wine that we finished, and he ordered another one."

"But you don't drink red wine…"

"Anymore." Rene corrected him. "He started telling me how

beautiful I was, and he put his hand on my knee." She squirmed. "It was as if I was instantly sober. I came to my senses and told him it was getting late. I stood up to go to my room—alone. But I had been drinking, and I was unsteady on my feet." Rene rose. "Doug, I don't know if I can continue. This is very difficult."

"Finish," he ordered.

Rene walked behind the granite topped island counter. "He said he'd walk me to my room. I told him that I was fine, but I was sensing things weren't quite right.

"I insisted that I was okay, but that if it made him feel better he could walk me to the elevator. I tried to walk a straight line as if I was a teen who had been drinking and got stopped by the cops. I didn't want him to know I was vulnerable in any way. I know I walked as if I was completely stone sober. I know I did."

Rene caught her breath. Doug stood there, looking down at her with his arms crossed in front of his chest.

"I walked to the elevator, but he followed," she continued. "When it opened, I went to shake his hand, but I was more drunk than I realized, and unstable. He put his arm around my waist and walked straight into the elevator with me. No one was in it. The door shut." She paused. "I've been over this next part a million times in my head. I keep wondering what I could have done differently." Rene paused. "The elevator opened. We stepped out. I told him I had an early morning drive to Dallas. I had my key out. In those days, there were still keys. It had the room number on it. He walked me straight to my room, and unlocked the door.

"I won't go into the details, but Doug, I told him no, but he wouldn't stop. I fought, I even screamed. I have never felt more helpless in my entire life…at least not until now."

Rene walked over to a chair and sat down. Tears were streaming down her face as she remembered. Doug remained silent, emotionless. "He raped me."

"I woke up a few hours later, the wine was wearing off. I showered. I bathed. I felt so…dirty. I just couldn't stay in that room. It must have been after five in the morning, but I packed my bag and left. I never wanted to see that man again. I never wanted to remember."

Rene was sharing words that she hid deep inside her for so long. She wasn't sure what Doug was thinking as his eyes drilled into her. "I got in the car and drove home. I didn't get home until you had already left with Vincent for the day. The first thing I did was shower again.

"I went to work. I told my boss I wanted off the account. He looked surprised. He had called. That man. He told me the client said he was excited to partner with us, and really wanted me to be in charge of the account."

"So that's why you went and got another job," Doug stared at her with a quizzical look.

She had expected that Doug would have lashed out by now. Since he hadn't, hope filled Rene that he might understand. "Yes! You know I loved that job, at least until then. I needed to leave that place. So, I took the first job that came along.

"My partner in charge, Mr. Martin couldn't understand my move. But I couldn't stay there. When I quit, I didn't know I was pregnant. I just had to leave. All I knew is I wanted to forget. I never wanted to see that man again. Then I found out I was going to have Sarah. At first I told myself she had to be yours. I wasn't sure. Not until she was born."

Doug was shaking his head. "I knew in the hospital she couldn't be mine because of her blood type," Doug said. "When they tested her, I was unsuspecting. I was curious if she was a B, like me, or an O like you. I remember my college biology. She was A. It was impossible."

"At the time, I didn't have the courage to face it. I considered telling you I had a one-night fling. Almost a year had passed since the night at the hotel, and I didn't think you would believe me about the rape....I suppose I didn't want to equate that brutality with the precious baby that we had been blessed with. The baby we had hoped for." She looked straight at her husband, "Looking back on it, I know I should have told you that first day I came home. But I feared so much — your reaction — my weakness being made public. Then, as time passed, it seemed easier to let that memory sleep.

"I got a new job, and I thought I was safe there. I stayed clear of my previous employer, not letting anyone know I was pregnant. For sure, I didn't want him to know." She swallowed hard.

"But at the hospital, when she was delivered, I got two dozen yellow roses with a card signed, 'remember me?' I have no idea how he found out." She looked at Doug. "They were delivered when you were in the nursery with Sarah. I had the nurse remove them right away, before you got back. All the panic came back, and when you confronted me, it seemed easier to say that that it was a one-night fling, hoping you'd understand. I was so confused. But damn it! Because of that, that man haunted me for years...."

Doug stood up and paced back and forth in silence as he wrestled with unresolved issues he kept locked up inside him. "That day, when I saw Sarah's blood type, I was so surprised. I needed to know the truth. I believed it when you said it was a one night fling. But now—I'm confused and not sure what's worse. I'm hurt because you couldn't trust me with the truth. All these years I've felt inadequate. God! If you had told me the truth…you know how much hurt you could have saved me? And you! Jesus Christ! You wouldn't have had to hide this goddamned secret." He paused. "I could have helped you heal. We could have done it together. Rene, you should have trusted me."

"Doug, it wasn't me not trusting you. It was about me, denying it, trying to move on. All I could think of is we finally had a baby. I wanted to get over it and build our life with our daughter."

Doug stood motionless and glared straight into her eyes. It took all his self-control not to lash out and kick something. "I can't handle this. I can't."

He left the room and she watched him walk away. Although it was hot and humid, she stepped into their screened in porch, not even bothering to turn on the overhead fan to circulate the heavy air. Rene just sat there for a moment – her thoughts fragmented. Her eyes began darting around the room, trying to focus. She saw a bright yellow object under the loveseat. Rene perked up. It was a lighter and a pack of cigarettes her friend Michelle left behind after last week's girl's night. That night was one of her few last nights of contentment. Four of Rene's best friends were there, sharing their lives' ups and down's, laughing and turning disappointing stories into comedy. It had been a fun night.

A faint smile began forming on Rene's lips. For a moment, she basked in her carefree memory. Then Doug stormed in, standing in the doorframe.

"Rene, I can't be here."

"You're leaving me now? Doug, you can't…."

"Just can't stay. I'm afraid what l might say."

Rene just sat motionless, completely speechless.

Doug hesitated in the doorframe. It was as if he was deciding whether he should stay. He paused, was still, then turned around and left.

Rene said nothing as she watched her husband walk out. Time seemed to have stopped. The realization of losing her daughter, and now her husband, was too much to bear.

She wondered where the police officers had gone, forgetting they had already left. Her eyes darted around the room, but they were drawn back to the yellow lighter and the pack of cigarettes. Sitting quietly, she reflected. Rene had been through so many heartaches. The infertility in her marriage, the issues with Vincent, the rape by Sarah's birth father, the cruel murder of her only daughter, and now her husband leaving her. Rene realized she didn't deserve it. She visualized her fate was a row of dominoes, and once the first one toppled, the others followed and collapsed.

Rene shook one out of the pack. Flicking on the yellow lighter a time or two until a steady flame appeared, she lit the end of the cigarette and inhaled.

As the smoke filled her lungs, she coughed, trying to catch her breath. She looked up at the ceiling and laughed. It reminded her of the first time she was offered a cigarette. Same thing occurred. Smoking didn't happen then, and at least, *that* wasn't going to change.

***

One the way back to the station, Pascoe asked Denise,

"What was with the question about what Vincent was wearing that night?"

"You always tell me how important it is to ask all the nitty-gritty detail questions as soon as possible—that's all."

"I sensed there's more to it than that," Reed responded.

"The Verge, the homeless guy, he said the perp was wearing a hoodie."

"Do you have your radar on this Vincent guy, or is it something else?"

"I don't know. It's an uneasy feeling right now. But, we can settle it by asking his employer for the security video and the record of Vincent using his security pass that night," she said. "Also, let's get a report on this Brad Lindgren. There could be something there."

Pascoe nodded.

These are just itches I need to scratch," Denise said.

14. CLOUDS

THE POLICE CHIEF STEPPED OUT OF HIS OFFICE AND LOOKED around. "Judson!" He bellowed. "Into my office, stat!"

Startled, Judson paused for a moment, trying to recall if he had made any foolish gaffs recently

"Seems in Kansas a very similar crime to our grocery store murders took place last night. Two young love birds caught in the act." The Chief didn't disguise his disgust. "Placed in a dumpster, only it was in Red Falls State Park, near a town called Brunswick. Apparently, they went there for one last fling before school started. Its schedule is a week later than here. The investigation there suggests the kids surprised the murderer. Authorities found a campsite. Unauthorized, secret. The camper took most of his stuff, but he left behind a plastic lighter."

"Prints?"

"Yup. ID'd them to an escaped felon from Louisiana. Armed robbery. Timothy Peters. He was on a chain gang picking up litter alongside a road that bordered a canal. A gator came up and frightened the bunch. Somehow in the melee he escaped. Damned if they didn't notice it until the next morning."

"When was that?"

"One week ago today. Plenty of time for him to make his way to Dallas, and do his business here. I know, it doesn't all match what we're looking at, but there are enough similarities that it needs checking out."

"Doesn't give him a whole lot of time to make his way to Kansas and set up camp, though."

The chief waved that thought away. "Not a lot of time. But enough. And that's all we need." The chief paused. "Marked differences, though. They were not shot execution style, and they were placed in the dumpster, not near it."

"What's next, boss?"

"I want you to talk to the investigators working the case in Kansas. We need to make sure we're not looking for the same perp. After that, a damned press conference. That's what. J Q Public wants to know this kind of stuff."

"Other than some similarities, though, what really do we have? Shouldn't we try to align our clues to prove our suspect is in fact the Teen Killer?"

"That's why I'm talking to you now. See what you can do, Judson, but first, notify Pascoe and Smith. They need a genuine, fucking break in this case."

"Well, first thing I'd like to get a picture of the guy. See if he resembles the one that the sketch artist drew from our witness."

"You mean the wacked out homeless guy?"

"Yeah, but I believe him. He wasn't just in it for the haircut."

"Jesus Christ, Judson. You didn't pay the witness off, did you?"

Judson squirmed. "The guy just needed a meal and a haircut, no biggie."

Chief Meadow's face was magenta red. "Goddamn, it doesn't

matter if that sketch is the goddamned spitting image of our Kansas felon."

"It was just a meal and a haircut—less than twenty dollars…"

"For a homeless man who has no idea where he's getting his next meal, it's huge! That might be enough to tell you anything." The chief calmed down. "Well, he's mentally ill, right? Not too reliable anyway…"

"But, he's not dumb. And when he's on his meds, he's just as normal as you and me…I believe him."

The Chief shook his head. "Notify Pascoe and Smith of everything we've talked about."

Judson slinked out of the room, feeling deflated. This was a full dose of the grumpy old man syndrome that hovered over the Chief when things weren't going his way. Judson had been there long enough to recognize it.

***

When Pascoe and Denise returned to the stationhouse, Judson told them about the escapee from the prison detail that the Chief found. "Do you have anything else I can work on while I'm here running this down?" he asked.

Pascoe said, "Yeah, if you don't mind—give this guy a call," as he handed him the business card from the owner of Zenon Technical Consultants. Denise wants to look at his security camera tape and the entry log from Sunday night."

The Chief walked into the squad room. "Pascoe, I got the forensics on the kids' computers." He handed the reports to Denise. "She's much better at this kind of stuff."

"I almost forgot," Meadows said, "the last page is the report on the security cameras where The Verge claimed he scavenged. You're going to be surprised."

"About what?" Pascoe asked.

"You'll see," the Chief said as he walked out of the squad room.

Denise gave Pascoe the page on The Verge and sat down on her desk. "Just what we predicted," she said. "Nothing—absolutely nothing. They both have some Sunday activity, but nothing about what might have led up to their murder. What's so interesting about The Verge?"

"His story checks out," Pascoe says excitedly. "He's on the auto-repair shop's camera at ten-forty. At six after eleven, he's on the camera at the drugstore on the other side of the street. That's a gap of twenty-six minutes, just enough time to witness the shooting and head back to the shelter."

Pascoe walked by Judson's desk. "When you get off the phone, join us in the Chief's office." Judson quickly hung up and followed them.

The Chief leaned back in his chair with a smug look on his face. "It looks like we're looking for a guy in a hoodie."

Judson inquired, "Are you saying this homeless guy—The Verge—that his story checked out?"

"To the exact time frame," Pascoe said. "Do you think you can arrange another meeting with him this afternoon? I think all three of us need to hear and see him. If we all get a good feeling about him, we need more details…like the color of the hoodie, the perp's height, hair color, weight…the works."

"What should I tell the press?" the Chief asked, "They're hungry for anything, and the Mayor desperately wants to get them off her back.

Pascoe said, "Don't say anything about The Verge. Let him and his illness be our secret. Just say we have a possible witness, but not an eyewitness, who heard the shots and saw someone running from the scene. Tell them we have a long way to go to find out the identity of the fleeing suspect."

There were smiles all around as Pascoe and the detectives walked out of the Chief's office. Chief Meadows was a patient man, content with the knowledge that he had a precinct filled with smart, capable, cops with good intentions and a dedicated work ethic. He knew the case that the press was calling the 'Teen Killing' had a long way to go, but he could sense that the tide had turned.

Judson pulled out his cellphone and Denise followed Pascoe into his office. She sat down in one of the chairs facing his desk, waiting for him to say something.

"It's looking more and more like we have a random killing by a stranger. This Kansas perp...I don't feel it." Pascoe said not so confidently.

Denise nodded. "I don't either. I want to go back to the video and what the Verge said. Just because he was wearing a hoodie doesn't make him a stranger—maybe just a loner." Denise paused for a moment. "But in this heat, you'd only put on a hoodie to hide your identity," she said.

"Let's see if we can get a picture of Vincent, even if just his driver's license shot. See if the Verge could ID him."

"Sure, this Kansas perp, and what about Lindgren, Sarah's birth-father, as well? Maybe get them all in one video, along with some random guys to see if he recognizes anyone." Pascoe rubbed his forehead. "What was that guy Meeker wearing when we caught up with him?"

"I think he was wearing a hoodie on the mall's security tape," she replied. "In August, but the mall can be cold."

Pascoe noticed Judson standing in the doorway.

"Zenon just emailed me the footage from their Sunday camera. It's on my computer. He says the log of the security card usage is in a computer data file. He sent me a transcript of whose cards logged in. Who are we looking for?"

As they walked over to Judson's desk, Pascoe answered, "Vincent Thompson,"

Denise clicked on the video record in Zenon's email. Judson scanned the list of card entries.

"Here it is," Judson said, "Card access at four minutes after nine Sunday night."

Denise scrolled through the video. Wearing a short-sleeved, plaid shirt and khaki slacks was the image of Vincent Thompson sliding his security card in the card reader. The time of day indicator in the lower right-hand corner read 21:04 hours, August 3rd, or four minutes after nine on that Sunday evening."

Judson said, "It says here he left at eleven thirty-one."

Denise fast-forwarded the video to eleven-thirty. A minute later Vincent's image reappeared, wearing the same clothes, swiping his security card in the card reader. Denise slumped in the chair. Pascoe thought she looked dejected that Vincent had an air-tight alibi. He also saw in her wrinkled brow what he had experienced in the past as a look of doubt.

"Vincent has an airtight alibi. Besides, Den, you heard the

Thompsons. Vincent worshiped his sister. No motive." Pascoe stood up. "Let's go."

Denise walked in a cloud of unknowing and unconvinced as she followed her partner.

Walking back to the evidence room, Pascoe and Smith picked up the tape and gave it to the technical specialist. He ran it, and they watched Carl, wearing a maroon-colored hoodie, as he sat on the mall bench. Pascoe said, "Denise, tell the guy in tech services to make a copy of this for us. Ask him to send the video to us by email and place the tape back in the evidence room. Then meet Branch and me in my office."

Pascoe found Branch at his desk in the squad room. "Gary, did you finish the follow-up on Carl Meeker?"

"Yeah, boss. It's in your basket," Branch said.

Pascoe gave him a hand signal like he wanted Branch to follow him to his office. Pascoe fished the report out of his basket and read it intently. Denise walked in a moment later and was about to say something when Pascoe said, "Wait, I need to read this first."

Pascoe looked up from the report and sat back in his chair. "Denise, Gary, this is my fault. I should have either looked in my basket or asked you personally about your report. We need to re-consider Carl Meeker as our prime suspect. Our eye witness says the perp was wearing a hoodie, and Carl's wearing one in the mall security tape. And, as you stated in your report, his alibi cannot be corroborated. This report is over a day old as we sit here. Gary, do you think you could try to find Mr. Meeker?"

"Yes, sir. I'll get right on it," Branch said as he left Pascoe's office.

Judson said, "The good news is that I've got us a meeting with The Verge at four-thirty. Stewart, the guy that runs the shelter, said he'd hold him there until we arrive."

Officer Worthy strolled in, oblivious to the mixed mood of the office and looked at Denise. "I've got this report on the child sex offenders you ordered."

The team looked at her, perplexed. "The one Detective Smith ordered," Officer Worthy opened it up to read the name. "Yah, a Mr. Bradley Lindgren."

Denise exhaled loudly. She threw her head back, as if asking for time to process the news before she provided an explanation. Perhaps she was embarrassed about not telling everyone about her hunch that he might be a person of interest, but she didn't expect this. Where he fit into the plot was a mystery. It did nothing to illuminate; instead the cloud of bewilderment grew darker.

15. A TURN FOR THE WORSE

PASCOE AND SMITH DROVE TO THE SHELTER IN SILENCE, both wondering if the rollercoaster ride of their investigation was about to become more focused. Doubts, however, filled their thoughts. Pascoe wondered how he could have been so wrong about Carl Meeker. Detective Smith, on the other hand, was wondering how her radar could have been so wrong about Vincent Thompson. She broke the silence with a thought, saying it aloud.

"If it's Meeker, why does he steal her diary and not her valuables? And if it's Lindgren, why murder your own birth child?"

"I think you're trying to make too much sense out of this one, Denise. Nothing so far, has made any sense.

***

Inside the shelter, Denise talked with the supervisor, Stewart, arranging to send him a copy of the video so he could display it on the shelter's computer. In the video were pictures of Meeker, Vincent and Brad Lindgren, along with others, using them as control subjects so nobody could claim any bias in selecting a line-up. Judson brought The Verge into the office while Stewart told him why the police were back.

"Virgil, Detective Judson wants you to watch a video," Stewart said. "He brought these other two policemen with him. They're all working the investigation together," Stewart explained.

"Sure, no problem," Virgil responded.

As the video ran Denise said, "We want to see if you recognize anyone in it."

After running the video, Virgil didn't change his expression. Denise asked Stewart to stop the video. "Virgil," she said, "did you recognize anyone on it?"

"No ma'am," and what was your name again?" Virgil asked as Judson and Pascoe slumped in disappointment.

"Detective Denise Smith," she said. "How about the guy sitting on the bench?"

"Never seen him before," he replied.

"How about the sweatshirt he's wearing? It's a hoodie like the one you told us about the other day."

"What is that color—red? No, that's not the guy and that's not the hoodie. The guy in the parking lot was bigger, his hoodie was either navy or black, and it had some kind of emblem or small design on the front on it. Besides, the guy I saw looked like the devil."

"One more favor, Virgil," Denise said as she laid the pictures of Vincent Thompson and Brad Lindgren on the table. "How about these two, could they have been the guy in the hoodie?"

The Verge glanced at them and said emphatically, "No, don't you get it? The guy I saw in the hoodie looked just like Satan. Hell, he could've been wearing a mask for all I know."

Pascoe, Smith and Judson walked out of the shelter dejected. "Back to square one," Reed said.

"Hell," Denise said, "we can't even find square one. We're nowhere. We've got a witness, who may or may not be mentally ill, but no suspect. Zilch!"

***

Next item on the Pascoe-Smith agenda, was their interview with Vincent Thompson. Denise called him to make sure he'd be there. They drove to Zenon Technical Consultants, his employer, not expecting much. "Why don't you take the lead on this one?" Pascoe said. "I'll jump in if it appears he'd rather talk to me."

It was mid-afternoon when they arrived unannounced, surprising the owner. After processing them through security, he led the duo to the operating manager, and introduced them. Pascoe explained that they were there to interview Vincent Thompson, to see if he had any information on the death of his sister. Pascoe's tone was flat, unemotional, revealing nothing, to avoid giving him an impression that their inquiry was more than routine.

"Vincent hasn't been himself since..." his manager said as he shook his head. "He's always been quiet, keeps to himself, and reserved." The operating manager paused. "But since it happened, I've overheard Vincent crying. I've told him to take time off, but he just shakes his head. Says it's better not to think of her, that work distracts him." They were walking down a long corridor that was not lit very well. "I can't imagine...."

The manager's voice trailed off as they stopped in front of his office door.

Imagine what? Denise wondered. She made a mental note to ask him what he meant if they came back for follow-up questions.

Vincent Thompson was in his office when they approached his closed door. The operating manager lightly tapped, a moment later it opened. A sheepish looking Vincent Thompson stood in the doorway.

"Vincent," his boss spoke gently, "Some officers are here to ask you a few questions about your sister." They walked inside. His office wasn't much more than a windowless storage room with computer equipment lining the shelves, blinking and purring. It was a little cramped, with no chairs other than Vincent's.

"I don't want you to worry about the time, or getting your work done," his manager said. "Just do what you need to do. You know I'm pulling for you." He turned to Pascoe and Smith. "When you're finished, please come and get me so I can take you back through security."

"Vincent, I'm Detective Denise Smith, and this is my partner, Lieutenant Reed Pascoe. First of all, let us express our condolences for the loss of your sister."

"I've been trying not to think of it," he said as he looked away in the direction of a coffee maker in the corner of the office. "Can I offer you a cup of coffee? I just brewed it."

"Thanks, I'll have one," Pascoe said.

"No thanks," said Denise as Vincent smiled and reached for the pot sitting on the burner.

"Cream or sugar?"

"No thanks. I take it black."

"We're sorry to bother you at work," Pascoe said, "But we have some routine questions and then we'll be on our way." He pulled out his notepad from his inside lapel pocket, revealing his holstered pistol. Vincent glanced at it, his eyes opened wide as he rolled his chair a little farther away, somewhat taken aback.

Vincent seemed to transform himself in front of their eyes. The quiet, expressionless man they saw when his manager was there, had turned into a frightened young man whose eyes began darting around, looking first at Denise, then Pascoe. He focused his stare on a spot on the floor. Then he grabbed a red stress ball from a drawer and began squeezing it. The expression on his face and his exaggerated breathing appeared as if the air got sucked out of his lungs.

"Are you okay, Vincent?"

He swallowed hard and nodded, still staring at the floor, gripping the exercise ball even harder. Denise paused for another moment. She looked at Pascoe who looked puzzled as well. After a few deep breaths, he seemed more relaxed, but still uneasy.

"We've been told the two of you were very close, and we understand this must be difficult for you. We just need to ask you a few questions. Is that okay?"

Vincent looked up at Denise with a menacing expression on his face, nodded, and returned his gaze to the floor.

"Can you think of anyone who was jealous of your sister, had a grudge against her or would have any reason to harm her?"

"Everyone loves Sarah." Vincent raised his head, wrinkled his brow, and stared up at the ceiling, still pumping the little ball. "You don't know her."

Denise was accustomed to hearing people close to a murder victim continue to talk in the present tense, as if they're not really gone. Vincent's doing it didn't seem so unusual, but something in his tone struck her as odd and threatening.

"Vincent, can you tell me what you were doing Sunday night?"

"Why do you want to know about me?" Vincent asked in a defensive tone.

"Routine," Smith responded. "It's okay. We're asking all family members and friends the same questions."

"I see," he answered, more relaxed. "I was at work. A customer needed adjustments to his system on Monday, and I wanted to make sure it got done."

"Can you tell us when you arrived and left?"

Vincent paused for a moment and then looked away, avoiding eye contact. "I was here from eight-thirty to eleven thirty."

Denise paused, wanting to ask if he was certain of the times, but her experience told her she would have another chance to dig further. She changed gears, hoping he would open up more.

"Everyone experiences grief differently," she said. "Some people need a time-out to mourn, and others need a distraction to avoid dwelling on the sadness. You've been back at work...."

"You can't imagine how I feel," he snapped. "We were close. She was always there for me—the only one I could talk to when I needed advice. Who do I talk to now?"

"I see," Detective Smith said. She glanced again at Pascoe, but he was content to say nothing, as if he'd rather watch her question him.

"I have another customer who needs adjustments to their system," Vincent said abruptly. "They're in a hurry for it." Vincent stood up, looking at the door. "You can go now. I need to get back to work," he snapped, looking away from them. "I'll take you to my manager." He walked to the door, and escorted the duo out. "Follow me," he said, quickly walking ahead. He stopped and stood at the side of the door to his manager's office. When the detectives entered, Vincent shut the door behind them and hurried back to his office.

"Vincent seemed to be in a hurry," Denise said to the manager. "Does he often work overtime or long hours?"

"Not often. Not in a while, really. Vincent is a brilliant trouble-shooter, but as you can see, he's—special. If we give him a stressful situation, he shuts down," his manager shared. "We appreciate his talents, but we try not to alter his schedule or give him anything out of the ordinary. We try not to pressure him. So far it's worked well that way."

Smith and Pascoe looked at each other, recognizing some inconsistences, and thanked the manager. They weren't satisfied with the interview with Vincent, but realized pushing him would be fruitless.

"What do you think? Does he strike you as odd?" Denise asked as they approached their vehicle in the parking lot.

"More than just odd," he said. "I'm assuming we saw a tech geek who's awkward, perhaps disturbed. Did you have a different take?"

"Not sure, but he's definitely peculiar. One minute he's a nice guy, and then the next, he's a nervous jerk. I also detected what might be something like an antisocial disorder. I'd like to speak with his parents to find out what it is."

Whatever Denise was feeling, it wasn't letting go. As she got in her vehicle, she sensed Vincent was watching them from inside the office. She wanted to turn and look, but resisted the urge. Another instinct of hers, suggesting it was better if he didn't see her seeing him, but she couldn't resist the urge. Sure enough, he was watching them from the window just outside his office. When she looked in his direction, he didn't try to move away. He just stared back at her. A chill ran up her spine.

***

They drove back to the precinct, and Denise tried to talk to Pascoe about the inconsistencies in the investigation. "Let's brainstorm about the diary and everything else that doesn't make sense."

"Not now," he snapped. "I'm getting a headache. I need some quiet."

Denise couldn't remember the last time Reed had complained of a headache, but she could see he was definitely bothered by it. It had been a long day, and quiet did seem like a good idea.

Back at the police station, Pascoe walked into his office and closed the door. Smith was talking to Judson about the inconsistencies when Chief Meadows walked by. "If you've got a minute, detective, follow me to Pascoe's office. Lieutenant Pascoe looked a little pale and said nothing when the Chief and Denise entered.

"Got a call from the Mayor," said Meadows. "She says what I gave the press about our witness was shit. It didn't satisfy them, and the community is going ballistic. Whatever it takes, we've got to find something, anything that points a finger at someone. The mayor doesn't care if we name the wrong perp. She just wants some closure. But I care. Call me crazy, but I have faith in you."

Denise had a sour look on her face. "Well, none of us are going to give up finding our guy. All we need is a little break," she said talking to the Chief as he nodded in agreement.

"Yah," Pascoe said. "It would be great if we could offer something new." His face was turning brighter, and he rubbed his head.

"Well, it's been a full sixteen hours since we've looked at the timeline," Denise said. "Another try?" Smith didn't give up easily.

"Let's hit the situation room again. Maybe after a fresh look something will pop out.

The Chief returned to his office and they went to the conference room. To the unexperienced eye, the graphic content of the pictures pinned to the back wall would have been nauseating: the victims, eyes frozen, as if suspended in time—marking the moment life became death. Pictures of their blood-stained hair plastered against their heads, then one of a blood drenched back seat of a Toyota Corolla. They also had clips from the supermarket's security cameras of all the people in the area from before the time of death until the truck driver found them. Everyone they interviewed was sincerely and believably mortified, with a strong alibi. Neither the detective nor the deputy had a feeling that any of persons caught on camera were responsible. Both Pascoe and Smith had an instinct, a sense about people

Both sat at the conference table, silent, as they poured over pictures, files, and interview transcripts. Deputy Smith felt as if there was some critical information, right in front of her, but that she was missing it. From the look of Lieutenant Pascoe, he was equally frustrated. His face was still all red, and he kept rubbing his forehead.

"If you don't mind, Denise, I'm going to take a break, take an aspirin and try to take a fresh look at everything."

***

Denise had never seen Pascoe out of sorts. To her, he was almost perfect in every way. A few minutes passed. She couldn't keep the image of a sickly-looking Lieutenant Pascoe off her mind.

Denise decided to knock on his door. He was bent over his desk. "Reed, are you okay?" He sat motionless and quiet. In an instant she was at his side. "Reed?" He struggled to lift his head. Drool was coming out of one side of his mouth. "Reed, tell me your birthday."

His eyebrows wrinkled. He tried to open his mouth. Only guttural sounds came out.

She'd witnessed a stroke in the past and immediately recognized the signs.

Denise ran out of the office, bellowing "Call 911 immediately!" She dug in her purse, searching for aspirin. She found Midol, a few tampons, some Rolaids.

"Anyone have some aspirin?" She called out. Within seconds, a few aspirins and a Styrofoam cup of water were put to his mouth. Struggling, she got the aspirin in the back of Reed's throat, and coaxed some water in him. He tried hard to swallow, and choked a little, but Denise thought he got them down. The ambulance arrived in less than five minutes. The entire time Denise was talking soothingly to her partner. He never lost consciousness.

***

As soon as Pascoe was wheeled into the ER, Denise phoned his wife, Cathleen. She was the rock of the family. Having flexible working hours, she was usually home for their kids. The moment she heard Denise's voice, Cathleen sensed something wasn't right.

"I'm at the hospital. Cat, Reed might have had a stroke. He's in the ER, and he's conscious and responsive."

"Oh my God. Tell him I'm on my way."

Denise hung up and went into the emergency room lobby. Through the diamond-shaped window, she could see everything going on inside. It brought back some difficult memories.

Zach, Denise's husband, had a hard time years ago with the demands of his wife's career. Denise could be single-minded, ambitious and sometimes obsessive. There were times they had spats. Sometimes they parted angry with each other. Denise's dedication to her job and the long hours were the issue. Early in their marriage, Zach chose to adapt. The flexibility he had with being able to work at home meant he ended up being the caretaker for their children.

Every once in a while, when they would squabble about her long hours, Pascoe would sometimes overhear their conversation.

"Den," he said, "take a deep breath. Look at the facts. Be objective. Just like in your work. Decide what his motive is. What's yours? When you have it straight, call him back." He looked at her with an exaggerated air of authority. "Now get over it so I can have 100 per cent of your attention!"

Denise now prayed for Pascoe. She felt it was a selfish prayer. She didn't want him leaving her.

***

An hour later, Denise and Cathleen were sharing a couch in the emergency waiting room. Cathleen said that their morning parting had been routine. "The last thing he said to me was he was looking forward to coming home...watching some baseball and getting to bed early." Cathleen looked over at Denise. "Then we kissed and said I love you. He went to work."

"Cathleen, what can I do?" Denise felt utterly hopeless.

"You know, Reed and I have always been a team." Cathleen was reassuring. "We'll be okay here. My sister is at the house with the boys. The doctors say it's just wait and see. I guess these next few hours are critical. Denise, go home. Go home to your family. Kiss them. Love them, appreciate them...please."

16. RUNNING ON EMPTY

DENISE RELENTED, AND SOON WAS IN HER OWN KITCHEN, alone. Zach was in the bedroom down the hall, snoring. She could hear him through the open door. Again, she knew she should be exhausted, but she wasn't. She was edgy, nervous, uncertain.

Her cell phone rang, it was Cathleen. "He's in recovery, and the doctors are optimistic. He may have had a stroke, but all the tests came back normal. He's sleeping now. I'll make sure someone calls you if anything changes."

Denise hung up the phone, relieved but reflective. *I don't know what I'd do without Reed,* she said quietly to herself. "Well, Denise. A glass of Malbec, or a run?" She whispered to herself. She didn't want to wake up Zach.

She walked into the bedroom, through the bathroom, and into the walk-in closet. She grabbed her shoes, running clothes and Garmin workout band. The evening would be perfect for some exercise, and she quickly changed clothes.

Before flying out the door, she climbed the steps to her children's bedrooms, in deference to Cathleen's advice. As expected, Zoe was sound asleep. Still in the first few days of school, she had her clothes all laid out neatly on the floor near her bed. A textbook was on her nightstand. She picked it up, "Texas History". Zoe was in eighth grade, and so unlike Denise, was over the top meticulous, taking great pride in her appearance and grades.

"Love you like a rock, pumpkin." Denise bent down and kissed her daughter on the cheek. Zoe took a deep breath and rearranged herself in her bed. Denise tiptoed out of the room, gently shutting the door. She looked across the hall and noticed Drake's light was on.

Gently tapping on the door, she waited for a low-voiced invitation to enter. Drake was at his desk, pouring over a book.

"Let me guess," Denise queried. "Math."

"AP Calc," Drake confirmed. "This stuff is crazy! What's more bizarre is to me it makes sense and I actually like it!" The boy smiled.

Drake was not a geek. He was a good-looking athlete who was well liked because he accepted everyone's oddities, including his own.

"Well, you need to get some sleep, buddy. Eight-thirty class is pretty early."

"Remember?" He looked at his mother and smiled. "I'm a senior now. Late start. Don't need to be at school until 9:45. I can sleep until nine!"

Denise put her right pointed finger to her head, pretending she had a gun, and with her thumb mocked pulling the trigger. "Silly Mommy! I forgot! How lucky you are!"

It was as if Drake looked at his mother for the first time, noting her athletic clothes. "Are you going running this late, Mom?"

"Yeah, tough day. Need to release some extra energy."

"What happened?"

"Lots of crap. Long story short, Lieutenant Pascoe's in the hospital. They think it was a stroke."

Drake swallowed hard and looked with concern at his mom. "Was it due to a gun fight?"

"No. He was in his office. We worked in-house all day."

"Mom, tell me again what a stroke is."

"Kind of like a heart attack in the brain. Blood is cut off. Brain can't work without blood."

"Will he be okay?"

Denise whispered, "Honey, I don't know."

"Shit." Drake said. "I wonder how Jim and Keith are doing." The two families had become good friends and got together several times during the year. Jim was a junior and Keith a freshman.

"Call them tomorrow, eh?"

She was beginning to leave when Drake said, "Mom, please wear a reflective vest when you go out."

Denise smiled, walked up to her son, kissing him on the forehead. "Ten-four."

After she shut the door to his room she nodded her head *My children are—despite me, not because of me.*

Not wanting to wake Zachery, Denise crept silently back into her closet and grabbed her reflective vest. She needed to escape for a midnight run. Tip-toeing through the kitchen, she noiselessly opened, then carefully shut the back door. She stepped out on the patio into the night, and stared up into the sky, noting the stars were dimmed by the beautiful full moon. The air was crisp and clean, and the cicadas were sounding their call. It was a normal life cycle; life continuing as usual in the universe.

The bright yellow running vest Drake insisted on her wearing was an added layer she didn't appreciate. It was not only constricting, but the plastic fluorescent vertical stripes going down the sides would eventually cause sweating. There was no doubt, though. She had to obey her son.

Sighing, Denise pressed the button on her Garmin running watch, starting the timer. It dinged. Taking a deep breath, she slowly jogged around the back path to the side of the house, then down her driveway, taking a left until she hit the stop sign at the entrance to their subdivision.

The streetlamps were on, and she could hear the insects buzzing and hitting the lights above. She decided tonight with the illumination of full moon she would turn right onto Blackburn Road, eventually running to West Lake Road so she could dart past the two little ponds the neighborhood so lovingly called, 'The Lake'. There were no street lights in that subdivision, but she thought the lunar glow would be enough of a guide.

The rhythm of her feet striking the street sounded louder than usual as she ran. It was because there were no cars out, no extra human noise other than the distant hum of air conditioners. Tonight it was just her and the world. She felt exhilarated, as if she owned the stars.

The conversation Pascoe and she had that morning with Chief Meadows sprang quickly to her mind, and for some reason, she felt the need to replay it.

How long had he been sick? Why hadn't they noticed how serious it was before?

Denise turned back to the present as she was running past the ponds. One side of the moon gleamed and reflected on the still water. On the right, the dark, split rail fence could hardly be seen. There was nothing but calmness and peace. No matter what time of year, or day, or weather, these sights always helped Denise keep her perspective and clear her thoughts.

She turned onto Ranchers West Road. This neighborhood of multi-acre home sites, with large, southern houses became pitch black. The heavily wooded streets blocked the moonlight from guiding her path. From here she ran on memory and instinct, hoping no rock, fallen branch, or snake would interrupt her from going forward.

Her watch chimed one mile. If she were worried by the conditions, she would turn back and go home. She was determined to forge ahead, full of energy yet relaxed, and for the first time in days she was able to look at the macro-view of her role at work and at home.

She thought of her own children, Zoe and Drake, and how they were safely tucked away at home. With compassion, she thought of Sarah's and Blair's parents, and the unbelievably large loss, and how there would be no more hugs and kisses goodnight, and how they were robbed of their future dreams for their children. These sobering thoughts slowed her down. Denise couldn't help thinking of everything like a puzzle, trying to make all the pieces fit. She reflected on her own life, educated by her dysfunctional upbringing, acknowledging the fact that not all the parts come together for a complete picture.

Turning the corner, leaving Ranchers West, she headed up Kempton Road, where there were lights. Once again Denise could see the street, the outline of the houses and trees that dappled the side of the road. The run felt good; as if the stress that started in her head was flowing down her core and out through the pounding of her feet on the pavement. Every breath in then out, exhaled self-doubt, fear and sadness, but the rhythm of her breath and her shoes hitting the pavement was calming.

Reed still weighed heavily on her mind. She couldn't imagine working without her partner. On the outside, their relationship initially seemed rocky and doomed. They were both alpha-cops which meant they wanted to be in control. In the beginning, there were loud arguments which caused their co-workers to hide. The police chief was getting tired of the conflict, and colleagues were betting when one of them would get sent to a neighboring precinct.

Denise recalled the conversation that ended most of that. "Pascoe, dammit! Don't push the witness so hard. You scared the crap out of him! How is he going to remember when you make him feel as if he did it?"

"How the hell do you know he didn't?"

"You think that kid in there is capable of holding a hunting rifle, and from half a mile, shooting his big brother dead? You're crazy!"

"No," Pascoe smiled.

"Well, thank God you shut up and let me come in. Did you notice how afterward I talked to him, his entire body relaxed?"

"Yes," a Cheshire grin spread across his face.

"So when the kid was relaxed, he was able to remember... able to remember which one of his brother's buddies hunted."

"So," Pascoe stood up, gripped his belt and hiked up his pants. He walked over to the coffee pot and poured himself a cup "I got this witness's adrenaline up, so he was on high alert, but your calming, maternal questioning calmed him down so he could recall. Am I correct in my analysis?" His eyes said it all: a laughter and a taunt, asking Denise to put the pieces together.

"You ass! So you scared that kid on purpose. You primed the pump!"

"So you could get what we needed from him to help find his brother's killer." Pascoe was serious now.

Denise just walked away, furious but thinking. At that moment, she hated that he was right, but had to respect his insight. Denise had good intuition. He was equally perceptive, but different. Then it hit her—they complemented each other.

It didn't take long until all could see how productive the Pascoe-Smith team was; they had a certain synergy that was obvious, almost a kindred spirit of ying and yang. Even if they worked on the same case alone, they didn't come near the sum of what they could accomplish if they worked side by side.

South Kempton Road had a steep hill, but the detective's mind was so focused, she didn't even notice the extra exertion. Instead, she thought of how Pascoe had become the good big brother she never had. She relied on him for all kinds of advice; in her marriage, her career, and even where to take in her broken-down car. Denise's own brother was such a mess—in and out of jail, or a mental hospital. It was comforting to have someone she trusted as much as her partner to lean on. Zach was a great husband and father, but he didn't understand police work, the internal workings of the mentally ill, nor could he see issues in her marriage like her partner did.

The final turn came up and she was back on Blackburn Road. It was a slight downhill grade until she reached home. Once at the bottom of her driveway, she stopped, put her hands on her knees and caught her breath, taking deep, jagged gasps. She realized she was crying.

What would Denise do without her most trusted friend and confidant? They could almost read each other's mind; so different yet complementary. *Dammit, Reed. You had better get better. Sarah and Blair need you to solve their case.*

Shit, Pascoe. I need you, too.

17. AFTERMATH

DETECTIVE DENISE SMITH ARRIVED AT THE HOSPITAL AT SEVen the next morning. Cathleen was standing in the hall just outside his room. She had just spoken to Reed's doctor. "Good timing, Denise. They just told me he's going to be all right. God, I'm so relieved. He's had at least three test procedures already this morning, and fell asleep once he got back in the room."

"That's the best news, I couldn't stop thinking of him all night." Then as an afterthought, "Did they say why he had the stroke?"

"I asked. They weren't sure. They found nothing conclusive. They said something about a chemical response in his body that I'm not sure I understand. But the good news is that he's going to have a full and fast recovery. He'll need speech therapy, and some motor rehab, but it shouldn't take long."

"The office will be so grateful to hear. I wonder what they mean by a chemical response."

"I don't know. I was so happy to hear the positive prognosis, I didn't ask."

Denise almost broke into tears, but was afraid Cathleen might not understand. "Have you seen him yet?" Denise asked.

"I'm going in now." Cathleen hugged Denise. "I'll tell him you were here. Tell everyone Reed will be just fine."

***

Reed lay in his hospital bed trying to wrap his head around the fact he had a stroke. *"How in the hell did this happen?"* The signs were infallible; the headache, blurred vision, tingling on his left side, and an inability to speak. The most puzzling was why. He thought he was in good health, with only slightly higher than normal blood pressure. Now he was in the hospital, with talk of rehab, and doctors' appointments. Frustration welled inside him. He had to get his life back.

Concentrating, he tried to move his left arm, full of pins and needles. What used to be taken for granted was now a monumental effort. He was trying to place it on his stomach, pairing it with his right hand. There was minimal cooperation, but better than a few hours ago. Reed was determined. He was going to walk out on his own accord, open the door to his home and sit down in his recliner. He needed to return to being a husband, father, and homicide detective.

Never one to sit still, he felt as if he wanted to jump out of his skin, shout, or punch his hand through the wall. But his body was not cooperating. He reflected on a few weeks ago lying in bed with Cathleen. They both had stressful days. She talked about how she relaxed in her yoga class, and began showing him some breathing and relaxation techniques. He smiled as he watched her. Rather than learning the centering practice centuries old, he became aroused by how attractive she looked in her black yoga leotard. He smiled because he recalled that they both agreed afterwards there were more enjoyable relaxation techniques not included in the instruction manual.

He recalled how their lovemaking that night was especially passionate, deliberate and tender. There had been stressful times in their relationship, but the last few years had been solid.

Reed's thoughts turned away from Cathleen and toward his job. He was a cop at a time when it was hard to be a cop. He was happy to be a plain-clothes detective. Back when he was in uniform, it seemed there were as many people who hated to see him as those who were grateful that he was around. He pondered who was to blame: the media, the public, or the cops themselves. It was all a mess.

No doubt, there were bad cops. Reed had seen them. He saw profiling, prejudice, and injustice in the system. It made him feel as helpless as he felt in the hospital bed that moment; unable to move out of the situation.

But he still believed most of the fraternity he belonged to were genuinely interested in the public good. He had also seen cops get jumpy after witnessing their colleagues get wounded or killed. Some changed after dealing with the dark side of humanity. But there was no doubt about it, some people were just bad apples from the get-go, and some cops were rotten, period.

While he acknowledged the Black Lives Matter movement was relevant, he also knew cop's lives mattered, too. As well as red lives, yellow lives, transgender lives…shit, all lives mattered. And there were "deplorables" in every nook and cranny of humanity. No one was immune.

He thought again about his 'Teen Killings' case. The net was drawn far and wide, but the lack of an apparent motive continued to impede his ability to get a hunch as to who might be the killer. And whoever it was, he or she knew how to be careful not to leave any clues. Perhaps, that's what bothered him the most. The perp was sophisticated about removing evidence and cool-headed enough not to make a mistake. That usually meant the perp was either a professional or a psychopath. The idea of either made him shudder.

Pascoe noticed he was beginning to tense up again, and his deep breathing had stopped. He began to refocus on relaxing, starting with calming thoughts and trying to relax the tension in his face, neck, and working down to his feet. The discipline of the exercise began clearing his thoughts, relaxing him. He realized that although currently incapacitated he wasn't in any pain. Closing his eyes, he began assembling facts and details in the case. In his mind, he was having a conversation with his partner, Detective Smith.

"Smith, what do we have?"

"Either a premeditated murder, or an act of passion, as if the victims surprised him."

"Don't think it was a random act of passion. Appears too deliberate."

"Ok, then premeditation. Someone they knew. Maybe jealousy. Or for all we know, maybe the victims held something over the killer's head."

"Blackmail? Nah. Don't see that, Den."

"Jealousy?"

Pascoe pondered. He could buy that.

"Let's look at the candidates. Schoolmates?"

"Maybe, but who? Haven't we talked to them all? I didn't see any that resembled a candidate."

"Okay, an old flame or a secret admirer?"

"I'm sorry. I just don't see a high school kid sophisticated enough to pull it off without leaving a clue."

"That's not leaving us much to go on."

"Tell me about it. We've checked out Sarah's brother, and he has an iron-clad alibi. It can't be a parent. They wouldn't kill their own child."

"Reed, what are we missing? There's got to be something we're overlooking or something that isn't what it appears to be."

"Damn these selfie conversations," Reed thought. "She's right—I'm right."

The fact remained that Reed was in no shape to work, physically, at least not yet.

Getting ready for the fight of his life, Reed closed his eyes, and concentrated. Desiring a real-time conversation with Denise, he wondered when he would see her.

18. WHAT WOULD PASCOE DO?

WHEN DENISE ARRIVED AT THE POLICE STATION, THE CHIEF and the entire homicide squad were waiting for her report on Pascoe. Chief Meadows took the floor and announced, "Detective Smith is going to be interim homicide lieutenant until Pascoe resumes his duties. Miles Judson will assist." That announcement brought cheers, but Denise wasn't smiling.

Remaining professional, Denise never shared her distaste for Judson with anyone. First of all, he was as far removed from Pascoe as possible. Where Pascoe understood her femininity added a depth to their combined experience, Judson found it to be more of a distraction. The fact that Denise was married only made a Deputy Smith seduction more appealing for Judson. Her rejections only made his determination stronger. Secondly, Judson was known for bragging about his sexual exploits.

Pascoe was humble; Judson was arrogant and abrasive. The only thing the two had in common, and Denise had to relent, was they were both good cops, with remarkable records. They could get the job done. The Chief gave her his praises and walked out. And then it occurred to her, *just do what Pascoe would do.*

That worked, and in no time the squad was giving their reports and their two cents worth of opinion on the investigation. "What's the latest on Carl Meeker?" she asked Detective Branch.

"The latest is that he's AWOL," Branch replied. His mother kicked him out of the house, he's been a no-show at his jobsite, and his cousin and his friends say they haven't seen him in a couple of days. I'm not giving up on him, but it's looking like he's on the run."

"Gary, when you're not working on that, we need to canvass all the businesses around the supermarket for their security camera tapes for Sunday evening. The perp had to park somewhere and walk to the store and back. No one can be so smart to know where all the cameras are."

Branch said, "Almost forgot this—the evidence team found a bracket attached to the undercarriage of Sarah's BMW. Late yesterday afternoon, they showed it to me. I didn't think much of it until they found what it was used for. It is solely designed to hold a GPS tracking device. Here's what's so weird about it. Mrs. Thompson told us the other day when we returned to get Sarah's belongings that she and her husband had that feature on their cell phones. Why have both?"

Denise walked over to the dry erase board, it was their place to put what appeared to be irrelevant facts or questions, and began writing, *ask the Thompsons about the bracket.*

Judson said, "I stopped by the front desk and talked to the clerk that's been holding all the transcripts of public calls. There's about sixty, three of them are interesting. One looks decidedly different than the others. It's anonymous and untraceable. We need to hear the recording. The transcript says—*"her brother is more than a little creepy."*

Denise turned to Officer Elizabeth Worthy, the homicide squad expediter. "Beth, see if you can find out what Zenon Technical Consultants does. I want to know who their clients are."

Everyone looked confused. Denise noticed their bewilderment and said, "It's where Sarah's brother works."

Judson said, "You keep going back to him. What do you see in him?"

Denise, somewhat annoyed said, "Other than this anonymous message, nothing, except a feeling that I got when we questioned him. Besides, him still living in his parent's home gives him access and opportunity to the diaries. Anything else, Miles?"

Judson was quiet, so Denise continued, "Judson and I are going back to the school and Sarah's church. Maybe we'll find someone who knows something, but hasn't said anything yet. Tomorrow morning is the funeral for Sarah and Blair's is on Saturday. I'll be at Sarah's. Who is willing to go to Blair's?"

Branch said, "I'm working Saturday. I'll take it. What do you need?"

"We need you to bring your camera and to be on the lookout for any unusual emotional displays. I want everyone who attends in your photos."

***

The meeting broke up, but the desk clerk was waiting just inside the squad room, waiting for Denise. "The boy's father is the waiting room, Mr. Rogers, I believe. He said he wants to talk to Lieutenant Pascoe."

Denise closed her eyes and sighed. "Thanks, I'll take him, please escort him to Pascoe's office. She motioned to Judson to come with her.

David Rogers was not taking his son's murder investigation well. He looked like a time bomb, about to explode. Narrowing his eyes at Judson he said, "You're not Pascoe—where's the lieutenant?"

"He won't be here today, Mr. Rogers," Denise turned his attention to her. "How can we help you?"

Rogers paused for a moment. "I want to talk to the lieutenant, and if he's unavailable, I want to see your chief of police."

"The Chief is tied up with the District Attorney. What can we do for you?"

Rogers looked at Denise, then Judson. "Look, too much time has passed. I know the rule. If the police don't have a prime suspect within forty-eight hours, the chances are poor they'll ever find one. So, I figure you have one…and you're not telling anyone."

"I've heard that saying before," Denise said. "But like all such sayings, it's rarely that simple. We told you we'd let you know if we had something worth telling you. In short, we don't."

"You know, this isn't the City of Dallas. This is Thomas Glen. If I don't get any more than that, your chief might need to start looking for another job."

Denise looked at David Rogers as if they were facing each other in a staring contest. In her case, she was thinking how Reed would react to that kind of remark. She ran through potential Pascoe replies.

"Mr. Rogers, I bet you haven't thought that through. Where do think that kind of remark will get you? I'm going to forget you ever said it. I suggest you do the same. We're working as hard as we can to find out who murdered Blair. The time we're spending here is taking us away from our job." Denise changed tones. "We understand this is a difficult time. Now go home to your family."

He seemed to be mulling over his options, appearing somewhat weary. Denise walked over to Rogers, and placed her hand gently on his back as she walked him to the door. "We know you're upset," she said. "I can only imagine how difficult this is for you."

They walked out of the bullpen and down the hall in complete silence. Denise sensed that he got what he needed to say off his chest. She could hear the despair in his voice and words, deepening her resolve to help this father find some answers so he could begin healing.

Just as Pascoe would have done. Judson, in the meantime, was impressed by her ability to turn him around. It was his "aha" moment that Detective Smith wasn't just a pretty cop.

*****

As she headed back to her desk, Denise noticed Rene Thompson sitting in the waiting room. She immediately wondered what the odds were that both parents would walk into the police station unannounced. *Is something going on that I'm unaware of?* She asked herself as she walked up to Rene.

"Hello, Mrs. Thompson. What brings you here today?"

"He left me. Doug packed a bag and left."

Denise paused, looking a little shocked. She had witnessed what

149

must have been a wedge being driven into the Thompson marriage the last time she was at their home.

"But I'm not here because of that," Rene said. "I got inside Vincent's room. I thought you should know what I found."

"Come on in and we'll talk in Lieutenant Pascoe's office."

If Denise had her own office, it would be just like Reed's, neat and bare; no color drawings, family pictures or ivy vines in the corner. A white board, wiped clean. An old, darkly stained desk. A computer left on and humming and whirring, a reminder that it contained valuable information.

She ushered Rene in, and had her sit at a rolling, vinyl chair with a high back. "Rene," Denise spoke softly looking into her eyes. "I know you've suffered a lot of loss. I am so sorry. But if there's information that you have, we want it to be complete and accurate. Because of that, do you mind if I record this?"

Mrs. Thompson nodded in agreement. Denise turned on the recorder and spoke into it. "Today is Thursday, August 7th, at 2:38 pm. Can you tell me your name?"

"Mrs. Rene Thompson."

"Mrs. Thompson, are you aware I am recording this conversation?"

"Yes."

"You came today to tell us you had some important information that may help us in the case related to your daughter. Is that correct?"

"Yes. Only my husband didn't think…" Denise cut her off. She only wanted facts, not personal opinions.

"What information do you have, Mrs. Thompson?"

"I wanted to see what Vincent had to wear for the funeral, so I went into his room, in his closet and looked." She stopped, thinking very hard. "I saw a nice suit, and started looking for his black shoes. I found one, but didn't see the other. They needed to be shined. I knew as he was busy working, he wouldn't take the time or even think about it. Besides, I needed something to do."

It was as if Rene was apologizing, Denise thought to herself.

"I looked around the room for his missing shoe," Rene continued. I looked under the desk, behind the door, in the bathroom. Finally, I looked under his bed. I found this."

From her large handbag, Rene removed a photo album with a red leather cover, and handed it over to Denise. Denise slowly opened it, and on the first few pages were pictures of what appeared to be Sarah as a little girl, and sometimes an older boy, assumed to be Vincent. It was all very sweet. Denise looked up at Rene, sensing in the next few pages this feeling would change. Very deliberately and respectfully Denise turned page after page filled with photographs.

Soon Sarah was older. She was no longer a little girl, but a young woman. The pictures appeared to be more sensual and candid. The first questionable photo was of Sarah lying at the pool in a lounge chair, sporting a white bikini, looking sound asleep as she sunbathed. Other pictures were of Sarah coming out of the shower, covered in an oversized towel, oblivious to the camera.

Denise spared Rene the embarrassment and did not look up as she turned each page, each one being more secretive, more private than the previous page. There were pictures of Sarah in the back seat of cars, making out with boys.

Detective Smith intentionally closed the photo album and put it on the desk between the two of them and looked at Rene. "Mrs. Thompson. I understood why you feel sharing this album Vincent kept of Sarah is important." Denise was speaking not only to Mrs. Thompson, but for the record of the tape recorder as well. "At first the pictures are very sweet, when Sarah is young. It appears as Sarah matured, Vincent, her adopted brother, secretly took private pictures of her."

"Let me tell you, I have a degree in psychology. This kind of sexual interest between siblings, especially non-blood siblings, is not unusual. This alone does not indict your son in any way."

Rene Thompson sighed. "That's what Doug said. Honestly, I never saw this from Vincent. I was shocked to see that he seemed to be stalking her in the latest pictures. I didn't like it one bit. They made me realize how little I've been paying attention to him. He is my son, and I love him. But I also loved Sarah. It just felt as if I was holding something back, not being honest." Mrs. Thompson looked determined. "Given everything, I have decided to be forthright in every way I can. Detective Smith, I need to live with myself, get rid of all secrets if I'm to move on."

Denise, trained to listen, remained silent, allowing Rene to continue, "Losing Sarah has been devastating. But I will not lose my soul. I'm telling you, Detective, I want to be a survivor, not a victim. I want to honor Sarah; I want her proud of me. I want her up in heaven not to see broken people, but people who loved and cherished her. I want us all to remember the Sarah we lived with for over seventeen years; her laugh, her smile, her grace. Not this horrific crime. I want Sarah's legacy to be full of dignity, joy and goodness."

"I've been thinking about a lot of things lately," Rene said. "I know it won't bring Sarah back…but…" she tried to continue, but tears got in the way. Denise gave her all the time she needed to compose herself.

"Thank you, Rene."

Rene smiled, looking at Denise with appreciation. "I think that's all I came here to say," Rene said with a sigh. "The best way I can honor her is to help you find the monster who killed her."

Denise suddenly remembered to ask her something. "Rene, one thing before you go. We found what appears to be a bracket for a GPS tracking device under the bumper of Sarah's car. What was that for?"

"You're sure?"

"Yes, I looked at it myself."

"That doesn't make sense. We used that App on our phones that's supposed to tell us where her car is. Except, as you know, it wasn't working properly that night. We bought that car new. I don't understand why it was there. I guess you need to ask Doug what he might know."

They walked out of Reed's office, the album still in Rene's handbag. Denise accompanied Rene out to the parking lot.

"Rene, I want you to know this case is personal to me for a number of reasons. I want to find who killed your daughter so we all can rest."

"Right now, I feel as if that's impossible."

Denise could only give her a look like she understood.

"You know, you wake up one day and you realize that what you thought were your big problems are nothing, really. And you wonder how you can wake up the next day and the next." Rene paused. "My head knows the sun will rise again. My work is for my heart to feel it."

"I wouldn't say this to everyone, but Rene, I believe you will feel it."

"I just need to get through this next hour, day, week…But, thank you Detective." The women parted, each feeling connected in a unique way.

19. DOUBTS

NO PARENTS EVER WANT TO PLAN THE FUNERAL OF THEIR child, and David and Victoria Rogers were no different. Still not comprehending how their son could have been murdered, the house had been consumed by a painful tension. Vickie couldn't get past what she felt was God's indifference toward her son's life, her faith and her husband's devotion to him. Victoria Rogers was a sincerely observant and devoted Christian. Until now, she never had a reason that her faith wouldn't always be rewarded.

Sighing, Vickie walked around the living room tidying up. Their pastor would arrive shortly so they could begin planning the unthinkable: a final goodbye for their son.

Towards her husband, Vickie remained stoic, reciting but not believing, the words in the scriptures. Over and over she pleaded that Jesus would give David the strength to forgive and for her to understand. Putting up a front, she recited His teachings, about how we must choose mercy, forgive others so God would forgive us, about how Blair will rise again, and at the rapture they would all be together.

Was it all insincere piety for the sake of her husband and children, she wondered. Her children just didn't understand any of it, while her husband was wrapped in hate and anger. Vickie tried to soothe David, so they could all begin healing. No matter what she said, how she said it, or what she did, his response was always the same: he was furious and convinced Blair's killer must die.

Vickie didn't understand why God would take Blair, and at the same time, transform her husband into a man full of hate and vengeance. This was not the man she was used to sharing her life with. Vickie was struggling with doubt. She kept asking the same questions over and over.

Why did God allow this to happen to Blair? Are we being punished for something we had done wrong? How can I ever feel at peace again? Isn't God supposed to send some grace to help me through this? Where is it?

Vickie knew her husband was battling with his faith as well, but at a different level. David's Jewish prayer book was on his desk, and on top of it neatly assembled were his father's prayer shawl and little hat. She knew after his father died, he had also taken these items out. Years ago, when he agreed to become a Christian, she thought he had signed over his heart too easily to her faith. Maybe he had given her lip service without a true conversion.

Vickie's own crisis of faith appeared insurmountable to her. It was too painful to imagine that her son would never walk into their home again. Blair was her blessing, a first born with a heart of gold and a boast-worthy character. She was proud of Blair and doted on him, and he on her. She couldn't believe that she would never see his smile, hear his laughter, or hold him in her arms again. Blair was irreplaceable.

There had been so much sacrifice and hard work for her children. Again, she began questioning. *Was it all for nothing? Am I merely running on the hamster's wheel, sweating, straining, pushing harder yet never moving? I don't want to doubt, but God, what is the point? Why give me this perfect child, only to take him away?* She wasn't perfect, but her heart was a seeking one that wanted to please God and do his will.

The truth was crying out to her: Victoria Marie Rogers was in doubt that there was a merciful God, that her son was truly in a better place, and that she would ever feel complete again. She doubted there was even a heaven, where there would be no more pain, tears, and the wolf would lay down with the lamb. A place where she would meet her son again.

As if it were as easy as waving a tablecloth full of crumbs clear, she shook her head in attempt to clean all the confusion and doubts away. Pastor Dan was coming soon. They had to be ready. She could hear her husband next door in his study, pacing. Weary, she tiptoed to his study and gently tapped on his door, reminding him of the pastor's visit to help them plan the funeral service and choose scriptures.

His anger was getting out of hand. He had become belligerent. For the first time since they had the news of Blair's death, she petitioned God to send some grace on her husband. It was a selfish prayer. She needed peace. Peace from David's anger.

***

Pastor Dan expected this meeting would be difficult. He had dealt with parents who had lost their children to horrific accidents and disease, even suicide. But never cold-blooded murder. He wondered what he would find in the Rogers. Although not always, but often, he saw those deep in their faith make that transition quickly. He was optimistic that Vickie would be able to reach forgiveness, and hence, some peace, but he had absolutely no read on her husband, whom he knew was raised Jewish. In previous years, Pastor Dan had wondered if Victoria's husband ever accepted full communion with Jesus. The pastor's doubts were due to lack of participation in the bible study discussions and overall disengaged impressions. Reminding himself that Mr. Rogers's faith was not his to judge, he told himself his work would be to serve the hurting parents.

This will be delicate, he thought to himself. Before ringing the doorbell, Dan prayed that the Holy Spirit would fill him with wisdom, counsel and knowledge. All gifts he desperately felt he lacked at the moment.

"Thank you for coming, Pastor," Victoria said in the brave front she put on with her welcoming. She ushered him into the living room where her husband was pacing.

"So sorry for your loss," Dan extended his hand.

"Exodus 21, Pastor," David didn't pause his pacing, nor look the pastor in the eye. There was no accepting the pastor's hand.

"Pardon?"

"Whomever strikes someone with a mortal blow must be put to death."

Pastor Dan felt a deep and urgent need to calm him down. "Let's sit down, David."

"It's an eye for an eye. Blair needs justice." It was as if Mr. Rogers was on a military march, heading for battle. The pastor didn't think Mr. Rogers had even heard his invitation to sit.

In all his years as a pastor, Dan had never felt so helpless as he came to a quick evaluation. David Rogers needed more than he could give. His immediate concern was Mr. Rogers might need psychiatric care.

Then the pastor looked over at Mrs. Rogers. The look on her face showed equal concern for her husband.

"David. Stop it. Stop this self-pity and talk of revenge. I won't have it!" For a usually soft-spoken, gentle woman this boldness surprised both men. She walked over to her husband, grabbing both his arms, looking him in the eye. "Look at me. There are two roads we can take with Blair's death. And that is love or hate. And this isn't about God, this is about us."

He was now looking straight at his wife. Vickie continued. "I know you're having doubts with your faith. I am too. But let's think of what Blair would want. He wouldn't want you on a revenge-fueled rampage. He wouldn't want you embracing death and this consuming hate," her voice diminished to a whisper. "Blair would want us to embrace forgiveness, to support each other."

David shuddered. Slowly the grimace on his face dissolved. He closed his eyes and gently wrapped his wife's hands in his own, silent for what seemed like several minutes, breathing deep. Then tears emerged, slowly trailing down his cheeks. In a whisper he pleaded, "Oh, Vickie. I don't know if I can do it. How can we live without Blair?"

"With love, and sharing our fears together. David, I don't know how I can go on either. But I do know what Blair would want. And it's not vengeance. It's not hate. Blair would want us to live, and work, and remember him by caring for each other." Her husband nodded, unable to speak. "Let's make Blair proud of us. Let's send him off in a celebration of his life, not a retribution to his killer."

David clung to his wife, as if a child. "This hate. This anger. I feel as if I'm betraying Blair if I let it go."

"No, David, no. The best way to honor Blair is by forgiveness. Believe me, I'm not there either. I'm mad as hell, but that has to be our destination. Let's work together. Together we can do this." The couple looked at each other, then she turned her eyes on Pastor Dan, who slowly nodded his approval.

"I wanted that son of a bitch to die," David cried out.

"If I'm honest, me too," she said. "But this is what civilized people do who have faith in God."

They held each other and wept.

Pastor Dan decided to leave and return later.

"Pastor Dan," David spoke up. "Don't leave. We need to do this right. We need to honor Blair."

The pastor returned to the couple. The three of them gathered in a huddle and Pastor Dan looked up a prayer.

"Just a minute," David spoke and the pastor held his breath, "Let me get the other kids. We need to do this together."

David ran upstairs and retrieved the younger children. For the first time since Blair's death they were focused as a family. They spoke of joyful times with Blair, remembering the love he gave them and the spirit he exuded with every adventure. They even laughed with tears in their eyes at some of his silly antics and his sense of humor. They celebrated his life and said goodbye. By all appearances, the healing had begun.

20. FINAL GOODBYES

MOUNT BETHEL BAPTIST CHURCH SAT ON TOP OF A HILL IN the middle of forty acres in the growing northern Dallas suburb. Outside it was hot, clear and breezeless, as if God was holding his breath, waiting. The service for Sarah was to begin at ten in the morning. Private security officers were in a huddle taking orders from Judson. The uniformed officers were an additional deterrent in recent years to compensate for the increase in hate crimes.

Days earlier Pascoe had talked with the pastor, the principal, and both sets of parents. All agreed on one thing: Given the nature of the murders, and the lack of a credible suspect, they would bring in portable metal detectors as the mourners arrived.

"Think this will freak the kids out?" Pascoe asked days earlier as they acknowledged the necessity. "No." Denise was positive. "This is the post 9/11 generation. They've grown up with this. May even find it comforting."

As usual, Smith was correct. The teens, parents, friends and family began arriving just after nine. Without discussion, the teens placed their purses and back packs on the table as the security officers very thoroughly inspected them, before walking through the metal detectors.

Detective Smith arrived after Judson. With an air of authority, she assessed the tables, the metal detectors and nodded in approval. Judson was pacing nervously back and forth in the atrium of the church, watching the people filter in. He knew the perpetrator would sometimes go to the funeral, affirming the success of his work or reveling in the power he had to destroy the lives of others.

Denise stood in one spot, directly opposite the metal detector, observing. She was looking for anyone appearing out of sync with the mood. The teens walked in, somber and sad. Upon recognizing their friends, many of them stopped and hugged each other, with some escaped sobs. The comments she heard were consistent. This was not fair. It didn't make sense. This was not supposed to happen to one of their own.

One young man was waiting his turn. Denise noticed he dressed differently, had a different air about him. He seemed older than the teens, confident and sure of himself. He showed little emotion. It was the Goth kid in the photographs.

His dress was black from head to toe, but this was not funeral black. Denise had a feeling this was typical for him. He had long, dark, nearly purple dyed hair, parted on the side, straight down to his shoulders. His brown, deep set eyes rested above a sharp nose and chiseled cheeks. By any accounts this was an attractive young man, and he knew it. A deep red tattoo of a cross dripping blood was on his right forearm.

Denise immediately zeroed in on him, watching him carefully. She could see Judson in the corner of her eye watching him as well. Neither was surprised when he passed through the metal detector and it beeped.

"Jameson must have his blade with him," Denise overheard a

tall, athletic boy mutter to his group of friends. She noted that he was being frisked, and Judson was heading in his direction. She easily entered the group of teens.

"So Jameson usually carries a blade?" She looked at the boy.

"Yes, ma'am, but he's harmless," a pretty blond girl spoke up.

"He uses that as an excuse," another girl interjected.

"An excuse?" Denise invited.

"He's a total loner. Wants to be by himself," the athletic boy decided it was okay to talk with Detective Smith.

"If he's a loner, why is he here?"

The blond girl spoke up again, "He was in our band class. Plays the sax and the drums."

"And he's brilliant on them!" the other girl added with an admiring flush in her cheeks. She was wearing a purple flowered dress.

"He's pretty smart with anything he decides to do," the boy added. "He's also our best cross country runner."

"But he's a loner." Denise wanted the blanks to be filled in.

"Ok. I'll give you the skinny on this guy. His name is Jameson McGladrey. He lives with his mom in some apartment. Smart, but not college-bound because of her. She's not all there, can't hold a job. I think she's a little off, you know." The girl in purple pointed to her head. "He's extremely quiet, but you know he's thinking. What's that saying? Still waters run deep?"

"Sarah had a soft spot for him. He reminded her of her brother. She was one of the few people Jameson trusted and talked to."

"Jameson's okay," the jock defended him. "He's just quiet, but he adds something—a dimension—character to our school."

"We all like him," the blond girl said. "Even if he's weird. He's just part of us."

Denise thanked the teens and walked over to Judson. "Another person of interest," she whispered. "I'll tell you about him later."

When the police took away Jameson's knife, he maintained an audacious and cool manner. The officer looked at Denise and she waved him through. As he walked into the sanctuary, Denise quietly followed him in.

Standing in the rear of the church, Denise looked around, assessing those present. The large sanctuary was full of teens, parents, and other adults she couldn't identify, then near the front, Sarah's family. There was a murmured hum as people softly spoke. Denise wondered if she was the only one who knew Doug had left Rene the day before. But, there the two of them were, standing next to each other. A few rows behind Mr. and Mrs. Thompson were Blair's parents, both of whom looked as if they wanted to flee. She couldn't blame them. They knew tomorrow would be their turn. Denise wondered if they felt as if this was a dress rehearsal.

As if from heaven, organ music sounded from above in the balcony. The pastor walked down the aisle, then the pallbearers, one of them being Sarah's brother, carrying the white coffin. His face appeared grey, drained by grief.

All rose to say goodbye to Sarah Elizabeth Thompson. Whimpers could be heard from the congregation. Denise caught a glimpse of Rene, visibly shaken. Call it women's intuition, but Denise sensed Rene was struggling to keep her wits. Something was going on beyond having to bury her daughter, even beyond her husband walking out on her the day before. The source of this agitation was something else. She saw Rene speak to her husband, and look over at a man near a rear door. She grabbed her husband's hand and had a look on her face as if she'd just seen a ghost.

Looking at the man, Denise saw he was tall, thin, with grey hair and high cheek bones. He wore an expensive double breasted black suit with a coral colored tie. She texted Judson to make a note of him.

Being in the back of the church, Denise walked around outside, then entered a door on the opposite side to be near this man who caused Rene to shudder. Denise stood next to this man with confidence that he wouldn't suspect why she was there. He immediately looked over at her, assessing her, then moved closer to her. Denise began to feel uneasy. Her female radar was on alert. She pulled at her necklace, her arm protectively over her chest. Even though this man was impeccably dressed, and by any standards an attractive man, but there was something dirty and ugly about him. Denise could feel it.

As the pastor began his eulogy, Denise scanned the room. Most of the teens were holding hands with friends, crying, or trying to present a brave front. Denise realized how hard death was for teens, who somehow believed they could live forever. Raw emotion and sadness could not be hidden from view in the hurting community. Everyone seemed genuinely mourning.

Then her eyes landed on Vincent. His face was stoic and somber. While at work the other day he seemed distracted and distant, but today he seemed razor focused, impassive and in control. He did not display the same pain everyone else seemed to possess. Thinking of her own brother, who could seem to turn his emotions on and off, she assessed Vincent had the same skill. No one was going to read his mind and know what he was thinking.

With the eulogy over, and teens were invited to come to the front and speak their memories of Sarah. The man that gave Denise the creeps was getting antsy, and she wondered if he knew Sarah and was going to speak. He looked at Rene, the coffin, and the pews full of teens. Rene was watching him. He noticed and he stared right back. She shook her head, as if telling him he wasn't welcome. The moment of connection passed when Rene looked away.

The final announcements were made, and the organ played a recessional. Denise turned to the man. "This is so sad," she said as if she knew him.

He appeared to welcome her conversation, slowly turned to her, and raised his left eyebrow. "Indeed. How senseless."

Denise turned to look at him, and they held each other's gaze for an awkward moment. She was observing. She felt there was something familiar about him, and as she looked at him, she had a feeling she had seen him before, but she couldn't place where.

A moment later it came to her. He had bright, sky blue eyes, deeply chiseled into a face of perfect symmetry. Denise knew where she had seen them: in the photographs on the fireplace mantle in the Thompson's living room.

There was no doubt. This man was Sarah's biological father, Brad something or other. If she was right, then her instincts were also on target. Her first reaction was that there was something creepy about him, and now that made sense, being that they recently found his record where he was listed as a registered child sex offender.

What could be the motivation for this creep to be here? Did Sarah know him? Did Rene stay in touch with him? Detective Smith missed her partner's point of view. She wanted to look in Pascoe's eyes. Instead, she followed her intuition and began making conversation with whom, she was pretty sure, was Brad.

"I'm sorry to meet you under these circumstances, but I'm Den-

ise. A friend of the family." She offered her hand. Greedily, he took
it.

"Brad Lindgren. I'm a very old friend of Rene's."

Denise had prepared herself for this confirmation, and her emotions did not betray her.

"Do you live in Dallas?"

"I drove up from Austin. I heard the sad news on TV. I had to
come and say my final goodbye to Sarah."

"Did you know her well?"

"No. Not at all. Really, it was her mother I knew. Many years ago."

Denise remembered the conversation she had with the Thompsons.

"Denise, nice to meet you. I wouldn't mind seeing you again."
He opened his expensive double breasted suit jacket, took out his
wallet, and with manicured hands, retrieved his business card and
gave it to her. "Call me anytime you're in Austin and we can have
lunch. But please excuse me. I want to go to the graveside....my
last vision of Sarah." Denise nodded and smiled. When he turned
around and left, she looked at the business card in her hand.

Bingo. Getting that contact was easy, Denise thought to herself
as she opened her purse, dropped in the card Brad gave her, and
texted Judson to put a tail on the guy.

***

The burial was very sad, but nothing out of the ordinary, other than
Sarah's brother seeming so detached. Judson would be observing

Brad, so she let him go, for now. She had to get ahold of the young man who had been detained with the switchblade. As the teens were walking to their cars, she spotted him.

"Hello, Jameson," she said, startling him.

"Uh, hello," he replied. "Do I know you?"

"You shouldn't. I'm Detective Denise Smith, Dallas County Police. I hear you knew Sarah pretty well."

Jameson's eyes teared up. That surprised Denise.

"Yeah, I guess you could say that." He looked up to the sky in apparent agony, wiping his eyes with his hands. "She was my best friend; maybe my only true friend. I can't believe I couldn't see this coming."

"I'd like to talk to you about that."

"Well, I don't think I can go back to school today. So I guess this is as good a time as any."

Denise signaled to Judson to come over. "Miles, this is Jameson. Would you mind continuing to observe the scene while I talk to Jameson in the squad car?"

Miles nodded and Denise led Jameson to the Crown Vic. Once inside the car, Denise carefully measured her words to gain the boy's trust. "It's not difficult to see that she meant a lot to you. I have to admit, this case has been the most difficult of my career. Sarah had everything going for her. She didn't deserve to leave us, especially this way."

"I still don't understand how I didn't know she was in danger," he said. "We talked that Sunday. She was nervous, so not like her."

"What was she like, Jameson?"

"There were two Sarah's. One Sarah was the perfect child, sister, student, and friend. The other Sarah was tired of trying to be the person everyone wanted her to be. Her life wasn't as charmed as everyone thought. I got to know her in our sophomore year. I guess I can tell you a secret she made me keep. Can I trust you to keep it private, and that I told you about it?"

"Absolutely. We have a system for keeping confidential information under lock and key. We won't disclose it to anyone that isn't in law enforcement and not committed to keeping it confidential."

"She had been shagging with the dad of a family she babysat for. I never asked her who it was, and she never told me. After she met Blair she tried to end it. She wanted to put it behind her. You know, bury it. The only way she got away from it was by threatening to tell his wife if he didn't stop calling her."

"Did you have a sexual relationship with Sarah?" Denise asked softly.

"I guess," Jameson looked at Denise with trusting eyes. "We were each other's 'first', so we had this special bond. Texted every day. We really never dated. Somehow, we realized we're better friends that were never in love together. I guess you could say that we were both confused about it. We promised to keep it our private secret. That was the way she wanted it. But whenever we were suffering, we always were there for each other. It seems the times we helped the other get over a bad stretch…it ended, you know. I can't explain it, except that I've always had feelings for her. I don't know if I'm ever going to get over her being killed."

"Tell me about the past few weeks."

"She began texting me a lot. She said her brother was getting under her skin, and she was annoyed. But she thought he began acting funny lately and she wasn't sure if she could trust him anymore. She also said the last time she came home from school, she thought someone had been in her diaries; she said they seemed to be messed with, and since then she thought her mom was acting weird to her, so she assumed her mom had been snooping. But, I have a theory. I don't think it was her mom, I thought it was someone else.

"Okay," Denise said, trying to be patient, waiting for him to continue.

"I think it was Vincent who was reading her diaries. It's my gut feeling that he said something to her mother–something he read in the diaries. I've seen Vincent a couple of times when I was with Sarah–never at her home. He looked at me funny. It gave me the creeps. It was like he thought he knew something about me that he shouldn't know. I even asked Sarah if she told him about us. She said she never told anyone about us."

"Anything else?" Denise asked.

"Well, I suppose I should tell you that I called the police. I did it from my computer. I've got a program that'll disguise my telephone calls from my cell phone. I think I said something to try to make you investigate Vincent. I can't remember what I said."

"I think I saw that call. You must really have a strong feeling about him."

"He's a computer nerd like me. Sarah told me once he was a conspiracy freak that was into stories about criminals who could make the truth disappear. I never really understood what she meant. When I heard about what happened to her and Blair, I began to look into the websites that talked about criminals that got away with murder. It's all about covering your tracks."

"He works for an IT firm that specializes in security systems. Sarah told me he already had figured out a way to look like he was working when he wasn't. She said he thought he was so brilliant, he'd get work done quickly, then go home and play video games, or just stroll at night because he could get away with it. Sarah said he was all about getting away with things. Trust me, if anyone could cover his tracks, it's someone like Vincent."

Denise was writing on her pad, looking down. She noted Jameson's remarks, but changed the subject. "Where were you Sunday night?" Denise asked.

"I was wondering when you were going to ask me that. I was at Lindsey's house — Lindsey Gardner. We've been dating over the summer. Her sister was there."

Denise had more questions for him, but held back, fearing she might be asking too much too soon. She wanted to follow up on and verify what he had told her, then return, hoping to ask more specific, pointed questions.

She sensed there was something about Jameson, something real and sincere. She felt he could be a valuable source of information about an investigation that was growing ever more complicated and confusing.

21. A NEW DIRECTION

ON THE RIDE BACK TO THE STATION, JUDSON AND DENISE stopped for a quick lunch. "I'm afraid, you're the only one who spotted anything remarkable," Judson said with a mouthful of hamburger. "What did the Goth kid tell you?"

"I've been wondering if what Jameson said was crucial to our investigation, or if it's merely confirmation of what I've been thinking all along," she replied.

"And that is...?"

"He thinks our perp is the brother, Vincent." Denise said.

Judson became more alert. "Yeah? What's he got?"

"Nothing concrete. Just a gut feeling. He thinks Vincent's the one with Sarah's diaries."

"Then it's time to shake up this Vincent guy," Judson said excitedly.

"I don't know," Denise said. "It hasn't even been a week since she was killed. I think it's a little early to get that aggressive with the grieving family."

"Before you do that," Judson said, "I'd like to confirm the rest of what he told you. I'll check out his alibi for Sunday night."

"While you're doing that," Denise responded, "I'll find out from

Rene or Lily who Sarah babysat." Denise didn't mention it, but she knew she needed to ask Rene about Brad Lindgren's presence at the funeral.

***

Smith and Judson rode in silence the rest of the way to the station. Once she got inside the stationhouse, Denise called Cathleen Pascoe, and got permission to come by after work. She wanted to get her partner's thoughts on what Jameson told her.

Denise would rather call Rene Thompson to confirm who Sarah babysat for, but felt that call would have to be very delicate. She decided Rene probably had family at the house, since today was Sarah's funeral. Instead she chose to call Lily, Sarah's best friend.

Lily didn't pick up, so Denise left a voice message requesting a call back. Denise was still sitting in Pascoe's office, wondering about Jameson when the Chief walked in smiling. "I just saw Miles in the hall. He's all excited about some kid you made contact with at the funeral. Care to fill me in?"

"It's very premature, chief," she said. "Judson and I are checking out his alibi and confirming some of what he told us. If he checks out, yeah, we might be onto something."

Denise's phone rang. The caller ID said it was Lily. "Can't talk anymore, Chief, one of my confirmations is calling me." The Chief sat down, making it obvious he wanted to hear it firsthand.

"Detective Denise Smith here," she said after swiping her I-phone's answer indicator. "Hello Lily, we're expanding our circle of Sarah's acquaintances and neighbors. Do you remember who she babysat for over the last few years?"

They talked for another minute or two, and the entire time Denise was scribbling on her legal pad as Lily answered her questions. When she hung up the Chief was sitting like a bookie waiting for the results of a horse race,

"That was Sarah's best friend, Lily Evans. She confirmed the boy's story we heard at the cemetery. Apparently, our sweet victim, Sarah, stopped baby-sitting after her junior year in high school, and her primary client was a neighbor whose wife was good friends with Sarah's mother. Lily said Sarah told her she was never going back there again, but wouldn't tell her why. Sarah apparently didn't tell Lily this, but she told the boy, Jameson, that she had a sexual relationship with this dad. He wasn't happy when she ended it. She threatened to tell his wife."

"Jesus Christ," the Chief said. "I guess you've got a motive and a suspect, and a delicate one at that."

"Don't go thinking in that direction just yet," Denise responded. "Judson needs to check out his alibi. We'll get it in due time."

***

Denise looked at the notes she took during her call with Lily. The name of Dr. Phillip Edwards and his wife Claire, had not come up before — she was certain of it. While she was looking to see if he was in the registered sex offender's database, Beth Worthy, the homicide squad expediter, appeared in the doorway. Somehow there was an

odd parallel to Brad Lindgren. They were both successful business-
men, both attractive, yet both preyed on vulnerable individuals.

"The judge won't grant the search warrant for the Thompson
residence without a 'show-cause' hearing in his chambers, and you,
the D.A., and the Chief are on the invitation list," she said. "He's
available at three-thirty this afternoon or tomorrow morning at
eight. Do you want me to tell the Chief?"

"Please, Beth. Thanks for your help," Denise said

Back to looking at the sex offender's database, there was no
Phillip Edwards that matched Sarah's neighbor. A moment later
the Chief walked in. "It's two o'clock now—how about we see the
judge today?"

"Yeah, that works," Denise said.

"I'll tell the D.A.," he said.

After the Chief walked out, Denise recalled the times she assist-
ed Lieutenant Pascoe when he needed a warrant. He was almost always successful, and she wanted to emulate his process. In her head,
she began to picture it. She role-played. He often said, "You've got
to stress the risk of losing valuable evidence, and list all the indica-
tions that he's your prime suspect. I always write it down in bullet
points."

On her legal pad, Denise began to write down what came to
her mind. She sat back a moment just to relax. It was kind of a Zen
exercise to clear her mind and focus.

Judson came in and sat down just as Denise was performing
the last phase of her routine, doing stretching exercises, rolling her
neck, interlocking her fingers, and raising her hands high above her
head in a yoga-like pose. "Jameson's alibi checks out," he said. "I
spoke to Mary Ann Gardner, the mother of Jameson's girlfriend.

According to her, he's over there a lot when he's not at school or working."

Grabbing her legal pad and her pen, Denise looked up at the ceiling as if someone up there was talking to her. Without saying what she was doing, she added the final bullet point to her list of reasons why Vincent was her prime suspect–she was relying on a statement by a key informant–Jameson McGladrey.

"I'm on my way to Judge Carlyle's office. He won't grant our search warrant without a show-cause. Do you think you can make us an appointment with Sarah's babysitting client, the dad? He's an orthopedic doctor off Heritage Mill Boulevard. He might want a reason, so tell him we need to interview the victim's friends, teachers, classmates and associates. If he's our guy, we don't want him to prepare for our questions about Sarah or destroy any evidence that's still laying around."

"That's a Roger, Detective Smith," Judson responded somewhat sarcastically, appearing unhappy with her need to remind him how to approach a potential perp. "I thought you didn't want to get tough with the family so close to the funeral," he retorted.

"Getting the warrant now isn't so much about doing a search today, rather, it's about having it ready if we need it," she countered.

***

Before Denise, the Chief, and the D.A. began their argument for the restraining order, the judge had said, "David Rogers, the boy's father, visited me the day before. He demanded that I give a green light to every request for orders that landed on my desk for any-thing involved in the investigation of his son's murder. I'm sorry, but I wanted it in the record that no favors were given. Let's do this right." The court reporter took it all down and the judge granted the order.

It had already been a long and taxing day, and Denise returned to the station to gather her things and make sure she didn't leave anything that needed attention. She lingered at the station longer than she needed to. She had promised Pascoe's wife she would visit after her shift. Cathleen had called her earlier in the day, sharing the good news that Reed was being discharged from the hospital. She said he was anxious to hear updates on the case, but Denise wasn't sure that was a good idea.

There were a few reasons for Detective Smith's reluctance. First of all, she didn't want to stress him with the lack of progress on the case, and secondly, Denise was worried about what she would find in her partner. Her last visit at the hospital was sobering. The Lieu-tenant was not the way she was used to seeing him. Although much improved, his posture and poor speech still betrayed his ill health.

She understood the ravages of strokes very well from her par-amedic Army days. But damn, this wasn't supposed to happen to her mentor, partner and friend. He was only forty-three, fit, healthy and in the prime of his life. Denise also knew Pascoe would be impatient and frustrated. For the first time in memory, Lieutenant Reed Pascoe was not in complete control. As hard as it was for Den-ise to witness her partner, she knew it had to be more difficult for him and his family. She swallowed hard and made her way to the Pascoe residence, grateful for the slow traffic and extra distance to gather her thoughts before her arrival.

***

Denise rang the doorbell and Cathleen answered. Always composed, beautiful and shining, today was no different. The look on her face was one of complete gratitude as she hugged Denise.

"Thanks for coming. Reed needs all the distractions he can get."

"How are you holding up, Cat?"

"Honestly? I'm physically exhausted," She looked at Denise, "but full of hope. We have an excellent prognosis. Reed will have to work hard in rehab, but they expect a complete recovery very quickly."

"Well, if anyone can give 'em hell, it's Reed. Do you have a PT coming here to the house?"

"We sure do! Starting tomorrow— PT and OT—and they are forewarned. They will not be getting the typical patient. In the end, we'll see who will be working who!" Cathleen and Denise smiled and understood. The unsuspecting home health care providers will have one of their most ornery, challenging cases in history.

Soon the children filtered in from watching TV to greet her, and they exchanged hugs. Denise could see worry and fear on their faces. "Your dad's a fighter. He'll be throwing that football in the backyard with you before you know it! What does he call it?"

Ian's eyes lit up and the corner of his mouth twitched to a faint smile, "The Pascoe Pass!"

"That's right!" Denise raised her hand to a high five, and Ian eagerly met her hand. A lightness returned to the room, Cathleen beaming brightest.

"Denise, when you speak with Reed," Cathleen said, "what

we've found works the best for all of us is to ask simple yes or no questions. That way he can nod his head."

There he was in his pajamas, appearing comfortable in his Lazy Boy recliner. Resting against the arm of the chair was a walking cane. His face, pale but smiling a crooked grin because of partial facial paralysis, was a welcome sight to Denise.

"I came straight from the stationhouse," Denise said. "You look good. Are you feeling okay?"

Reed nodded, but in a manner Denise didn't recognize.

"I bet you'd like to hear the latest on our case?" Denise offered.

He nodded again, but this time more energetically, with a twinkle in his eye.

Denise knew she could not be condescending to her boss, so she was straight forward, treating him like she always treated him: full of respect, equality and a little deference. Quickly and efficiently she related all the recent developments. He was quite intrigued with Rene's visit, and disappointed about not being able to attend the funerals.

Reed reached over to her, and put his left hand on hers, displaying a noticeable weakness in his right arm, but the crooked smile on his face warmed her.

"Go home now," he said clearly. "I'm going to be just fine.... The worst part," he mumbled, "I want to be there...with you and the team."

Reed's smile was a reluctant one, showing the disappointment of his condition, but at the same time Denise could feel an underlying commitment stirring in her partner. He was not going to be down long.

***

In another corner of the world was Sarah's and Blair's assassin, smugly satisfied with himself.

I am too resourceful for my pursuers. This Lieutenant thought he was smart enough to catch me. What a joke. Mortals have been trying that for centuries.

This guy keeps his medication in the center console of his car. When he wasn't suspecting, I got inside his car and found blood thinners, aspirin and meds that expand the arteries. He's a perfect candidate for a stroke or heart attack. Endothelin is a drug that constricts the blood vessels. It looks just like aspirin. I found everything I needed on the dark web. I just mixed in a few with the aspirin, a couple more in his coffee, and bingo, he's off the case.

Let's see how smart his understudy is. It might be quite enjoyable watching little Denise try to catch me. I have to admit, though, she looks quite chic in her pants suits, but those black running shoes she wears have got to go.

22. LOOSE ENDS

THERE WAS NO ALARM CLOCK BUZZ TO WAKE DETECTIVE
Smith this day. She didn't stir until it was past eight o'clock. Only
the sunlight unblocked by the window blinds illuminated her bedroom. She picked up her IPhone from the night stand and checked
her calendar before pulling off the covers. Her calendar was empty—no need to rush to meet an appointment or deadline. She
couldn't remember the last time she was able to sleep in and also
had a restful sleep, free of tension and worries.

Denise hoped the day would be an opportunity to be distracted
from her career and unsolved homicides, and press the reset button.
Memory clutter is the curse of crime detectives. Denise felt that
if she could purify her mind for a day or two, she could find the
thread that ties the teen killings to the right suspect. Although it
was hard to resist the pull for her to go to Blair's funeral, she knew
her family needed her attention.

Being the interim lead investigator, she delegated the weekend
investigation chores to Judson and Branch. Together, they would
work the funeral of Blair Rogers, taking photos and notes of those
who attended or were conspicuously absent. They would report to

her the highlights of what they felt were noteworthy and call her if they needed her opinion. Nothing they sent her on that matter suggested she needed to insert herself.

There was no sign of Zach in the room, so he was apparently up and active. She found Zoe in the den talking on the phone with one of her schoolmates and Zach at the kitchen table with a cup of coffee in one hand and morning newspaper in the other.

Zach looked up and caught Denise's gaze as she surveyed the scene. "You look rested," he said.

Denise gave him a quick kiss on the lips as she made her way to the fridge. "I slept like a baby last night. It feels so good to have a day with nothing that I have to do. Where's Drake?"

"He left with Rick. They've arranged a pick-up basketball game at the park's courts."

Sunday, August 10, one week out

Judson was able to get a Sunday afternoon meeting with the father of the children Sarah babysat, Dr. Phillip Edwards. He called Denise while she was in the backyard with Zach, setting up for a sleepover party Zoe had planned. Judson couldn't arrange a meeting more suitable to her schedule because Edwards was leaving town for a medical conference in the morning. She wanted to confirm for herself that the doctor and Sarah had a sexual relationship, and she felt it was her job to lead the interrogation, advising Miles Judson and Gary Branch that she wanted them to be there to assist her. The interview was scheduled for two in the afternoon. Denise expected

Zach might be disappointed that she had to go to the precinct for an hour or so, but she didn't expect an argument.

"That's just great," Zack said upon hearing the news. "I thought we were going to do some yardwork together and take the kids out for hamburgers."

"We can still do that. I'll help you with the front yard, and while I'm at the stationhouse you can mow the backyard. I'll be back in time to help with the gardens and trimming the shrubs. Then we'll all go out to Mike's with Zoe and her sleepover friends for hamburgers.

"That sounds easy now, but it never goes as you predict. As usual, we'll get the short end of the stick."

"That's not fair, Zach. We're talking about two hours, tops."

"Suit yourself. We'll be here when you see fit to grace us with your presence."

Judson and Branch met Denise at the station early to set up the interview room for a tape recording and to plan how they wanted it to proceed.

"I want the two of you to watch and listen to us from the viewing room. See if I miss anything. Feel free to come in if there is an important question I'm missing. We're a team here, and I don't want to have to bring him in again."

Dr. Edwards was accompanied by his attorney, Grayson Crawford. Denise was familiar with his solid reputation as a trial attorney. Crawford looked to be a prematurely grey-haired man about fifty, and very dapper. Dr. Edwards was a slender, fit-looking man, no older than forty. He wore a yellow polo shirt, khaki slacks, loafers without socks, and a sweater draped over his back with the sleeves tied loosely around his neck. After cordialities and gaining permission to tape the interview, Denise used the early questions to gain comfort with the doctor and his attorney.

"We've asked to talk with you, because you're friends of the Thompson family. If you've been following the investigation, you're aware that we haven't found a prime suspect. As a result, we're trying find out as much as we can about the Thompsons, and why someone would want to murder their daughter. Do you remember when you first met them?"

Dr. Edwards took a deep breath. "Let's see," he said, "It must have been about five years ago. My wife, Claire, came to know Rene because of the neighborhood tennis team. They were teammates and became close friends. We've had them over to our home several times and we've been to their house a lot over the years."

"How about their children," Detective Smith inquired.

"I haven't seen much of the older boy. What's his name?"

"Vincent," Denise said.

"Yes, Vincent. He always seemed shy around us. Sarah, though, was quite friendly. She seemed to have a good head on her shoulders. She babysat our children for a few years. They adored her." The doctor's body sagged. "Such a shame. I expected a bright future for that young lady."

"Did she continue to babysit for you this year?" Denise asked.

"She told us that between schoolwork demands and her boyfriend she no longer had time. We had to find another babysitter."

"Did you have much contact with her?"

"I was the one that drove her home most of the time. It's about a mile between our houses. Sometimes her parents would drop her off or Claire would pick her up, and the other times she'd walk here, but I didn't want her walking home late at night in the dark."

"How would you consider your relationship with her?"

Edwards glanced quickly at his attorney, which Denise recognized as a "tell", a term used by poker players indicating a gesture that, in this instance, signified stress or lack of confidence. "I would say it was cordial," he stated, blinking several times, another "tell" confirming his discomfort with the question.

"Would you consider her affectionate?" Denise asked calmly.

Edwards cleared his throat and responded, "What do mean by that?"

"Just what it means," Denise said. "Would you consider her an affectionate girl?"

Denise glanced at his attorney, who was squirming in his chair, but refused to look back at Edwards again. Denise considered his silence or failure to intercede as his best effort not to give Denise the satisfaction that she was asking the question that probably led to him being hired to accompany his client to the interview.

"What are you getting at?" Dr. Edwards replied.

"Her boyfriend's father–the boy who was murdered along with her in his car–he thought Sarah was demonstrably affectionate, maybe clingy. I was wondering if you noticed the same thing."

Edwards seemed to relax a little, breathing more easily. "No, I don't think I ever noticed that."

"Had you seen her with her boyfriend?"

"I don't think so."

"How about Jameson McGladrey?" Denise asked.

"Who's he?" Edwards replied.

"He's a boy she dated before Blair Rogers. I think he's been over to the Thompson home with her several times."

"I can't say that I have. In fact, I don't think I've ever seen Sarah with a boyfriend. Do you think an old boyfriend may have killed her?"

Denise didn't answer. Instead, she cleared her throat stared at her notes, searching for the right words to catch the doctor off guard. "When did Sarah tell you she didn't want to have sex with you anymore?"

"What?" the doctor shouted. "Where did you get that from?" His face turned red, the veins in his neck popped up, as he slammed his hands on the table. His attorney restrained him, preventing him from standing up.

"It's okay, Phillip," his attorney said. "Take it easy. Come on."

Dr. Edwards calmed down and his attorney released the bear hug that was needed to keep him from going after Detective Smith."

"Look, Detective," Crawford said, "I'm advising my client not to respond to such groundless accusations."

Denise shrugged off the comment by his attorney and continued as if he had said nothing. "What if I told you that Sarah kept a diary? Dr. Edwards, I also have a close friend of Sarah's who said you two were having an affair, and she recently told you to stop hounding her. This friend also told us that she threatened to tell your wife if you didn't leave her alone."

"That's bullshit," Edwards shouted as he tried to stand up again.

His attorney had to restrain him again, but Edwards vigorously resisted. As the attorney wrestled with Edwards, he said to Detective Smith, "This interview is over." The attorney guided him to the door

Denise stopped the men. "This interview is over when I say it is. Unless you want me to make a big deal and get a subpoena, repeating the same questions over and over, I'd advise you to sit down." Her tone was no nonsense, and the men retreated to their seats.

"Doctor Edwards," she continued, "we have excellent sources which point to this affair between you and Sarah. That alone does not make you a killer, but certainly a person of interest. You are to remain in town. Your attorney can advise you that we are well within the law to require you to do so.

Judson and Branch entered the interview room as back up for the detective, if she needed it.

"All lies," Edwards said as his attorney motioned him to be silent. "Lies, I never touched her."

"Detective Smith, I suggest that we end the interview now. My client is too distressed by your accusations to remain here and take this abuse without time to think clearly. I am instructing my client not to respond to any more of your questions. When you have something substantive, please contact me."

"Go, but stay in town," Denise ordered. "And Dr. Edwards… this is not over, and I won't be going away. If you're innocent, you need to help us, and if you can think of anything Sarah may have told you that would help us find her killer, it'll be in your best interests to do so."

The pair got up, breaking the high tension in the room, and walked out.

"Jesus," detective Branch commented, "You could have told me what you were going to ask him."

"What do you think, Gary?" she asked. "Did he act like it never happened?"

"You got me."

"What if you had a relationship with a minor girl and the police accused you—how would you react?"

Detective Branch paused. "Probably the way he did."

"Yeah, I thought so," Denise said. "If you didn't do it, you'd be insulted, but in control of yourself."

"By the way, when did you find her diary?" he asked.

"Who said I had it?"

"But…"

"Listen to the recording of the interview, Gary. All I said was that she kept a diary. I didn't say I had it, or had read it."

The two men looked at her and realized why she was the one chosen to substitute for Pascoe while he was convalescing.

***

Patrolwoman Elizabeth Worthy was waiting for Denise to return from the interview. "Detective Smith," she said, "Harry Richardson is waiting to see you. He's in the lobby."

Denise rolled her eyes, worried that she might be in for another diversion she didn't need, and Zach would be gloating about her underestimating how long she would be away. She made up her mind it was going to be a very short meeting. Worthy led Harry into her office.

"I heard about Lieutenant Pascoe having a stroke. He's a good guy—I hope he's doing okay," the reporter said.

"Thanks for asking. He's doing well. With his determination to get back to work and a little luck, he might be back in another week." Denise didn't doubt he meant well, but she sensed that the real reason he was in her office would soon be revealed.

"I also wanted you to know that I'll be doing a couple of minutes on Monday's six o'clock news about the families of the victims. I've spoken to both sets of parents. There's nothing controversial in the piece. It's a human-interest story on how the tragedy has changed their lives. They're frustrated by not knowing who did it, but Blair's father has calmed."

"Will I be allowed to see it before it airs?" Denise asked.

"Sure, I'll email it to you before noon on Monday," Harry replied.

"Anything else on your mind, Harry?"

"Just one other thing. I was wondering if you're any closer to identifying the guy in the gun shop surveillance video."

"Afraid not."

"I just can't wrap my arms around a killer being so skilled at leaving no evidence or even clues to who he is. It's very disturbing."

Denise contemplated saying nothing, not wanting to give in to his probing for her suspicions. After a pause she answered, "We're all disturbed, and we're doing everything we can to find something that will put us on the road to the killer. It hasn't happened yet."

Harry Richardson was not getting what he wanted out of Denise, which was more inside scoop on the police's progress. He suspected she wouldn't cooperate, so he went to Plan B. "I'm not sure I agree with your theory that the killer knew the kids. We could have a psycho or serial killer. Maybe the kids just happened to be in the wrong place at the wrong time."

Holding a straight poker face, Denise replied, "I kind of doubt it," Denise responded. "But you do what you have to do, and you're welcome to speculate."

Sunday pm

The next day Denise stopped at the Pascoe home after a short meeting at the stationhouse. He was talking with only a slight slur and walking around with a cane. "I need you on my side, Den. I've got to get back on the job. I can't stand it anymore, sitting here doing nothing while we have a murder to solve. The Chief says I need my doctor's okay. He said I'd be limited to desk duty. I don't think I could sit at my desk."

"Whoa, partner, aren't you putting the cart before horse?" she said. "When do you think you'll get the okay from your doctor?"

"I'm seeing him tomorrow morning. If he won't approve it, I'm going to find one who will."

"Reed, I'd love to have you back, but only with your doctor's okay. We don't want a relapse. But you know I want you back."

"Thanks, Den. I wouldn't say this to anyone else, but coming back anything less than I was–that's not an option for me."

There was a noticeable break in his voice.

"One thing I know, Den, I'm nothing if I'm not a homicide detective. I have to get back on the job."

She hugged him and they squeezed tightly to each other for a few moments. When they separated, both noticed that their respective eyes were filled with tears. That made them laugh and they embraced again. They were more than partners. They relied on each other for emotional support.

She didn't stay much longer. She knew they said everything there was that was important.

In her mind, her promise to support him getting back on the job had reservations. She was thinking, *if they were going to be riding together in the squad car, he needed to be able to do more than walk with a cane. Sure, he could be helpful in the precinct, but a liability in the squad car.*

Cathleen always knew her husband was ambitious, but she had no idea how driven he was to be successful. He started with the physical exercises and regimens and moved on to the speech therapy, the whole time thinking about the killer. Finding the perpetrator was always his obsession. Without the hunt, he was ordinary. Being a detective, though, completed him.

Monday August 11, one week from the discovery

At Pascoe's Monday morning doctor appointment, the tests came back normal and his speech and mobility were on track for a quick recovery. With reluctance, his doctor gave him his blessing to a light job workload of desk duty. After a call to Chief Meadows to get his approval, Cathleen drove him to the precinct station for a short day of work.

Buzzing with well wishes, there was an air of hope in the bullpen. Cathleen pulled Denise aside.

"Say, when Reed is ready, could you drive him home? I really need to get to work," Cathleen said.

"How are you doing, Cathleen, you look tired."

"I am. I must admit, as much as I love Reed, now that we know he's going to be fine, it's as if my body is telling me I need a rest now. Going to work for a few hours seems a complete blessing."

"It's been a really tough week, but look at him!" Denise and Cathleen looked at Reed, smiling, laughing, telling off color jokes to the guys.

***

Reed was in his office reviewing the daily reports, although he knew he was far from fully recovered and knowing there was plenty of rehabilitation in store for him, he was almost giddy with being back. He looked with distaste at the cane that was needed for stability. He chose one from the drugstore assortment that resembled something Sherlock Holmes might have used. His phone rang, interrupting his file review, and he picked it up. It was Victoria Rogers. She wanted to talk to Detective Smith. He felt like, during the interim, he and Denise had switched places. He shrugged the thought away and punched the intercom button on the desk phone. "Pick up on my line, it's Victoria Rogers."

Denise picked up the call at her desk in the squad room. "Would it be alright if David and I came by the stationhouse?" Victoria Rogers asked. "We want to express our apologies for all the drama. When would be a good time?"

"I'll be here for a couple of hours, if that fits your schedule," Denise replied.

"Yes, that would be perfect. We should be there within a half hour."

Denise walked back into Pascoe's office. "Are you in the mood to talk with Mr. and Mrs. Rogers?"

"I guess," Pascoe said. "What's on their mind?"

"Mrs. Rogers said they want to apologize for their behavior."

Pascoe gave her a quizzical look.

"I know," Denise said.

"I'm skeptical, but you've still got nothing. Right?"

"That would be accurate," she said. "I take it we play it straight, hoping they've got something new to consider."

"Yeah, sure," Pascoe said. He paused and asked jokingly, "Are you sure you don't want to continue the call in the privacy of your new office? I can get comfortable in the bullpen."

She smiled back at him while shooting him a bird. Pascoe laughed. He was grateful to be back among his colleagues

***

The meeting with Dave and Victoria Rogers was a little strange. They didn't have anything new. They simply wanted to get their disappointment with the investigation off their chests, revealing their faith crisis. The meeting lasted no more than a half hour, and they were out the door,.

"We've seen it before," Denise said, "but not quite like this."

"The questions, the doubts, they've been a part of me ever since I became a homicide cop," Pascoe said. "How can you try to make sense out of something that isn't supposed to make sense to us? We accept the senselessness of it all. It comes with the job. But to those who've never had to deal with it…it's tough, real tough."

"By the way, did the Chief say anything about your being back on the job?"

"Desk duty for now. I think I can stand it for a few days. Don't worry about me."

Pascoe was the kind of guy who made good on his predictions of what he could accomplish. However, Denise was a little worried he might be rushing it. She didn't want him trying to fake a full recovery. Until he was at least eighty percent of what he could do before the stroke, he'd be a cop who couldn't get out of harm's way.

23. THE CHASE

DENISE KNEW SHE WAS SHORTCHANGING HER FAMILY DUR-
ing this investigation which monopolized all her time. Even when
she was home, she was preoccupied with it. Usually on high profile
cases, the intensity lasted only a few days until the suspect became
obvious, then she could wind down and split her attention more
evenly between work and family. There was a gnawing feeling inside
that this case would be different, take longer, and she may need to
multitask at a far greater level than ever before.

Zachary was always the first to be neglected. Being hyper-focused on cases meant nothing else was on her mind. Their inti-
macy suffered. While Zach intellectually knew this had nothing to
do with him, Denise could sense that when she recoiled from his
touch it bothered him and he took it personally. She couldn't help
it. Making love was the last thing on her mind when she was processing facts, trying to align timelines, and behaviors, and analyzing
gut feelings. After big cases were put to bed, she in turn, made sure
Zachery knew where her heart was. He even joked that closed-in-
vestigation sex was even better than make-up sex. For Denise, when
she wasn't distracted, and she felt like celebrating, making love with

her husband was the perfect finish. The two of them did everything to keep this special tradition between them strong.

This night was different, filled with tension, Denise went out for another run in the dark of evening. It had become her habit lately, enjoying the solitude and the quiet. There were few cars, and she hardly ever saw any one out walking, running or biking.

It was after ten, the stars were out, and the air crisp. A perfect night for releasing steam. She could sense Zach's disappointment when he curled up on the sofa as she prepared for the run, lacing up her shoes. She promised to be back soon. "I'll only do the loop, I'll be back in less than thirty," Denise said, gliding out the door. The loop was three miles. Just enough time to get a good sweat going. She knew tonight would be a night she would have to multi-task with Zachary, so she decided to make this a speed run.

Soon after beginning, in her hurry, Denise realized she not only forgot her running watch, but her phone. Often she left the watch, leaving the pace, heart rate, and other statistics behind on purpose. But she never forgot her phone. Her phone was her best defense if she was ever injured, or if she came across something that needed attention. Knowing this would be a quick run, she quickly dismissed it and relaxed as she ran along the road, sparsely lit with street lights.

She noticed a man walking two dogs a couple of houses ahead of her. It was Scott Rand. She grimaced. There weren't many people Denise disdained, but this person was one, along with his entire family. From the few times she saw his wife, timid and fearful, Denise strongly suspected she had been bullied, not only by her husband, but her grown sons. Both the boys had been arrested for drug possession, and everyone in the neighborhood looked at her for words of help, guidance, or explanation. This she found annoying. There was nothing further Denise felt she could do to prosecute them or protect the neighborhood. Perhaps they were petty criminals with bad habits. Fortunately, the past several years had been quiet, as they realized they had better not practice in their own backyard.

Rumor had it that the Rand dogs, one a pit bull, and the other a German shepherd, where groomed to protect the family business, which speculators claimed was something illegal. Denise never wasted her time on this kind of gossip, although she knew the dogs to be fierce. It was no wonder that Scott walked them at night, and on leashes.

As she caught up to them, running from behind, the dogs began to growl, then calmed down after their master turned around and greeted Denise. "Well, hello, officer. Mighty fine night. Are you sure you're safe to be out here?"

Scoffing, Denise knew she had to answer. "I'm fine, Scott. Especially with you right behind me. Take care."

She ran ahead and down the hill. Keeping to her plan of the short run, she turned left, but away from the street lights. There were two ponds, one to her right and one to her left. She wanted peace and solitude, and she was pretty sure her neighbor would stick to the street that was lit.

The stars reflected in the water, and it was a sight out of a fairy tale. Peaceful, calm and clear. She breathed deep, relaxing. She didn't notice it, but her pace had slowed considerably. She began letting go of her day at work, and began thinking of getting back to Zach at home, in bed.

Denise picked up her pace. Soon she was in complete darkness. Auto-pilot directed her feet. She felt strong, and for the first time in several days, hopeful.

Then, out of nowhere, someone or something grabbed her from behind and pulled her to the ground. She got to her knees, but he was behind her with his arms around her, twisting her one way, then the other way. Instinctively she fought back, swinging her elbows at his face, but missing every time. His size and strength prevented her from getting back on her feet, and his grip was such that she couldn't pry his hands apart. She was fighting a losing battle so she did the only thing that was left. "Let go of me right now," she screamed aloud. But all that came back was emptiness, not even an echo.

His reaction, a punch in the back and a knee to the hamstrings of her right leg. It stunned her, and he rewrapped his arms around her. She couldn't move, and her size and weight were an easy match for him. She tried to smash the back of her head in his face, but he anticipated it, moving his head out of the way.

He laughed as if amused. "Capturing you is way too easy."

Denise's skin crawled. The guy sounded crazy. "Let me go, you asshole," Denise shouted. She dug her fingernails in his arm. That loosened his grip for an instant, allowing enough time to thrust her elbow at his groin. He flinched, and she hit his gut instead.

"You bitch," he shouted back. He retightened his grip around her, squeezing the breath out of her. Seconds passed and Denise began to feel dizzy. She tried kicking him, but he used his weight to pin her to the ground, face down, squeezing her harder, robbing her of breath. "You're simply not strong enough. I've got you, Detective." He was powerful and he knew what he was doing, staying on top of her, using his weight and his arms to force the air from her lungs.

She was helpless and losing consciousness, but she could feel his mouth at her ear. "It won't be long, detective. You're mine," he whispered, feeling his tongue on her neck.

Denise quit fighting. Perhaps overconfident, thinking she had succumbed, or wanting to prolong the torture, he eased up and raised himself. She gulped in some air and regained her wits. Breathing hard she gasped out her words, "Who are you, and what the fuck do you want with me?"

The man cackled. It sounded menacing and evil. "Detective Denise Smith, your problem is you think I'm like every other idiot." He laughed even harder, louder.

The voice wasn't familiar. He eased his hold on her a little more so she could take a breath. She speculated she was in the grasp of the Teen Killer. Physically he was stronger than her, and if the profiler was correct, he was a sociopath with no remorse for murder. But he could have ended it earlier, and he didn't. Her training told her to drag it out, distract him, and wait for him to make a mistake. Digging deep down she began processing how to talk this guy down if, in fact, he was the guy who murdered Sarah and Blair.

"What's your plan?" she egged him on while gasping for breath.

"Plan!" He squeezed her harder. "I put your partner out of commission, and you're next, that's my plan, my pretty...."

The sound of barking dogs stopped him, and then he loosened his grip on her.

Before she could decipher what happened, she saw the Rand dogs attacking and biting him, as he held onto her with one hand and fighting off the dogs with the other. They were vicious. He let go of Denise, deciding to make a run for it. The dogs ran after him.

Without thinking, Denise began running after him as well. She could hear the dogs barking as they pursued him, and in the darkness of the night, that was the only way she could follow. The one thing on her mind was not losing him, but in the dark, there was nothing but confusion, shadows, and the barking dogs.

Some homes in the neighborhood had outside lighting, and with the barking, more lights began turning on. It helped her see where she was going, but the perp was too far ahead to get a look at him. Suddenly the barking stopped, turning into snarls and growling. It sounded as if it was just beyond the home in front of her.

"BLAM!" The unmistakable sound of a gunshot stopped her in her tracks, and a dog began whimpering. In the ensuing silence, she ran until she found one dog, shot dead, with the other one licking the fallen animal's face. She stopped for a moment, then kept running through the yards, and back onto the street. She soon realized that she was running deaf and blind. She could hear no steps; she could see nothing. In the distance, she heard the sound of police sirens wailing. She stopped, resigned that the perp had eluded her.

Denise walked back to where she saw the dead dog. Scott Rand was there, kneeling by the fallen animal, stone quiet and still. Finally, he spoke. "I heard you scream. My dogs are trained to attack the aggressor. I let them go, to protect you...."

Denise put her hand on his shoulder, "Scott, I'm so very thankful. You saved my life; your dog saved my life. I cannot tell you how sorry I am...." The sirens were getting louder. "Scott, are you okay?"

He nodded. She walked out of the yard, and into the street. A police patrol car was driving toward Denise, and stopped when they saw her. Down the road, she saw another car approaching as well. It was Zach.

Denise didn't recognize the younger officer in the car, but she addressed him with authority. "Detective Denise Smith. Sorry, I don't have my I.D. While running I was attacked by a man, about six feet tall, wearing black clothes. Strong, excellent runner. Did you see anyone?"

He opened his car door and stepped out. "Negative. You're the first person I've seen. I was responding to a call from the neighbors about a disturbance. Are you all right?"

Denise hadn't noticed, but somehow, she had been scratched across her cheek and was bleeding. She touched her hand to the wound, felt the blood and asked the young officer for a tissue. By that time, Zach had gotten out of his car and approached them.

"What the hell happened, Denise?" Her husband did not sound happy. "Are you okay? When I heard the sirens, I had a feeling you were involved."

Denise was still panting as she raised her hand and gave Zachery an 'in a minute' nod and turned to the patrolman. "There's a dog that was shot and killed behind this house. The dog's owner is with him. Please call a backup unit. We need to take the animal in and do ballistics on the bullet. It might be from a gun used in an unsolved homicide."

Curiosity was beckoning the neighbors out of their homes. As she looked at the onlookers, one at a time, she began walking toward the vehicles. She winced. Who she needed to address right now was Scott Rand — and her husband; not curious bystanders.

Denise looked at Zach while the patrolman was using his radio to report the incident and relay her instructions. The look on her husband's face was incredulity.

"Zach, I'm sorry about this. During my run, Scott Rand's dog attacked someone, and the animal has been shot dead. Scott is with the dog, Let me go there to see if he's still okay. You know how he was with his dogs."

"You're kidding, right? The local drug dealer gets what he deserves and you're feeling sorry for him?" She recognized the tone and the body language; he was furious.

"It wasn't like that. Trust me. I'll be back."

She turned around, seeing Scott carrying his dead dog, heavy in his arms, the other animal following close behind him, whimpering. Between the car beams and the house lights, she could see the sadness on her neighbor's face. They looked at each other and she knew they would have a bond uniting them. Her life for his dog's life. A life for a life. The concept was spinning in her head. Where would she be right now if not for the man she had labeled as an undesirable neighbor?

"Scott. I'm so sorry. Are you all right?" He didn't answer, but she recognized the look–he was already grieving the loss of his faithful companion. Even Zach stood back, not saying anything, noticing the man's grief.

Scott slowly began, "We trained him for protection—to do just what he did. I should feel success right now, right?" Scott looked back and forth from Zach to Denise. "Denise, are you ok? Did they find the man who attacked you?"

"Denise, what?" Zach was dumbfounded. "Attacked?"

Scott continued, "Yes. I was walking the dogs, when I heard Denise scream. We ran as fast as we could, then I let them loose. They tore into that guy. A slender built man, dressed in black...who could run fast, very fast." Scott turned towards Denise. "You were pretty brave, running after him, especially after he shot Hawkeye." There was a new respect between the two.

Zach looked as if he was going to explode in disbelief at Denise. A second patrol car pulled up. It was Detective Judson. She left her husband with Scott, and walked over to him. "A young man about six feet tall attacked me during my run. He said he would put me out of commission just like he did my partner. Then my neighbor's dogs came and attacked him, and he took off running. The attacker shot one dog dead before we lost him. We need ballistics to take a look at bullet that killed the dog. Also, I think the perp was bitten. Maybe we can get his DNA and the bullet from the dead dog?"

Judson couldn't believe Denise's calmness, getting back to business so soon after such a terrible assault. Matching her coolness, he offered to call ballistics and take the dog to the lab.

"Also, the guy said something about putting Lieutenant Pascoe out of commission. Ask the M.E. if he could have done something to Reed that could have induced a stroke," she said looking at Judson.

"Then help with the crowd control, partner." Denise turned around, getting back to Zachary and Scott.

"Scott, they need to take Hawkeye into the police station to perform ballistics tests. They need to see if they can identify the bullet, and see if there's any DNA from the attacker on him. Hawkeye is now evidence. I'm sorry, but we'll get his body to you as soon as possible. My partner, Detective Miles Judson, will give you the paperwork to fill out," she tilted her head toward Judson, still on the phone.

Scott nodded, walked over to the other patrol car. It was time for Denise to face Zachary now.

"'Nice, please tell me you really didn't put your life, our lives, in jeopardy over a dead dog, a dog of an alleged drug dealer?" Zachary was still upset.

"There's a lot more to it than that," Denise was matter of fact and businesslike with her husband. "He said he had put my partner out of commission and I would be next. Zach, I think this was the Teen Killer."

In her honesty and eagerness to placate him, she had disclosed too much information for her husband to handle. He turned around raising his arms up in anger, muttering to himself. Zach turned back to his wife. "Denise, you're telling me that this twisted sonofabitch who killed those two teens did something to Reed, and now is stalking you? Whose next, Denise? Me, one of the kids? He obviously knows where we live." Zach was more than agitated. "Jesus Christ! I know your work is important to you, but this?"

Denise was fearful as well. But she would not give in, or give up. Zachery was right about one thing, there was more at stake than just her reputation. There were serious implications that there was a crazy man out there with no compunction for killing.

And Denise was the best–maybe the only one at this point–capable of figuring out who the bastard was.

24. REQUIEM

AFTER RETURNING HOME AND TRYING TO CONVINCE ZACH
that he was overreacting, Denise sat quietly alone in the den after
everyone else was asleep. His point of view had begun to sink in.
The Teen Killer was no ordinary bad guy. He was a sadistic devil
that took everything as a personal insult. On top of that, he had
twisted notions of avenging anything he considered a crime against
him, and now she was his adversary. Denise was reaching the conclusion that she had underestimated the depths to which the killer
was willing to go.

She was right. Whoever or whatever the killer was or might have
been, he was now on a path of irretrievable malevolence. He had
crossed the line of madness into the abyss of calculated evil, where
he had talked himself into the role of God, deciding who deserved
to die. Now only days after he did the deed, he was reliving every
moment, playing back the event in his mind, savoring every detail
as if it were the climax of his life. It was his rapture.

In a dark, private place he was wrestling with his demon. He
never expected the rush, the exhilaration of the conquest. He came
to realize that gaming was counterfeit and artificial, he discovered
the actual act of taking a life was far more satisfying. Although he

neither welcomed nor sought his first encounter, there was no denying it was his destiny. Recalling the moments before, then the
instant of realization that another's life lay in the balance, the struggle—hand to hand, soul to soul, and then the BANG, feeling the
recoil of the pistol, the blood splatter; and finally, the realization
that he came out unscathed, as if God had guided him.

*I thought my eyes would pop out of my head. And even with the
pillow, the sound of firing the weapon was remarkable. POW! I can still
hear it as if it was a moment ago; I recall the vibration moving down
my arm from the residual of the backfire. It's been over a week now.
I miss it. It's calling me back. I need that high, the sensation that my
heart has stopped, when my victim's does. Then suddenly my heartbeat
returns. I feel invigorated, reborn. I have conquered death as my heart
regains its rhythm.*

*I need to seize and conquer death again. I need a new target, only it
can't just be a random stranger. I need more of an intellectual challenge
than that. I need to create a master plan with a connection, with an
element of risk and danger. Maybe it could be someone that has killed
before. I must make this a part of the game; the hunt. I am an eagle. I
will find my prey and fly away.*

*Could the newspaper be a source? No, too few stories are newswor-
thy on a given day. Ah, the internet.*

After a few searches, he didn't find enough detail about anyone
who might be a candidate for killing. Next he searched the local police website. There were several investigations underway, including
the mention of his, but all the dangerous prospects were in jail, awaiting disposition. There were others mentioned that seemed promising,
but the police were withholding details for unspecified reasons. He
imagined there were candidates there, hidden from the public.

Then it dawned on him. *Shit, I bet I could get inside their system.* Searching the dark side of the internet, travelling in lowlife malware, phishing, and hacking sites, he queried chat rooms for experience in getting into the computer records of a police station. He didn't wait long, but the source needed a quid pro quo. That was no problem for our killer; he had a steady supply of infectious and sought-after programs and made the trade. The source's advice was useful in discovering the "backdoor" of the Dallas County Police records. A quick search of the active cases displayed nine investigations, and one was the murder of Sarah Thompson and Blair Rogers. He couldn't resist a peek inside.

Reluctantly, he turned to the other cases. One stood out, the rape of a college student by a middle-aged, degenerate with a record of sexual assault. He was walking free because the identification from the victim was hesitant. The investigating officer wrote in his report he was certain the rapist and prime suspect was a Mr. Jack Arnold. That was good enough for our killer. The report listed his current address and what areas he trolled to prey on young women.

Now the fun can ensue, he said out loud. *Yes, let the games begin.*

***

Perhaps the Jack Arnolds of the world should face justice, and be put to death or incarcerated for most of their life. By the standards of the American justice system, this would be harsh punishment for a rapist if he was convicted by a jury of his peers.

Deciding that Mr. Arnold didn't deserve a fair trial was a

preemptive move of irrational consideration. The Teen Killer stalked Arnold, an alleged serial rapist, as if he was playing a video game. He assumed himself superior and the decider of Arnold's fate. The only thing left was to find out if he was a worthy target, a valid prey. To make it more interesting, he chose to wear makeup to create the cartoon face of Satan, leaving Arnold with a last impression that befitted his crimes. Yes, he would be on his way to hell.

Like him, Jack Arnold was a creature of habit, leaving for his hunting trips as darkness fell upon the city. Invariably he took a route he used the days before, not far from the subway depot near the campuses of a university and a junior college.

The killer had determined where to do the deed, that is, assuming Arnold chose to park near the three-block redevelopment zone as he did the previous day. This section of Industrial Avenue was in the demolition stage of construction, leaving empty lots on both sides of the street in rubble, with poor lighting. A good place to attack a preoccupied young lady, and, therefore, also a good place to shoot a man dead and get away unnoticed.

As Arnold slowed down and pulled his van alongside the curb to park, his stalker passed him by, only to turn at the next side street on the right and park where an opaque construction fence blocked the view of his car. It was another hot and muggy evening, a thin crescent moon barely lit the sky, further muted by the humidity. In the midst of being replaced, there were few street lights, and those that remained were almost a block away. The darkness provided a perfect cloak to shield his movements.

He calmly put on his grey, polypropylene gloves to avoid leaving finger prints. Armed with his pistol and bolt cutters, clad in black jeans and a black hoodie that covered his head, Arnold's would-be executioner cut the clasps that secured the nearest gate and crept along the inside of the fencing toward the main gate, not far from where Arnold parked. He had to walk through mud and tall thistle weeds that scratched his clothes to get to the gate's location, just beyond Arnold's van. With the bolt cutter, he cut through the padlock that secured the gate. Leaving the bolt cutter behind, he crept on his hands and knees toward the back of the van.

Now, resting against the back of the van, he scraped the mud off his shoes with a stick he picked up along the way. He was surprised to find that Arnold had not turned off the motor. The van sat there, idling with the lights off, somewhat like the German U-boats that lurked in the waters off the coast of Europe during WWII.

Satisfied that his once muddy Nike's wouldn't impede his moves or prevent a quick getaway, he crouched low and crept toward the front door of the van on the passenger side, out of the range of the rear-view mirrors. At this point the killer reached into his pocket and pulled out two ear plugs to protect his ears from the blast of the pistol.

Inside the van, listening to heavy metal on his playlist, Arnold's focus was on the view ahead, looking for coeds. Occasionally, he would glance in the rearview mirror if headlights indicated an approaching vehicle, trying to tell if it might be a cop car. Even if his executioner was careless, it would be unlikely that Arnold would suspect he was in danger.

Slowly the assassin positioned his head so he could see into the van's passenger side window with one eye, expecting the dark of the night and his slow movement would not alert his victim. There Arnold sat behind the steering wheel, eating a cookie of all things, while he waited for a damsel to pass his way walking from the college to the rapid rail. The assassin raised his gun to where its barrel was about an inch above the window's doorframe. He took a deep breath to calm his nerves and steady his hand. When he closed his eyes, he pulled the trigger. The recoil and the shards of broken glass surprised him, but he opened his eyes to see he hit Arnold in the torso, but not fatally.

Standing up now, holding the pistol with one hand, he pointed it at Arnold's head and opened the back door of the sedan. Arnold's face wore the look of horror as he watched his executioner. Between moans and sounds of anguish Arnold asked, "Who are you? What do you want?"

"I'm the angel of death." the killer said no more, sliding behind Arnold, aiming his pistol at the back of his head. With a slight squeeze of the trigger, Jack Arnold's life came to an abrupt end.

Blood covered the driver's side interior of the door and windshield. The assassin put the pistol in his pocket and ran to his vehicle. As he was about to turn the corner toward his old sedan, he spotted what appeared to be a woman or a girl about a hundred feet in front of him on the sidewalk, crouched low as if trying to appear invisible. Rather than continue and get to his car, he chose to stop and then run toward her. She obviously noticed him, turned and ran the other way in fear.

Seeing her run away, he stopped, satisfied she wouldn't see him get in his car and leave, and thereby identify it and its license plate. Inside his car, he cranked the engine without delay.

He pulled away from the curb and onto the road with the gas pedal pressed to the floorboard. He took a gasp of air into his lungs to settle himself, and an instant later he backed off the gas, bringing the vehicle closer to the speed limit. "WOW", he cried out loud,

"What a rush." His heart was pounding and he was perspiring. The glow of accomplishment took over his emotions as he drove toward home with a smile on his face. *This,* he thought to himself, *was a defining moment.*

25. SOMETHING OR NOTHING?

BEFORE CATHLEEN BROUGHT REED INTO THE OFFICE, DEN-
ise, Judson and Chief Meadows met in his office early Tuesday
morning. The Chief spoke up, "Folks, we need to gather all the
intelligence, and try to...."

"Make some intelligence out of it," Miles Judson snickered.

"There's a lot of stuff out there, and we need to assemble and
organize it. Keep the good stuff, flush the crap," the chief said, ig-
noring Judson's remark. "How are you doing, Denise? Feeling okay
this morning?"

The two men looked over at Denise, noting the scratch on her
left cheek, a reminder of the crazy guy they were dealing with.

"A little sore around the ribs, but I'm fine."

"I mean your head. Are you still good? Is this too personal now?"

"Jesus Christ, it is too personal. But I'm in. Now that I've had
contact with the perp, I feel it will only help me on this case."

"Or cloud you?"

Denise remembered her cloud of unknowing. She felt as if the
incident actually shed more light, helping to dispel it.

"Negative, Chief. I'm all about getting the right guy, not just
any guy."

"Got that, but Denise, if ever you feel less than objective, let me know."

Pascoe sauntered into the office, barely using his cane. The smile on his face and his light step, put a smile on everyone in the squad room. Rather than park himself in his office, he headed straight for the Chief's office, interrupting the discussion going on.

Strangely, this was a gift to the three public servants in the room. "I'm baaack!" Pascoe sang out.

"What a sight for sore eyes," Judson said.

"What?" Reed shrugged his shoulders. "I've only been gone since three yesterday. Did anything happen?"

"Shit's happened, Reed. Denise got attacked last night."

While looking at Pascoe, Judson cocked his head toward Denise. Reed saw the scratch on her face. "Damn! Den, what the hell happened?"

"Got a visit from a friend. Says he put you out of commission, and I was next."

"Out of commission?" Pascoe looked confused.

"Your stroke may have been chemically induced, Reed," the Chief said.

"What?" Reed was incredulous.

"Yeah, that's what the doctors told us at the hospital, but we never understood what he meant. Got a call into the M.E. for the blood work. They suspected something at the hospital. Truthfully, in all the commotion, we kind of pushed it aside." Denise apologized. "We should hear something soon."

Pascoe sat down. "This is one crazy fuck we're dealing with."

"I've got more," the Chief said. "And you're not going to like it. We have another murder."

"Not more children?" Pascoe said. His face was white, not wanting to hear it.

"No. The ID on the vic was Jack Arnold. He's the guy Branch investigated on the rape case last month. Miles, I want you and Branch to lead this one."

***

Denise and Pascoe spent the morning going over the facts and the suspects in the situation room. White boards lined one wall with pictures of all four of the victims affixed to them: Sarah, Blair, and the two from Kansas. Calls to the hospital about Reed's chemistry tests were not returned, so the threat that the attacker made the previous night was still on "the parking lot" section of the white board: the place they kept unconnected evidence and facts, and were not sure where they fit into the puzzle.

Around three in the afternoon, Pascoe was crashing and Denise drove him home.

***

When Denise got to her home, she didn't expect to see Zach packing a bag, which sat on their bed next to some folded clothes. In a surprised tone she asked, "Where are you headed, Zach?"

He didn't expect to see her, either. "Home early for the first time this year?" he asked sarcastically. What's the occasion?" He was walking between his closet, his dresser, with open drawers, filling his suitcase.

She recognized the tone, something was wrong. "I just lost an account because the client needed me to be more available," he yelled. "How can I be more available when you're married to the job? I'm stuck doing it all."

"What?" Denise said

"And now this crazy killer attacks you while you're running in the neighborhood. Do you knows what this means?"

"Of course, I do. This guy saw my name in the news. He looked me up on the internet. I get it. He stalked me. He knows where I live."

"Where you live—you? This lunatic knows where our kids live. Think he might come after them next?"

"Oh, Zach…."

"I called my mother, and we're staying with her in Flower Mound until… until we figure things out." He stopped long enough to hold her eye gaze. "I'll be meeting with a very important client and management all day tomorrow, and I can't be distracted," Zachary paused his packing, and looked up at Denise. "You do know you're not the only one with a career that's important to them, right?"

Denise remained silent. Although she wanted to, she could not blame Zach for his actions.

"We can talk later, but you need to figure out how to make this work better. We can't go on like this."

"I thought you worked this out with your boss," Denise said. "I had no idea this was happening all over again."

"Look, Denise, I don't have the latitude you think I have at work. You've been taking me for granted. And now you're on an investigation where some psychopathic nut case knows where we live, and who the hell knows what that asshole is thinking. Can't you see how crazy this is?"

Zach turned from his suitcase and walked into the bathroom. Denise followed him.

"I'm sorry, Zach, but I didn't expect this either. It will pass once we get this guy."

"Yeah? And what about the next fucking lunatic you're hunting? And the next?"

Denise was speechless. Why hadn't she seen this anger building sooner?

Gathering all his toiletries, Zach headed back into the bedroom. He put them in the bag and zipped it up.

"Denise, this has got to stop." He picked up his bag, ready to walk out the door. "The kids have already packed their bags this morning. I'm going now to pick them up from school.

"We'll be staying at mom's house until this animal gets caught. You can stay wherever the hell you want." The look on his face was twisted with anger. "But understand this. I don't want the kids to see us fighting. And don't try to talk me out of this."

Denise was caught off-guard by what Zach was saying, especially the suddenness of it. She couldn't think straight, and she feared she might say something she'd regret later. But the competitor in her wouldn't let it go without a fair fight. "You must be hurting so bad," she said sarcastically. "You do remember we've had this conversation before, don't you?"

He had no response other than the scowl on his face.

"You said you would let me know if you were starting to have such thoughts again. That was supposed to give us time to work things out. In your self-centered world of feeling neglected, you seemed to have overlooked that part. And now that we're on the subject, why can't you imagine what I've been going through?"

"This is no ordinary case I've been working on. Some really good kids, children like our children, living in a neighborhood we would love to live in, have been taken from us. Their parents aren't perfect, but they're good people, too. They're really hurting, confused about what's supposed to be the path for God-fearing parents who have done everything right. The entire community is scared because the monster who did this is still at large, lurking in the shadows, ready to do the same to them.

"Don't you get it? If it was one of our kids, murdered like this, we wouldn't want the police to rest a minute while the killer was running free. And are you so inconsiderate not to imagine what it's like almost losing your partner, your mentor to a stroke in the middle of the investigation?"

"It's always something, Denise." He stood nose-to-nose and said, "Decide Denise, decide."

Zack slammed his suitcase shut and left without letting Denise go any further. She stood in the bedroom without moving, more from shock than anything else. She never saw Zach so mad that he wouldn't talk to her. Denise had felt the tension rising ever since she was on the teen killing case, but she never realized it would come to this.

Denise collapsed onto the edge of the bed, still staring out the doorway, wishing Zach to return, and knowing he wouldn't, at least not today.

She couldn't help acknowledging the parallel, to some extent, her family had become another victim of the teen killer.

Stubborn, Denise refused any responsibility for this critical state of her marriage. At least not yet. Maybe tomorrow. Denise pushed aside her frustration and tried to figure out what to do. Nothing was coming to mind. Every idea ended up senseless and discarded. She needed someone to comfort her and give her advice. Nobody seemed right, except Pascoe. She picked up the phone several times and put it back down, debating whether it was a good idea, and if he would understand why she was asking *him* for that kind of advice.

After the second full glass of Merlot she pushed the *Send* button on her phone. When he answered, she said, "Reed, this is Denise, your partner."

"Hey, Denise. I think I remember you." Reed responded, tongue in cheek.

"Huh?"

"Den, are you all right?"

"Yeah…I mean…no," she said. "Zach took Drake and Zoe with him to stay with his mom."

Providing comfort and empathy wasn't Pascoe's strong suit. He paused, searching for something to say that would make her feel better. The only thing he could think of was to offer to come over there. "Den, I'm only fifteen minutes away. How about us talking this out at your place?"

Denise wiped the tears from her blurry eyes. "You'd do that?"

"I'll always be here for you."

Somehow, hearing him say those words was what she needed. "Thanks, Reed. I needed to hear that. I'm going to be alright. You stay there with Cathleen and the kids. I'm good now. I'll see you tomorrow morning."

"Are you sure, Den?"

"I'm sure. Don't worry. I'm fine. See you in the morning."

Denise was telling Pascoe the truth. Just knowing that he'd jump in his car and come over was reassuring. She still had unresolved feelings for him, but for now, she could convince herself he was more valuable as a friend and partner.

Denise decided to go into work as if she'd not called Reed the night before. *He'd want that,* she thought to herself. She called her husband and surprised herself by remaining composed and civil.

"Zach, I'm not going to share my thoughts with you about this tonight," she told him. "Let's just agree to talk tomorrow. I just need for you to know that we're going to come to some understanding on how to proceed before the kids come home from school tomorrow. Be prepared to get used to them staying here, with me. They're old enough to get ready in the mornings and come home without either of us being here. This will not be negotiable."

She put the phone down and realizing she was a little harsh with Zach, she knew in her heart of hearts that it was better that he knew she would fight him. She was also confident that he knew he couldn't expect to beat her if she would fight him. Her cell phone rang. It was Zach. She let it ring while she made herself a cup of coffee.

***

The next morning Denise dressed in a hurry to get out of the house, which lacked Zach and the kids. Their absence was difficult for her to ignore. She couldn't help thinking of the adage, *you don't know what you have until it's gone.* There was no way for her to minimize the impact on her thinking. Her morning routine was so disjointed. Everything took longer and she ended up doing the same things more than once, unable to remember what she had done a moment ago.

The only thing working for her was distraction. She knew she had to work even harder now to wrap this case up to get her family back, and to protect the public from this crazy killer. She could sense he would strike again at any time, probably sooner than later.

Denise arrived at the stationhouse a half hour early to complete her paperwork, prepare her progress reports and to talk to the Chief, who had left her a text message that there was something she needed to see about the Jack Arnold homicide.

She didn't have time to make a cup of coffee before she noticed Chief Meadows lurking in the doorway of the breakroom.

"Good morning Clifton. How's everything?"

"Life sucks," the Chief replied.

"Don't tell me—let me guess. It's the press?"

"Nope. And don't try guessing anymore, you'll never get it. Remember me telling you I gave Judson and Branch the Jack Arnold investigation?"

"Who is Jack Arnold again?" she asked.

"He was the victim found shot to death the other night. What's changed everything is the preliminary ballistic report on the bullets we removed. They appear to be from the same weapon that killed your teenagers last week, and the dog."

"What?"

"It's not official, but the striations on the bullets appear to be identical under the microscope. Whoever killed Sarah, Blair, and your neighbor's dog killed our victim the other night."

"Jesus Christ, Chief. Do you think we've got a serial guy or a vigilante?"

"Search me. Whoever it is, I'm guessing he's not done."

The Chief walked away, leaving Denise's psyche in disarray. She wanted to call Pascoe, even though he wasn't supposed to report for work until ten, doctor's orders. She chose to ignore what the doctor said and called her partner.

It was half past nine in the morning, and Pascoe was reading the paper when Denise called.

"Hey Reed, am I interrupting anything?" she asked.

"Not hardly. I just picked up the Sports section of the paper. The Rangers defeated the Braves. Nothing new. What's up?"

"Do you remember the investigation of the rape Gary Branch was working?" she inquired.

"Yeah, sure. What about it?"

"The gun that killed him was the same one that was used on Sarah and Blair."

Pascoe paused as his mind tried to fathom the connections. "Reed, are you still there?" Denise asked.

"Yeah, Den, I'm here — thinking, trying to figure out what we have. I'm wondering if we've got a killer that thinks he's some kind of judge and jury. You know, maybe he thought that Sarah and Blair needed to be punished for something. He might have thought the same about the alleged rapist. But I've got to tell you, Den, I don't get how he knew about Gary's investigation. The name of the prime suspect in the rape case was never revealed. We don't do that unless we've indicted someone for the crime, and that never happened."

"That's why I called you. I knew you'd see it the way I was seeing it. What do you think is going on?"

"Let's parse it out, Den. On one hand, there's a rape victim who gave the sketch artist a description of the perp. Branch's investigation finds a match, and he had a record of assaulting young women, but he had an alibi. The alleged rapist had been scratched by his victim, but the victim had showered so thoroughly after the rape that there was no DNA. The scratch wounds on the suspect matched the description she gave, but she wasn't certain about the identification in the line-up, so it remained under investigation in our records. I don't get it. How does the killer of the kids know about the rape investigation and Arnold, and what's his motive if he does?"

"I'm wondering if he considers himself some kind of vigilante." Denise said.

"Yeah, I understand, but how does he know about the other prime suspect? He'd have to be a party to both crimes or their investigation, or, he's got a buddy in the precinct that had access to the record room."

That was a lot for both of them to digest.

Denise was of a different mindset. She was focused on finding the one thing that might connect the killer to both crimes. Her intuition told her that the killer didn't know both the rapist and Sarah or Blair. The crimes were committed ten miles apart, the ages were all different, and the crimes were not similar. She knew, however, that she had to rule out that suspicion first before any of it could make sense.

Looking out the window of Pascoe's office Denise could see Branch at his desk in the bullpen. She walked over to talk to him. "Gary, do you have a minute to talk about the rape case," she asked.

Less than a minute later Gary handed Denise the file folder, and she scanned each piece of paper. She wrote down all the names connected with the case, employers, and relatives. Nothing stood out to her. The victim, Lexi Meisner, lived in an apartment not far from Denise's subdivision.

"Gary, you've been helping out with the Teen Killings—have you seen any connection between the crimes, the suspects, the contacts or the victims?"

"I was totally surprised when ballistics came back with a bullet match," Gary replid. The cases have nothing in common besides the bullet. I mean nothing. I've been wondering if it's a random coincidence."

Denise paused, gathering her thoughts. Have you or anyone else shared the file contents with the outside world?

"Not that I know of. The victim wanted us to keep it as confidential as possible until we were certain we found the perp and had enough evidence to charge the crime and convict him."

"Who else besides the Chief had knowledge of the details of the case?" Denise asked.

"The only other person that knew what was in the file was the rape counselor," he said. "The victim and her mother chose Dr. Richter at the Women's Advisory Clinic. Her report is in the file."

"Thanks, Gary. That's all I have."

Denise knew that she still needed to ask the rape victim if she knew anyone named in the Teen Killing file. She suspected it would only be a formality that wouldn't provide a connection, but it had to be done to rule it out. She didn't waste a minute. She called the victim and arranged a meeting in an hour. After she hung up, Judson walked in. They discussed the connection of the bullet.

He asked, "Why didn't you ask the victim if she recognized any of the names over the telephone?"

"You know me. I like to see them when I question them. My dad taught me how to read a person's reactions to stimuli–especially how they react under stress."

"Are you good at it?" he asked.

"What do you think?" She sat poker-faced at first, then a smile curled up on her lips. "I think I'm right more than I'm wrong. Do you want to go to the morgue with me? I need to take a look at the body."

Judson shook his head. "I'll be in ballistics. I want to see the film on the slugs."

No one had told Denise about the body. When the medical examiner pulled the sheet off, she gasped. Two gunshot wounds, one bullet hole...in the back of the head. "Jesus Christ," she shouted. "Couldn't someone have told me he was executed like the kids?"

Denise was pissed. She barged into Chief Meadow's office not expecting someone was with him. She was startled to see the mayor there. "Just the person I wanted to talk to," Mayor Coleman said.

"Oh, sorry to interrupt," Denise said.

"No...no, Detective Smith. We were just talking about you. The Chief and I noted that it's August, and we had three murders, total, in our precinct since the first of the year. All of a sudden, within ten days, we have three more...and they're connected. The press is going to love it. And if we don't have some answers, they're going to make us look like fools. So, what answers do you have for me?"

"I'm afraid we only have questions so far, Mayor."

Mayor Madeline Coleman wanted to offer a snide remark, but

she liked what she knew about Denise. She held her tongue and shook her head as walked out of the Chief's office. Once she was out of hearing range, Denise turned to the Chief. "Don't you think you could have told me Arnold was also killed execution style?"

"What difference would it have made, Denise? The bullet told us the perps were the same guy. Saying they were killed alike was simply redundant." But the chief was covering his ass. After she pointed it out, he knew yesterday as they were discussing everything he should have mentioned it. He looked back at her sheepishly. "My bad. Sorry, Detective."

"Oh, men," she said sarcastically as she marched out of his office.

***

Denise was anxious to get home. One quick stop at Lexi Meisner's place and she'd still have the afternoon to figure out what to say to her husband. It was weighing heavily on her mind as she arrived at Lexi's apartment. Zach had a point; but she had a job to do. She pushed the issue aside once more.

A twenty-something woman answered the door, and they talked at her kitchen table. Except for offering Denise a soda, she didn't appear to be very talkative.

After opening the case file folder, Denise said, "Lexi, I don't want you to relive the crime, I'm only interested in finding out who might have killed your attacker. Can you tell me who you might have told about the attack?"

"As few people as possible. Except for the police, I didn't want anyone to know about it. I'm an only child. My father divorced my mother years ago, and I don't even know where he might be. I told my mother, the rape counselor, Dr. Richter, and the police. That's it."

Denise paused, hating to ask her next question. "I've got to have the answer to my next question for the case file, I hope you understand. A man named Jack Arnold was shot to death two nights ago. What were you doing between the hours of eight Monday night and six o'clock yesterday morning?"

"Monday night I was with two friends from school. We went to a movie at the mall and ate in the food court. I got home about ten-thirty. I stayed up a couple hours—you know screen time on the phone with friends. Then about midnight I crashed. I got up this morning about eight."

"Did you take revenge on your attacker, Jack Arnold?"

"No, ma'am. I wouldn't do that. But, I'd like to know who you think might have done it."

"I have two teenagers, a boy and a girl, shot with the same weapon that killed your attacker. Let me show you a list of the names of the victims and everyone we've met in connection with that investigation. Tell me if you recognize any of the names."

Lexi took less than a minute to read the list and said, "I don't know any of them. Which one owned the gun?"

"We don't know. We haven't recovered the murder weapon," Denise answered.

Lexi started to cry. "I've been trying my best to forget it ever happened," she said. "I thought I was over it, but I guess not. I'm sorry, is there anything else?"

"No, that's all, Lexi. I'm sorry for putting you through it all again." Denise reached to shake her hand, but they ended up in a hug.

***

The drive home filled Denise with more questions. She was having trouble focusing on any of the issues plaguing her, but at the top of the list, she expected that Zach and the kids would not be there. Once inside, the sheer quiet of the house was profound. It occurred to her that it might be similar to what the parents of Sarah and Blair must feel.

Lexi's account of her experience was what Denise suspected. No relationship to the Teen Killing. Except for the matching bullet, the rape and Arnold's murder were outliers. She thought to herself, *the killer is either toying with us, using the Arnold murder as a distraction or he's developed a taste for killing, and he wants to appear noble or charitable by killing someone he feels deserves it.* Dammit, that still didn't answer the biggest question, how did he know about Arnold?

Earlier she had left a message on Dr. Richter's answering machine to contact her about the case, hoping she would call back soon. Denise placed her cell phone on the kitchen counter as she opened the refrigerator, looking for dinner options. It rang, half scaring her out of a daydream about peace and quiet. It was Pascoe.

"I'm sorry to bother you, Den. I've been thinking about our last conversation, and I think your intuition might be right."

"What do you mean?" she asked.

"Answer this first, have you been able to find a leak in the precinct?" Pascoe asked.

"No, but I haven't heard back yet from the rape counselor. She's the only person left that could have leaked it," she replied.

"That's what I figured. What if our killer is a super geek with computers? What if he hacked into the police files? What if he hacked into his own company's security surveillance records?"

"Do you really think it might be Vincent? What would be his motive? By all accounts he worshiped Sarah."

"How about the oldest motive in the Bible–jealousy," Reed said with a tone of confidence.

Denise was mulling over Reed's words. She had been fighting off her suspicions that pointed to Vincent, not wanting them to influence or divert her attention away from the evidence. *But what evidence was there?* She asked herself quietly. *All they had kept pointing to Vincent.*

"Den...are you still there?" Pascoe asked.

"Yeah, sorry partner."

"I think you might want to ask Chief Meadows if he would try to convince the mayor to have that Israeli firm that we use for IT solutions to see if our computer has been hacked. If they find something, then we should be able to convince the chief to look into the security system at Vincent's employer to see it it's been hacked."

"You don't think we're moving too fast on Vincent?" Denise asked.

"Come on, Den," he said. "I may have had a minor stroke, but I didn't forget what you've been saying. And I know you too well. You've been on this Vincent guy all along."

While Denise paused, mulling it over, Pascoe said, "Oh by the way, can you pick me up tomorrow morning on the way to work? It'll be the last time. Cathleen can drive me until the doc gives me clearance."

"Sure, I'll see you tomorrow," she said before hanging up.

She knew her partner was right about finding out if they've been hacked as soon as possible. In an instant, her mind was wandering, and settled on her quiet, empty home. The void hurt, as she thought about her last conversation with Zach before he took the children to his mother's house.

Denise refocused and walked into her study, sat down with her laptop to hammer out an email with a formal request to the Chief to contact the county's computer hacking firm. While she was on the precinct website, she checked out her email inbox, like she always did.

There was an email from an unfamiliar source, not a city or county employee. She wanted to open it, but her suspicions were still raging. *If our system's been hacked, the email could contain some kind of malware*, she thought. She decided to wait until morning, when she could show it to their system tech.

26. A COLLECTION OF ODDITIES

DENISE WAS REVIEWING ALL THE POTENTIAL CANDIDATES that were on her suspect list. Many of them had their quirks and flaws, but none stood out as something that would motivate them to commit the execution of two teenagers. She admitted to herself that she was fixated on one of the suspects, for no other reason than a hunch based upon what she called his "creepiness quotient," Vincent.

Vincent Jerome Thompson was a collection of oddities. First, there was his physical appearance, which he did nothing to improve. He had a high widow's peak of dark hair, wearing it in a buzz cut, which framed his face in cartoon-like fashion. For years, his sister begged him to grow out his hair long and part it on one side, camouflaging his particular hair line, but Vincent refused. He said he couldn't stand hair in his eyes, and with the hot and humid summers in Texas, he preferred less hair. Nature was complying. At twenty-one his widow's peak was already receding, enhancing his already high forehead and accentuating the point of the peak. In no time, he would be considered bald.

Vincent's eyes were an interruption in his narrow face. They were small, near set with one green and one blue eye, which was unbalancing. The blue eye was a bright, clear blue, with the green nearly hazel. One had to get to know Vincent a long time before this wasn't a distraction in his looks. That seldom ever happened. He had no friends.

His nose was pointed, with slender nostrils looking like train tracks in the middle of his face, and his mouth was too small for his teeth, despite expensive orthodontics.

He was six feet tall, but he was pencil thin with a concave chest. Most people thought he was taller, because he gave the impression of being a vertical pole.

In short, Vincent Jerome Thompson appeared harsh, almost birdlike, and the way he turned his head or looked downward, was off-balanced physically, giving the sensation that he was under some sinister spell.

His personality accentuated this feeling. Vincent was a compilation of all that was socially awkward, anxious and introverted. In social settings when people asked him questions, he paused an unusually long time before responding. People assumed he was slow or dense, but that was far from the case. His parents had him tested in the third grade, with an I.Q. of one-hundred and forty-two. He was so good at all the mathematics and computer classes, he was considered an equation savant. But that didn't translate into his social or academic work. First of all, he was so oblivious to his peers, he often spoke to himself out loud, rocked back and forth in his chair, or tapped his pencil during quiet time. This was disruptive in class, and his fellow students teased him and called him unkind nicknames. Although the teachers suspected he suffered from autism and Attention Deficit Hyperactivity Disorder, he was so uncooperative in all areas of school and classroom management his teachers quickly labeled him defiant and showed him little compassion.

Vincent took to computers at six years old, and by the age of ten he was an internet prodigy. At first he was saddled to his parent's computer, so he had to learn how to hide his activity. His parents were computer illiterate, using it for recipes email, and online purchases. In no time, he mastered the skills of becoming completely untraceable on the internet, allowing him a secret life online, creating false personas on social media and dummy email accounts. He delighted in sending threatening messages or pornographic websites to individuals he found particularly objectionable. But that paled in comparison to his ability to write system crippling viruses he knew would completely paralyze computers not only for individuals, but for companies as well. For Vincent this was pure justice, accounting for his unfortunate social circumstance, and providing him a vehicle for revenge.

He did little to compensate for his shortcomings. He knew he was different, and accepted it. He reasoned that as his own biological mother had rejected him at birth, and because his adoptive parents were so damn desperate to have a child, they compromised and adopted him with great regret. This, of course, was Vincent's assumption. His parents always treated him well, offered him many opportunities, but Vincent never let them cross the vast chasm that separated them emotionally.

What his parents didn't tell him was that his birth mother relinquished her parental rights with extreme anguish. Although having some mental illness issues herself, her intent was to be a strong, caring and providing single mother. But she was only eighteen, and after the birth of her son, she went into serious postpartum depression. She self-medicated and began using drugs. Her parents intervened, coaxed her into placing her son, then named Jerome, up for adoption before he was a year old. Enter the Thompsons. They were ready, willing and able for Vincent and his birth family to have a relationship, but his mother soon overdosed and died.

His grandparents simply evaporated from their lives. All his adoptive parents told Vincent was that his mother loved him very much, but became sick and died. They withheld from him the details, and Vincent sensed they were hiding valuable information. Since he didn't know specifics, and never had the courage to ask, he completely assumed he was a cast off, when in fact, that was the furthest from the truth. He was loved, wanted, and adored. Unfortunately, his poor social skills blinded him from seeing that.

When Vincent was four years old he formed his earliest and brightest memory. That was when they brought home his sister Sarah from the hospital. He immediately bonded with the pink bundle of tears, wet diapers, and complete dependence. She was helpless, and Vincent understood that.

When Sarah was small, Vincent was very protective of her. Rene and Doug Thompson, to Vincent's complete obliviousness, were relieved. Their son was not so strange after all; he had made that human connection that had evaded them from the day they brought him home.

Doug had been a serious athlete, playing baseball in college, and had dreams of playing catch with his son in the backyard, coaching little league, and eating hot dogs while watching the Rangers at the ballpark. It didn't take long before Doug Thompson let go of that dream. His son had no interest in the game, or in other sports, except for distance running and physical fitness training.

Vincent drew cartoons and read a lot. Even at a young age, his cartoons were of dark anime figures. He colored them in with a strange mash-up of colors, revealing Vincent was color blind, yet another trait that separated him from his peers.

But as Sarah grew up, Vincent glowed in her presence. She lovingly called him VJ, and before school began for her, the two were inseparable. She followed him everywhere and he taught her how to draw his anime figures, build Lego space ships, and play his favorite video games.

Vincent found a treasure in Sarah. It was the best time of his life. However, when Sarah was unavailable to him in times of need, he became vindictive and had temper tantrums. That's when she also became his defender and advocate.

As Sarah grew up and began her school career, her interests matured. Unlike Vincent, Sarah was well liked and adjusted effortlessly to any social situation. She had many play dates, was gifted at gymnastics, dancing, and music. And as she grew older, she gravitated toward her own special interests, including boys who competed for her attention.

Vincent and Sarah remained close, but Vincent became more introverted as he matured. His parents were not clueless about his lack of social development, but they also knew his computer and math skills would be his ticket to independence and success. They enrolled him in Saturday school UT Dallas where he enhanced his computer skills and excelled at programming and graphic design. To all, it appeared to placate Vincent's need for attention and accomplishment. Sarah was usually busy on Saturdays, but this outlet for their son led to peaceful harmony in their home.

Sundays were always a family day for the four of them. They went to church, then out for brunch and often did things like bike in local parks, visit botanical gardens, go to museums or to the movies. Rene and Doug were a pair, and Sarah and Vincent were a pair. For years, this was another harmonious arrangement. When Sarah got older, her time for her family, as well as her interest in it, waned. Sundays became difficult for Vincent. Once Sarah was given a cell phone, her time for Vincent decreased again.

Vincent sharply felt how his collection of oddities separated him more than ever from the outside world—and his precious Sarah. Vincent withdrew even farther into his dark, chosen world of loneliness and solitude, hiding in his room with his computer and the door locked. When Sarah began dating, Vincent dove deeper into his various internet lives, writing malware, and frequenting those dark websites so many lonely men find as substitutes for human companionship.

Vincent Jerome Thompson certainly was an eccentric anthology of unfortunate peculiarities. He knew it, and by the time he reached his twenties, he realized he was destined for a much more difficult life than most.

27. STRANGE DAYS

THE NEXT MORNING BROUGHT THUNDERSTORMS AND HIGH
winds. Tornado warnings filled the airways, but at the moment
Denise arrived at the Pascoe residence, there was an eerie calm.
Cathleen greeted Denise at the door with a dishtowel in her hand,
"Hello!" She motioned Denise in, giving her a welcoming hug.
"Reed is in the basement. He should be finishing his rehab exercis-
es." Cathleen smiled, but there was an air of urgency, "I'm in the
middle of making him a healthy breakfast. I can't leave the stove."
She quickly walked Denise to the basement door and beckoned.
"Go on down, Reed needs the break. He has been working so hard,
probably overdoing it–you know Reed."

Denise walked down the carpeted steps, wondering why Reed
wasn't ready to leave. When she peeked around the corner, she saw
a well-appointed home gym. The room was quiet and still, so Denise, tip-toed silently, and looked around. When she finally spotted
Reed, she smiled. There he was, sound asleep in an overstuffed arm
chair.

At first Denise felt a maternal glow. She was motionless, gazing
at her partner in his workout clothes, tightly tailored to his slim phy-
sique. But as he sat asleep, Denise sensed she was seeing a fresh side

of him. In a T-shirt and gym shorts, she saw Reed's muscular body that could only have been maintained by a routine of daily workouts.

Being honest with herself, Denise realized she was jealous of Cathleen. Cathleen had a husband who was sensitive and passionate; a husband who understood her and what made her tick. Denise felt her own husband lacked those qualities, Denise wondered if Reed understood her better than her own husband, Zach. That realization hurt.

Perhaps she was seeing Reed differently now that she and Zach were going through a rough patch. Zach could not understand her passion for her career, or her need to focus on a case until it was solved. Their marriage had recently become work and a chore.

Denise understood that being attracted to your work partner was a recipe for disaster in police work. Perhaps that's why it took her this long to notice how appealing Reed was. She had been putting such thoughts out of her mind. But now that they had escaped the bottle, like a magical genie—she had to find a way to get the genie back into the bottle.

That thought conjured up an image in her mind—a row of dominos falling after the first one gets a gentle tap. She took an inventory of those taps in other peoples' lives. Rene Thompson wished she could undo a momentary regretful moment in her marriage that was now threatening it. Same thing with the Rogers; his conversion from Judaism to his wife's faith was threatening their happiness. She and Zach had put off resolving their family responsibility issues to the point where now he's considering divorcing her. *All of us, our lives appear ideal, we appear so perfectly happy, but our happiness can be threatened by events that occurred a long time ago; things we assumed would stay swept under the rug. Perhaps we can't put the genie back in the bottle unless we face them head on.*

Reed began stirring, realizing he was not alone. "I must have dozed." Reed shook his head, clearing the fog from his brain. "Damn workout isn't quite the same as before the stroke."

"Looks like it's working, though." Denise's words were timid and quiet.

Reed sat up. "Deputy, what say you? Anything new on the investigation?"

"Nothing since yesterday when we talked," she said.

"I guess I dozed off. Do you mind waiting in the den upstairs while I shower?"

"No problem," she said, and they went upstairs. Denise sat on the den sofa, waiting and looking at the room where Reed and Cathleen spent most of their time together. She put her new feelings about Reed aside, conceding that they were mere fantasy at a time in her life when she was vulnerable to thoughts of things gone wrong and what might be.

***

On their way to the precinct, Pascoe was energized and in the mood for conversation. "How was your evening last night?"

She shook her head. "I don't know. Zach is still mad at me."

He recognized her tone as serious, not just small talk.

"Is it still the safety issue?"

"Yah, could be," she replied. "He's still got the kids at his mom's. Insisting he won't be back until we get the killer."

"Sorry, Den."

Denise looked at Pascoe. "It just makes me work all the harder to get the perp."

Reed had seen and heard it all before. The two things that break up a marriage on the police force are the constant risks and close calls together with the long, unpredictable hours.

"I'm sorry. Are you and Zach going to be okay?"

"I don't know. I think I'm more worried about how it might affect Zoe and Drake. I don't want them to see us fighting about it." Denise was suddenly uncomfortable talking about the state of her marriage.

Reed sensed there was a sensitive nerve exposed so he directed the conversation to the case. "Den, thinking about that attack on Monday night; whoever he is, he thought he could scare you off. One thing I learned the hard way, if your pursuer is serious about killing you, he won't be saying much—he'll just do it. The opposite is true if he had no intention to hurt you. Yeah, he wanted to intimidate you."

"Why? I don't get it," she said.

"This kind of killer gets off on it," Pascoe answered.

"And what kind is that?"

"The kind that thinks it's all a game. That's why I think the killings are related. He's doing it because of a self-imposed agenda. And that's the worst kind—dangerous because he's demented and unpredictable. They only way he's going to stop killing is by us stopping him, probably with a bullet."

When they got to the office there was a note on both their desks that Harry Richardson, the reporter, was in the waiting room, asking to speak to them.

Denise looked at her partner with a look that begged him to

deal with Richardson. "I've got an appointment with Dr. Richter so I don't have time," she said.

"I'll meet with him after I get my coffee and look at the overnights," Pascoe said. She walked out, and he leaned his cane against the credenza. The demanding physical training had strengthened his entire body, and now he could easily navigate without losing his balance, so long as stairs weren't involved. He encountered Judson and Branch who were sharing opinions about college football.

"You're looking pretty spry, Lieutenant," Judson said.

"You know Cathleen, she won't leave me alone," he joked. "Truth is, this physical trainer I'm working with really knows her craft. If you ever need one, I recommend her. Not bad on the eyes, either."

Patrolwoman Worthy interrupted the locker room banter. "Reed, Harry Richardson is waiting to see you," she said.

"Yeah, Liz, I saw your note. He's going to have to wait until I'm ready to see him."

When she walked out of the room, Gary Branch asked, "Did Denise talk to the counselor who helped the rape victim yet?"

"I think she has an appointment with her later today," Reed replied. "Gary, you saw the crime scene. What was your impression?"

"I have no qualms that whoever killed Arnold and the kids is the same guy. The crimes have got to be connected by something other than coincidence. I think we may have a vigilante out there. I may be the only one thinking this, but I wouldn't be surprised that in the mind of the killer, the teens did something just as despicable as Arnold, only we don't know it yet."

"Okay, we get that possibility, but how does he know about both without having eyes on our reports?" Reed asked.

"You and Denise seem to share the same theory that someone gave him that information," Branch said. "Remember our suspects. We have one that's a serious IT guy, the brother, Vincent. Judson told me his company specializes in security systems that prevent unauthorized access. Doesn't it make sense that they have to know a lot about hacking so they can develop that kind of security? My bet is that he hacked into our database."

"You're starting to sound like Denise. She won't say it, but I know he's her favorite."

"Why won't she say so?" Gary asked.

"This is solely my opinion, but I don't think she likes to admit to her 'women's intuition,'" Reed replied. "You see, Denise doesn't like to remind us that she's a woman."

"Huh? I don't get it," Gary said. "She's one classy lady. How can we ignore the fact that she's attractive?"

Pascoe smiled. "A woman like Denise resents anyone thinking she gets preferential treatment, and wants everyone to think she deserves her status on the basis of merit alone. Which, by the way, she does."

Pascoe returned to his office and looked at the overnight reports. One item caught his eye. Dr. Edwards called in at 6:35. He wanted to know if the police had followed him home. The note indicated that the duty officer assured him that no one had such an assignment. Pascoe couldn't help but wonder that if Gary's and Denise's suspicions about Vincent were right, Dr. Edwards might be next on the killer's list.

Pascoe spotted Liz Worthy standing outside his office through the window that looked into the bullpen. She was staring at him and mouthing, *Harry Richardson*, and pointed toward the waiting room. Pascoe nodded, and a few seconds later Richardson sauntered into his office and sat down in one of two chairs that faced his desk. "I was wondering if I needed to order in lunch," he said.

"Sorry, Harry. You know how it is. The murders are starting to pile up, and everyone wants answers," Pascoe said with a sigh.

"Tell me about it," Harry snorted. "I've been snooping around myself. Nobody seems to stand out. And that's why I'm here. Something keeps nagging me about the victim you all investigated the other night. What can you tell me?"

"I'm afraid I can't tell you a damn thing you don't already know. I can only say that he was shot while sitting in a vehicle parked off Industrial Avenue," Reed said.

"Come on, Pascoe. I know you've got to have ballistics by now. How many shots were fired, the kind of bullet, and if the vic had a record."

Pascoe paused. What Harry was saying brought to mind Branch's suspicion that somebody might have hacked into the police database. And now he's talking to a reporter who's asking questions like he knows what's in their records.

"Look, Harry, you know me and how this precinct works. We're not going to leak you anything. I'll make you a promise, though. As soon as we're ready to release information at a press conference, I'll call you."

Harry was visibly frustrated. He knew Pascoe was his best source at Thomas Glen besides patrolwoman Worthy. He was concerned that if he said anything more Pascoe might get suspicious about what information he already had.

***

About a half hour later Denise returned from her interview with Dr. Richter. She walked into Pascoe's office and sat down. "I expected it. The rape victim's version holds up, and Dr. Richter said nobody knew about her role as therapist other than Detective Branch and the victim's family. So, that leaves us with someone who has a snitch in the County Record Room or he's hacked into the department database."

Pascoe paused for a moment. "Branch suspects the same thing, and Harry Richardson knows more about the Arnold killing than he should. We've got a breach. Let's go see the Chief. You asked him to have an expert look into it yesterday, right?"

"Sure did. My guess is that if he had the results we'd know it by now. If he doesn't have it, he needs to realize how critical it is that we know what happened ASAP."

The Chief was hanging up the phone when they appeared outside his door. He waved for them to come inside. "That was the mayor. We've been on the phone with all the mayors in the county, their police chiefs, and their system analysts. You were right about the hack. The consultant couldn't ascertain the individual, his location or what he accessed, but it was done by using the same type of probing software that is attributed to a source in the Ukraine. And, we have an exact time of the breach, Saturday."

The Chief looked up at Pascoe. The implication was obvious. It occurred six days after the murder of Sarah and Blair, and two days before Arnold was killed. Denise stared at Pascoe as well. He wasn't saying anything, expecting that she would say it for him. She didn't disappoint.

"I think we can agree that the timing is not a coincidence with our investigation of their murders. It's our perp," Denise said. "I've got a lot of suggestions, and the first one is the arrest of Vincent Thompson. The second; we get a court order for our hacking expert to examine the cyber systems of his employer to see if he doctored the security entry records to create a false alibi. Depending on what we find will drive our next steps."

She had the look on her face that they both recognized. She was right. They knew it and she knew it. "Only one problem," said the Chief, "you've got the order reversed. We can't arrest the Thompson guy without evidence that his company's security records were altered. The D.A. is already working up the subpoena."

"We may have a collateral issue," Pascoe said. "Dr. Edwards complained that someone followed him home from work yesterday. It wasn't us. My suspicion is that it's our perp, looking for another vigilante-style execution. We need to arrange for a detective to shadow him."

"Sure," Meadows said. "I'll have Branch contact the doctor and get it done. In the meantime, I'll get a patrolman to find Vincent and shadow him."

***

Driving his Volvo to the medical park, the Teen Killer had noticed the black, Ford Crown Victoria that remained behind him for over a mile and two turns. He looked at his watch. He had enough time to figure out a plan to shake the tail, if that was what is was. To be safe, he turned into a self-pay parking lot and waited for the Ford to enter. When it did he found a space and waited. The Ford drove on the up-ramp instead of the down-ramp he took. He quickly backed out and headed for the exit, put his ticket in the reader, and left when the automatic arm lifted. The Crown Vic was nowhere to be seen.

At the medical quarters parking lot, he pulled out the diagram of the security cameras and retrieved the small stepladder from his trunk. Armed with his loaded pistol and wire cutters he headed down to the floor where his target parked in his reserved spot. Wearing his ball cap under his hoodie he looked around for potential witnesses. There was no one on foot. He placed his stepladder under the light at the deck's door and reached up, unscrewing the light bulb.

His next moves were aimed at the security cameras. He cut their wires and waited in the shadows. Close to forty-five minutes passed before his target unlocked the driver's side door of his Audi SUV. That's when the killer made his move.

***

After finishing dinner at home that night, Pascoe got a call from Detective Branch. "The Chief asked me call you when I had something worth sharing," he said. I'm parked at Wayne Medical Quarters parking lot waiting for Dr. Edwards to leave for home. The patrolman assigned to Vincent Thompson lost sight of him about an hour ago. WAIT! Got to go...."

Through the phone, Pascoe could hear Detective Branch shouting. Then he heard two popping sounds like a pistol firing in the background. Three more popping sounds, but this time they were much louder.

"Gary, what's going on?" Pascoe shouted over the phone. The only thing he heard was the sound of someone running. "Gary, can you hear me?"

A moment later, Pascoe heard someone breathing hard, almost panting. "Reed, are you still there? Dr. Edwards is down!" Branch yelled into the phone. "He's been shot. Get an ambulance over here for me... and back up. I'm after the perp."

Pascoe called an ambulance, and then called Denise as back-up. "I can leave right away," she said.

***

Denise arrived at the scene about thirty minutes later. The ambulance had already taken Dr. Edwards to the Parkland Memorial trauma unit. Detective Branch, Pascoe, and another man, Detective Peter d'Arnaud, were standing next to the open door of an Audi SUV. She overheard Detective Branch talking to d'Arnaud.

"Dr. Phillip Edwards was found in his car, in the parking garage. He was shot by an unknown assailant who escaped."

"Hey, Detective Smith," Gary said when he spotted her walking toward him. "Dr. Edwards was in the driver's seat when he was shot by a man in a hoodie. I saw it go down."

Denise looked inside the vehicle. The carpeting and floor mats were puddled in blood. Reed approached her as she walked toward the scene. "Denise, the City of Dallas Police have jurisdiction, and they've graciously turned over the lead to us, but they want to be a part of the investigation. I called the Chief, and he agreed. Their man Peter d'Arnaud. He's..."

"No need for an introduction, Pete and I go way back," she said.

Denise made her way toward the City of Dallas detective, and he walked up to her. "Denise, how are you?" he said as they hugged. "We finally get to work together."

Denise asked, "Which one of you got here first?"

"Other than Detective Branch, who was shadowing Dr. Edwards, I did," Pascoe said. Gary was on the phone with me when it went down."

"One of our patrolman was sent over here on a call by the woman who owned the car parked next to his," Pete d' Arnaud said. "She's gone home now, but we have her statement. She called 911 at six-forty-three this evening. We didn't have a connection to your investigation until Detective Branch called me while I was on the way here."

"As you know, Denise, I was assigned to the doctor this afternoon. I called Pascoe to report to him that the cop who was supposed to shadow Vincent Thompson, lost him. I was parked over there." Gary pointed to his white Ford Fusion parked just outside the sheltered parking spaces.

"It looks like Dr. Edwards got lucky," Pascoe said to Gary. "He was shot in the shoulder and forearm. Tell her what happened."

"Like the Lieutenant said, I was on the phone with him when I saw this guy running toward the Edwards car, pointing a pistol. I yelled for him to stop. He looked at me for a second and then shot into the Audi SUV. I shot at him and he ran. Before I chased after him, I made a running pass to look inside the BMW. The doctor was hit. I asked Pascoe to call an ambulance, and then I headed after the guy in the hoodie. I never found him."

"Anything else you can tell me?" Denise asked.

"This perp is athletic. He could really run. I didn't get a look at his face, he was wearing a baseball cap, and best of all, he wore a hoodie."

"How about the garage security camera footage?"

"That's the most puzzling part," said Detective Arnaud. "See the camera over in the corner, its power wires were cut. Two more cameras were found cut as well. We talked to the security custodian—he didn't notice the cameras were out until he heard the shooting. He said he came down here just a minute or so later. A patrolman has his statement."

Denise turned to Pascoe. "What's your take on the camera?"

Pascoe unfolded some papers he removed from his vest pocket. "The custodian left these diagrams of the two floors of the garage where the disabled cameras are. If it's the perp who killed the kids, I think he's been here before. He knew where Dr. Edwards parked, and he walked inside from the ground floor from right here, at this corner of the lot. He knew just how to move to the camera's dead spot, avoided being viewed, and then cut the wires. Next, he walked up these stairs, staying close to the wall to avoid the camera there. Out of the stairwell on the second floor, he cut the wires to the camera just over that door there, and then proceeded along this wall to cut the camera over there, in the corner. Here's the beautiful part of his plan—the perp had to be carrying a ladder with him to reach the camera wires."

Branch took over. "It's my gut that he waited near the corner camera until he saw Edwards come out of the elevator. Edwards doesn't see him approach or doesn't pay any attention to him because he doesn't recognize him. As soon as Edwards closes his car door, our perp sees me and opens fire on him."

How about you, Reed?" Arnaud asked.

"I can't argue with the theory. It would work, and it sounds like the precautions our perp takes."

"Shit," said Arnaud. "This case is something else."

"Tell me about it," Branch remarked sarcastically.

Denise needed a moment to process everything. She walked over to the parking deck's elevator, and then the corner where the security camera was. The beam from her flashlight illuminated the pavement floor under the camera. It appeared to have a thin coating of dirt. She walked back to where Arnaud was chatting with Branch.

"Pete, do you know if your cameraman shot the area under the security camera?" Denise inquired.

"To be honest, I don't," he replied. "If you'd like me to get him over here, I will."

"Please—I think I saw a shoeprint and the marks of a stepladder. Judson might be on the right track about our perp. If he finds the same thing, he'll need to shoot the pavement under each of the disabled security cameras and the perimeter of the first floor, where there's enough dirt to leave a shoeprint."

Denise was trying to imagine the shooter's process as the men filled in Arnaud about the other murders. If it was the same guy, probably Vincent, he had to be the one who has Sarah's diaries.

Rather than discuss it with Pete or Gary, Denise turned to Pascoe who whispered, "I can't believe this. He must have the diaries, or somehow know Sarah had been involved with him."

"I was the one who interviewed Dr. Edwards," she said. "There's nothing in the report about him having a sexual relationship with Sarah. Yeah, I agree with you."

Pascoe hadn't thought about it like that. Now *he* was getting a headache. Denise convinced him to visit the Edwards home with her now so his wife would know why he wouldn't be coming home that night. They left Branch and Arnaud to finish processing the crime scene.

***

It was disconcerting to Denise, driving into the same neighborhood to meet with another family who they had to break more bad news. At least this was only an attempted murder, without the perp succeeding. Both she and Pascoe parked their vehicles on the street. It was then that it dawned on Denise that Pascoe drove to the crime scene, apparently feeling strong enough to drive alone. It also occurred to her that the news about Dr. Edwards was bittersweet in that he would recover and could be eliminated as one of the suspects in their investigation.

The home for the Edwards family was equally as impressive as the Thompson's and the Rogers'. It was late in the evening, about nine, when they rang the doorbell.

A pre-teen boy answered the door. "Hello son," Denise said as she showed him her badge. "I'm Detective Denise Smith. Is your mother home?"

JEREMY LOGAN & BRENDA SEVCIK

He didn't give his name, but said, "I'll go get her."

Claire Edwards entered the foyer appearing as if she was auditioning for a part in *"The Housewives of Dallas.* She was a thirty-something brunette with long straight hair, a glass of wine in her hand, wearing an expensive matching yoga outfit. She eyed her unexpected guests from head to toe.

"What can I do for you officers?" she asked in a deep, raspy voice.

"May we have a moment in private with you?" Denise asked as she looked at the teenage boy hanging back in a far doorway.

"I think I know why you're here. Has Phillip been a naughty boy again?"

"I think it would be best if we discuss it in a place where we can talk confidentially."

Without saying a word Mrs. Edwards gave the universal gesture of 'enter' with a flare. Walking to an intercom on the wall next to where her son was standing, she pushed a button and some lights on the device lit up in red. "Julia, can you come to the foyer and take Trevor to the bonus room?"

The foyer was designed to compare with any opulent home in Hollywood, complete with white, Italian marble floors and a huge, crystal chandelier hanging from a sculptured ceiling some thirty feet above.

"Yes ma'am," said a young voice with a Spanish accent coming from the intercom.

An attractive, petite young woman, no more than twenty, appeared from a white, carpeted stairway. She whispered in the boy's ear and they walked up the stairs together. Once they vanished to the second floor, Detective Smith and Lieutenant Pascoe were led to what appeared to be a great-room.

254

"May I offer you something to drink?" Mrs. Edwards asked as she reached the island bar that separated the room from the kitchen. "No thank you, Denise replied. "We have some serious news regarding Mr. Edwards."

Mrs. Edwards took a seat on one of the bar stools and looked at Denise as if she was daring her to surprise her. "Dr. Phillip Edwards is at Parkland Memorial Hospital after being shot by an unknown assailant. His injuries do not appear to be life-threatening, however he's currently in surgery. He was shot in his car at his office parking garage."

Mrs. Edwards struggled to hide her expression, but she swallowed and didn't breathe for a few moments. When she tried to speak, she tilted her head and said in an even more raspy voice than before, "Did I hear you say that Phillip has been shot?"

"Yes, Mrs. Edwards–at the office in his car."

Mrs. Edwards snorted and shook her head slowly. Denise looked at Pascoe, and noticed his eyes were wide and frozen in time. Looking back at Mrs. Edwards, it appeared she was about to drop her glass of wine. Denise gently took the glass from her hand.

"I-I-I thought you were going to tell me that Phil had wrecked the car again. It would have been the umpteenth time. You said... shot?"

"Do you know of anyone who might want to kill him?"

"Are you serious?" she retorted, looking insulted. "Phillip can be overbearing at times, but he shies away from people in general. I've seen him argue with people, but it was never like he was a threat to them."

"Can you tell me if you know of anyone he might have been worried about lately?"

"I've noticed he was a little more edgy than normal, but he rarely talked about work, his patients or colleagues," she said.

"Did you know that he called the police station the other night? He asked if we were following him. Do you have any idea what that was about?" asked Pascoe.

Mrs. Edwards nervously fidgeted with her wine glass and turned away. "No, he didn't tell me about it."

"Did he tell you about us interviewing him last week, and that he brought his attorney with him?" Denise asked.

"There's a lot of things Phillip doesn't share with me," Mrs. Edwards said in a voice about to crack.

"We questioned him about his relationship with Sarah Thompson," Denise said as she stared into Mrs. Edwards' eyes.

"I've been broken up about her death and her boyfriend," Mrs. Edwards said. "She babysat for our children. I liked her a lot." Claire Edwards paused and closed her eyes.

"But since you only questioned Phillip, I suppose you wondered about why he paid so much attention to her. Yes, I knew about it, and I was worried about what it meant. He was so obvious. I asked him about it plenty of times. He always had a good answer. He's the same way with our present nanny. If you ask me, I've never seen anything between them. I've reconciled myself that he's just a harmless flirt. But what does that have to do with someone trying to kill him?"

"To be honest, Mrs. Edwards," Lieutenant Pascoe said, "others might differ. We have an acquaintance of hers who told us that Sarah said their relationship became sexual. That person also said that Sarah threatened to tell you about them unless he left her alone."

Mrs. Edwards looked away. She nervously pressed her thumb

and index finger against her eyes, as if trying to stop her tears. She appeared more in grief about these new developments as opposed to being angered by her predicament.

Denise finally reached out to her. "We're sorry about bringing this all up now, but to be perfectly honest, we don't have any evidence that points a finger to whoever is Sarah's killer or who might have tried to kill your husband. We have suspicions, but that's all."

Mrs. Edwards turned toward Denise. Her face was red and her mascara was smeared. "I hope you understand. I wasn't curious about how he seemed to be more interested in them than me. I was hurt. I didn't want to know. If I knew, I'd have to do something about it. It would destroy me if I didn't. The fact is, the romance in our marriage ended with the birth of our first child. But that, I could deal with. I couldn't deal with being a divorcee—a bitter, pathetic woman without the means to do the things I enjoy."

Mrs. Edwards stood up and raised her chin, showing a resolute strength to get past this hurdle in her life. "The answer to your questions is I don't have any idea about any of this. You see, my husband is a secretive person. He shared little with me other than our bed. To be perfectly honest, I don't give a damn about your investigation or him. Now, please excuse me. I want to be alone."

Once outside, Denise asked Pascoe, "Have you ever met a woman like that before?"

"Sad, isn't it," he replied. "From out here her life appears perfect. They live like royalty. She's very attractive and smart. She's married to a doctor and has young children who are probably happy and ignorant of their parent's shortcomings. You know, we all live in a house of cards... take the wrong one out, and our life could just collapse."

"Depends on what you built your house on," Denise said.

28. THE BIG DECEPTION

THE NEXT STOP FOR PASCOE AND DENISE WAS PARKLAND ME-
morial Hospital. Dr. Edwards was out of surgery and in the recovery room. The surgeon told them there should be no permanent
problems. And they would be able to ask him questions in about
an hour.

Edwards was medicated, but willing to talk to Lieutenant Pascoe and Deputy Smith who were given permission to visit with
him. But their hopes of getting a description were dashed at the
outset when Edwards said he never got a good look at his attacker.
That made the interview short and useless. Edwards noted his wife
wasn't there. That upset him.

***

The next morning at the stationhouse, Mayor Coleman, the District Attorney, Chief Meadows and Pascoe and Denise were in the
Chief's office with the door closed. "Chief Meadows advised me of
the latest details of the Edwards shooting," Mayor Coleman said

with a surly look. "Harry Richardson called. He's running a story airing on the six o'clock news. The drift of his report will question our inability to identify a prime suspect in the teen killing, and that the killer is acting as a vigilante, gunning down prey based upon his twisted notions that they deserved to die. Do you all realize how the public will react? I've also got Dave Rogers and now Doug Thompson complaining about your lack of progress. I just wanted you to know that I've lost my patience." The mayor walked out of the Chief's office in a huff.

"I don't care who you think our killer is, I want you to bring in all the suspects for another round of questioning," Meadows said. "The D.A. and I will look in. We'll seek an indictment from the best of them."

"I hear you, Chief," Pascoe said, "and you all have the right to make that decision. That's your call. I have no comment."

The Chief knew Pascoe well, and he knew his response was the most polite way of saying, "Fuck you." Pascoe and Meadows had been friends for years, so he knew not to push him any harder. Denise remained silent.

But before Pascoe walked out of Meadows' office he stopped and turned around. "Chief, you know I won't go along with picking a suspect out of a hat so you can arrest him for murder. Look, I know you don't owe me any favors, but I need one. I'd like one more crack at reviewing the crimes scenes and the evidence. I think we can do it in thirty-six hours. After that we'll turn it over to the D.A. If she wants to take it to the grand jury to seek an indictment, we can be satisfied that we've done what we could."

The Chief paused to think about it for a moment, looked over at the D.A. who nodded, and said. "Okay. I'll call the mayor and beg her to grant your request. Now, get out of here before I change my mind. In the meantime, get cracking. I don't care if you have to enlist the help of the entire squad."

***

Reed put his arm around Denise's shoulders as they walked down the hall to the squad room. He looked at his watch and said, "Detective Smith, round up all the detectives and investigators and have them meet in the squad room in a half hour. Come get me from my office once you have everyone assembled."

"Roger that, sir." Denise had to resist the temptation to salute. Denise was confident that Pascoe got them the time they needed.

Reed wasn't in his office but a few minutes when the Chief walked in. "You owe me one, Lieutenant," he said. "The mayor will keep the hounds at bay for another thirty-six hours."

"I'll do my best." Meadows walked away and Pascoe looked at his watch. He had twenty minutes to come up with a plan.

Denise was waiting in the bullpen with the entire nine-member homicide squad. Reed walked in, stopped for a moment, and silently walked over to what they called "the investigation wall." The entire side of the room, perhaps forty feet in length, was made up of cork, except for a ten-foot wide dry-erase board at the end. He faced the assembled and gave Denise several sheets of paper he had been carrying. He kept one sheet and said, "Pass the rest around the room."

"These contain everyone's assignment for the next thirty-six hours. Report to me at noon tomorrow. We'll have the rest of the day tomorrow to make sense out of what we have and to give the D.A. our recommendation. But before you go, let's review."

Pascoe walked over to the far left of the investigation wall where there was a title block that read, Gold's Supermarket, August 3rd. It included the yearbook pictures of the victims, the photos of them shot to death next to the dumpster, their cars, inside Blair's Toyota stained in blood, and his cellphone found in Carl Meeker's backpack. It also included a list of missing items: Sarah's cellphone, the pillow used to muffle the sound of the gun shots, the murder weapon, and any fingerprints other than the victims.

"This is Day One of our investigation. I'm placing Miles Judson in charge of filling in all the missing pieces. Miles, your assistants will be Officers Brock and Worthy. They'll have new eyes and impressions. It would be a good idea to record their impressions. Just for starters, where's Sarah's cell phone, and what's the conclusion about the finger prints and crime scene evidence. The weapon, the pillow, the bullets and everything else except the bullet shell casings are missing—as well as a clear motive. Come up with an explanation or scenario of what the three of them did for the hours between the time the killer first arrived at the store and the time of death. Bring in 'The Verge' one more time. Show him everything and report on everything, all the video we have, etc."

Pascoe moved his attention to the section to the right of the first panel. This board looked more like a family genealogy tree. On the top was the title, "Suspects". It was mostly barren except for the pictures of Vincent Thompson and Carl Meeker. Making a list called "Honorable Mention, but Ruled Out" were the names of Sarah's school music instructor and Dr. Phillip Edwards. And lastly, the list titled, "Unlikely, Requiring Confirmation on Alibis" were the Kansas escapee, Jameson McGladrey and Sarah Thompson's biological father, Brad Lindgren.

"Next we have the suspects," Pascoe announced as he walked in front of the panel. I'm turning them over to Detective Branch. In your charge will be profiler Ramona Beamon and Officer Richard Duggar. Your assignment will be to review all the interviews and take any additional interviews that are warranted to clear up inconsistencies between what they said and the facts. For instance, the hacking into our records; Jameson's claim that Vincent could do it and that he has the knowhow to doctor his company's security records that show when an authorized employee enters and leaves. Where are Sarah's diaries? We've got a search warrant at our disposal. Use it if you have to. Find out where Carl Meeker is and interrogate him once more. Oh, I almost forgot to mention the Kansas guy that escaped–let's find out if we can rule him out."

Pascoe moved to the last panel titled "Collateral Crimes". Two photos, one of Jack Arnold and the other of Dr. Phillip Edwards, were below the title block, and below that were photos of the crime scenes.

"Denise and I will re-examine the Arnold and Edwards crime scenes for evidence," Pascoe said. "The perpetrator of these crimes was the same person who killed the grocery store kids. The bullets and shell casings link them all. We'll also be reviewing the gun shop video and interviewing the shop owners again. Finally, we'll be reviewing the matters you're looking at that we think are crucial. The rest of you, Officers Washington, McMackin and de Jesus, I need for you to canvas the areas around the crime scenes one more time. Look for anyone we might have missed who could have seen or heard something, and review all the other video footage from security cameras in the vicinity of the crime scenes. I want you to look for our guy with the hoodie. We need to see his face."

Pascoe looked around the room, "Any questions." Hearing none he said loud and clear, "Use email to report results and call either Detective Smith or me if you think you found something important that hasn't been reported. Be thorough and be suspicious. If we don't find anything better than what we've already found, the entire homicide squad is going to look incompetent. Godspeed."

***

The meeting broke and Denise pulled Pascoe aside. "Damn, you give one helluva pep talk, boss."

Pascoe smiled. "How about we check out the vehicles at the impound lot."

The evidence impound lot was only a half mile from the station. They looked at Blair's Toyota. Inside were wires that indicated the trajectory of the bullets originating from a pistol held by the killer in the back seat. Seeing a toy squirt gun representing the position of the pistol looked a little hokey to Pascoe, but the depiction surprised him.

"Den, don't we have all the suspects being right-handed?"

Denise looked at the suspect's notes and said, "Yes, that's right."

"If that's the case, then the shooter was positioned in the middle of the back seat when the first shot was fired. And the gun was only a foot from the driver's head, about shoulder high on Blair. Almost what you might expect from an executioner. But now look at the position of the gun and the trajectory of the bullet that killed Sarah. The gun is much lower and her head is not much higher than the center console between the front seats. Either there was a struggle or Sarah lunged toward the mortally-wounded Blair when the first shot was fired. She was shot in the back of the head, but it might not have been planned to be an execution-style killing. Her death might not have been intended by the killer at all."

Denise got in the back seat of the Toyota and examined what was the scene of the shooting. "I think you're right, Pascoe. Sarah might be dead because the killer was surprised by her reaction and squeezed the trigger by mistake. I don't think we can rule out the murders as executions, but it opens the door to a broader set of motives."

"Why do you think the killer took the pillow with him?" Pascoe asked as he looked at the pillow stuffing fibers in the car.

"It either could have been his, and he brought it with him," Denise said. "In that case, he left with it so it couldn't be traced to him. The other scenario is that it was already here and he mindlessly left with it. I don't think option two makes much sense unless he believed his DNA might be on it, and taking it with him was insurance that he left no evidence that could link him to the scene."

From there they walked over to Jack Arnold's minivan. They saw nothing that wasn't already in the police report. A shooter stood at the passenger side of the vehicle and opened fire through the glass window. The report indicated that there were no security cameras near the Arnold vehicle and no eye witnesses. Just like at the grocery store, there was zilch evidence to identify the perpetrator.

Pascoe's face mirrored dejection as the two walked out of the impound lot. "Now you see what I've been dealing with the past week. It's discouraging not seeing anything that might help.

Before they could visit the gun shop where the ammunition was purchased, Chief Meadows called to tell them to come straight to his office to meet with the firm that investigated the hacking of the police computer records.

***

Pascoe and Denise were met by the mayor, the Texas agent they met at the initial press conference and Dallas County Chief of Police–Randall Jefferson, his IT manager, Ron Garrett, and two members of the DeHack computer investigative firm. Garrett led the meeting, but it turned into a shouting match because DeHack investigators wanted to leave the hack active a little while longer so they could come up with what a layman might call a trace or signature of the person who compromised the system. The police wanted it closed immediately or to leave what might be considered a land mine, which is a file folder—when opened it would send a virus to the hacker's machine that would render it to nothing more than a useless doorstop.

Pascoe interrupted with, "Are you saying you haven't been able to identify the hacker?"

Garrett responded, "That's right. We've narrowed it down to six possible online identities, but the location of the hacker's machine is still uncertain. It's very complicated, but this guy is using very sophisticated masking networks. We won't know his true identity until he re-enters the system at least another two times. What's worse, he hasn't entered it in the last two days."

"We can't leave ourselves exposed that long," Jefferson said. "Who knows how adventurous this guy might be. He might want to access the most confidential files that aren't even related to your investigation."

"Well then," Pascoe said, "we'll have to give him an incentive to enter into our records a few more times, and do it quickly."

"I don't catch your drift," said Jefferson.

"Simple. A carrot we leak to reporters that we've found incriminating evidence."

"I didn't know we had any," said Chief Meadows.

"We don't," said Pascoe. "We'll have to lie."

Everyone quickly agreed with Pascoe's plan and he called Harry Richardson. Harry said he would be at the stationhouse within the hour.

The plan was to say that The Verge identified him when he viewed the videos of the suspects. Judson was to take The Verge to a safe house in case the killer wanted to eliminate the potential eye witness.

Harry Richardson met with Pascoe and Denise in one of the interrogation rooms. Harry was offered the recent fake evidence about the eye witness if he would hold off his story that was critical of the police investigation. "I can't authorize delaying it by myself," he said. "But if it is approved, we'll report on the eye witness and delay our comments on your investigation, but no more than forty-eight hours." A couple of hours passed when Pascoe heard from Harry that the delay was approved.

That was a complete victory for the police, but there was a snag with The Verge. He wouldn't leave the shelter or alter his routine. The fake report was filed anyway, with the Thomas Glen precinct providing around-the-clock protection for him. The morning news aired the fake police story as 'breaking news'. Within the hour after that all the news outlets had it, so did the killer. The story referred to a homeless witness. The headline read, "Eye witness says killer wore the mask of Satan, but he saw him without the mask on as well."

The fake report proved to be enough incentive for the killer to hack into the police records again to find out who he identified. The report was as vague as they could make it while also making it clear who The Verge fingered. It said the identification was made from viewing the videotapes of suspects interrogated on the Wednesday following the incident. The interrogation records in the police database were also easy to identify. They showed that the only witness who was questioned on that date was a homeless man.

Pascoe was rewarded for his plan within an hour after the story broke. DeHack had located the hack to a machine in the Dallas area. As soon as Chief Meadows was advised of this news, Pascoe put into motion the news story. He called Harry and said the eye witness would be placed into a police safe house to protect him from the killer.

After that, another fake police report was filed that detailed which safe house would be used for the eye witness. It was known as Resource Nine. Another fake document was placed into the records called Police Resources. Resource Nine was listed among eleven items as 1497 Lewis Farm Road. This resource was, in fact, a property recently condemned by the county. It consisted of eight acres with a farmhouse and barn. Night vision video cameras were installed throughout the property and at the most likely points of entry pointed outward. The cameras were so well disguised that the police had difficulty identifying them.

The killer didn't waste any time stalking the property. He showed up the next day, driving past the entry driveway several times in his vehicle. His face was clearly viewed, as well as the license plate, but the driver wore the Satan mask. The vehicle was a Volvo, and appeared to be identical to the one owned by Vincent Thompson, but the license plate looked like a dealer tag. The killer was simply too careful to allow himself to be identified with any certainty. In fact, Pascoe and Denise interpreted it as Vincent thumbing his nose at them.

The bad news kept coming. DeHack reported that the perp used another machine, which was also disguised by masked networks. A meeting with Meadows, the D.A., Reed and Denise ended in a unanimous belief that they were certain the killer was Vincent, but that they had a purely circumstantial case that was missing an identification. D.A. Holmes refused to take it to the grand jury without an eyewitness to identify the killer.

29. ROUND-UP

THE DA ADVISED THE INVESTIGATION TEAM THAT SHE WOULD not be going to the grand jury to indict Vincent until they had more hard evidence. Lieutenant Pascoe and Detective Smith were not deterred, only more determined to find something substantive. They were in Chief Meadow's office for a strategy meeting minutes after hearing the news to refocus on the case.

"Chief, we still have the search warrant for Vincent's home and possessions," Pascoe said. "We still can build a case for an indictment. The diaries are somewhere. So are the murder weapon and its ammunition. Any one of those, if we find them among his belongings, should be more than enough evidence on top of what we have."

"I get all that Reed," Meadows said, "but in the meantime, we'll be working in the middle of a shit storm of negative press."

Pascoe glanced over at Denise, who was patiently witnessing the kind of deal-making that goes on behind closed doors among stubborn people who wield the kind of power that changes lives. "That shit storm is coming no matter what we do," Pascoe said. "I've got a hunch we're going to find something with our search warrant and an intense interrogation. The Chief didn't share Pascoe's optimism.

He looked the part of a man who had gone ten rounds with someone and who had the crap beaten out of him.

Chief Meadows nervously began tapping the eraser end of his pencil on his desktop as he considered the consequences. Then, as if a bomb had exploded under him, the Chief stood up and shouted. "Dammit, Reed. You're going to do it anyway…. Yeah, use your little search warrant. Surprise me…and find something worth the bother. Now, get out of here."

Reed and Denise had seen The Chief in one of his shitty moods many times before. They didn't bother to comment on it, instead they retreated to the Lieutenant's office. "Den, do you mind calling Sarah's parents and give them a heads-up. I don't want to surprise them, and I don't care if their lawyer objects. We'll work our way through it. We can't have them thinking this is a sneak attack and say so to the press."

Denise agreed and made the call from her desk.

Detective Judson came over to her desk while she was on the phone with Rene Thompson. "I got the final word on that Louisiana felon that killed the two lovers in Kansas a week before the grocery murders. Their suspect, Timothy Peters, was captured on a Kansas bank's ATM camera the same day of our murders. We can now officially rule him out."

Denise grimaced and then smiled. "It's kind of bad news–good news," she said. We eliminate a long shot who could save us a lot of grief if he was the one that did our murders. But in the end, it just makes me more certain we've been on to the right guy all along."

***

The drive to the Thompson home was a quiet ride. Denise was dreading there might be an emotional scene. The flip side was Pascoe's optimism that they might find something useful. Three uniformed policemen arrived just prior to Denise parking at the curb. Just behind them was the panel truck the Thomas Glen precinct sent to every scene of a search warrant. It was necessary in case large, bulky items needed to be taken off-site, typically computer equipment, file cabinets and strongboxes.

Not unexpectedly, their arrival soon drew a crowd of neighbors, curious about the police action outside their door. Rene Thompson's reaction didn't surprise them. She answered the door without a complaint, allowing them inside as she retreated to the kitchen. She stood behind the large kitchen island that was a multi-purpose wonder of artistic design.

Lieutenant Pascoe and Detective Smith explained to Rene that Vincent remained a suspect, and that they had to rule him out. "The search warrant was for any place and anything that might hold evidence important to the investigation. "In particular, we're looking for Sarah's diaries," Denise explained. "By the way Rene, is Vincent at work?"

"He should be," she replied. "He left at two." She glanced at the clock on her stove. That was a couple of hours ago."

Pascoe's phone rang, and after excusing himself, he walked out of the kitchen.

Rene whispered to Denise, "I don't know much more of this I can take. I can't concentrate when I'm at the office, and in the evenings I get lonely with nobody around. People call me, and I don't what to say. How do I explain what's going on?"

Denise couldn't help but feel for Rene. Everything she had seen or heard from Vincent's mother appeared genuine and honest. Denise had met a lot of people during her years in law enforcement, but none had struck her like Rene, a woman much like herself, who simply got tossed a different set of dice.

Pascoe returned, cell phone in his hand. "Mrs. Thompson, it really is in your son's best interest to cooperate. We need to speak to him again. If you talk to him, tell him that I'll be here first thing tomorrow morning." Denise noticed the look on Rene's face as Pascoe was talking to her. Rene told the lieutenant that she would be calling their attorney to represent Vincent, and demanded that Vincent's interrogation occur only after her lawyer arrived.

Detectives Judson and Branch tried one more time to find Carl Meeker to bring him in. Denise arranged to bring in Jameson McGladrey. Since Dr. Edwards was now on the victim's list, they ruled him out as a suspect.

***

Patrolwoman Worthy escorted Vincent Thompson and his attorney, Arthur Benator, into the interrogation room. After a few moments, Smith and Pasco entered the room. The Chief added profiler Ramona Beamon to the group who would be watching the interrogation from the observation room, which already included Chief Meadows and Mayor Coleman.

Pascoe opened a manila folder. On one side were notes, written reports and evidence records. On the other side were clear plastic document sleeves holding photographs. Both Vincent and his attorney were immediately fixated on the photos, which varied in size, some in color and others in black and white.

As this was going on Denise explained, "Today's questioning, this August fifteenth, will be recorded and videotaped. It will be conducted by Lieutenant Reed Pascoe and Detective Denise Smith in the main interrogation room at the Thomas Glen Police Station in Dallas County, Texas. The person being interviewed is Vincent Jerome Thompson regarding the murders of Sarah Thompson, Blair Rogers, Jack Arnold, and the attempted murder of Dr. Phillip Edwards. Mr. Thompson is with counsel, Arthur Benator. It is five minutes past ten in the morning."

Pascoe glanced at Vincent, who did not look back. Instead, Vincent was fixated on the folder in front of the lieutenant. Denise was studying Vincent's expressions and demeanor. Vincent looked at her, perhaps only for an instant, and then back at the photos. The way Vincent was staring at the photos is what caught her attention. He seemed afraid. She thought to herself, *he's seeing them for the first time. How could this be the person that hacked into the police files? Surely, he would have looked at the photos in the folder of his crime.* Denise busily took notes of this paradox.

Meanwhile, Pascoe began his questioning, oblivious to what Denise was seeing. "Vincent," he said, "Where were you four nights ago between the hours of six and eight in the evening?"

Vincent looked into the two-way mirror and said, "That was Sunday. I went into the office for a little while after dinner to work on a customer complaint. I must have arrived about seven. After about a half hour or so I left. The complaint was more about the client not operating the system properly. It was a training issue, not a systems issue."

"When did you get home?" Pascoe asked.

"About nine. I didn't go home immediately. I drove by the cemetery. I was feeling sad. I miss Sarah."

"Did your route bring you anywhere near Industrial Avenue?"

"Not even close," Vincent answered. "That's in the other direction from my office."

"How well do you know Dr. Phillip Edwards?"

"I don't know Dr. Edwards. Sarah used to babysit for them. I've seen him at the clubhouse with his family, but that's about all."

"Were he and Sarah friendly to each other?"

"I guess so. But I think I remember her telling mom she didn't want to sit for them anymore."

"Do you know why?"

"I don't."

"Let's change the subject, Vincent. How many diary books did Sarah have?"

"I'm pretty sure she was working on the sixth or seventh diary."

"Do you know where she kept them?"

"Not really. I only know she kept the current one in her purse. She always told me they were private. She didn't want anyone to know where she kept them, not even me, mom or dad."

"If you had to guess where they might be, where would you look?"

"I don't know. When she was little she kept some things under her mattress."

"Do you think we might find them there if we looked today?"

"I don't think so. The police already searched her bedroom. If they were there, I think the police would have found them."

"What did you think of Blair Rogers? Did you like him?"

"I didn't know him. He was Sarah's boyfriend. I might have talked with him once or twice, but not like he was my friend or anything."

"Was he nice to Sarah?" Pascoe inquired.

"I don't know. I guess so. Why would she go out with him if he wasn't?"

Pascoe sighed. He wasn't getting anywhere with Vincent. He looked over at Denise. He read the look on her face; it was clear to him that she wanted to ask some questions.

"Vincent," Pascoe said. "If it's okay with you, Detective Smith will be asking you some questions."

Vincent looked at Denise, nodded and said, "Okay."

Denise took the clasp off the folder, the side with the photos, and laid them on the table. Vincent turned away immediately and said "No."

"I just wanted to ask you about the car," Denise said.

"Uh uh. Don't show them to me. I won't look," he said shaking his head vigorously. "You can't make me."

Denise looked at Pascoe who had a puzzled look on his face. She didn't think his reaction was consistent with a murderer, at least not like the one in their profile. It also occurred to her that he sounded more like a child than an adult. "Now, Vincent," she said, "how can we proceed if you won't cooperate?" She looked at his attorney, who was trying not to provide any body language that would reveal an impression. She paused, thinking of another way to approach him. "Let's talk about some of Sarah's friends. Do you know Lily?" She left the pictures on the table, hoping Vincent would return to looking at them.

"I know her," he said looking at the wall. "She's tall and pretty."

"That's right, Vincent," Denise said. "How about Jameson, do you know him?"

"Kind of," he said sheepishly. "I don't think he likes me. He was Sarah's first boyfriend. He asked her to send him some pictures of her half-dressed. Sarah asked me if there was a way to make them private, so nobody else could see them. I didn't think he should have been asking her to do anything like that. I sent him an old picture of her in a swimsuit from her email account, but I had loaded some malware in the background of the picture document. It really screwed up his system. Sarah told him I sent it. He was really pissed."

Denise was feeling she wasn't talking to a twenty-one-year-old man, but an adolescent. This wasn't the same personality they encountered at his employer.

"I just have a few more questions, Vincent—you drive a Volvo, isn't that right?"

"Yes. It's a tan sedan," he replied.

"Does it have any mechanical problems?"

"It leaks a little oil. It needs a valve job, but I haven't had the time to take it in."

"Do you carry your insurance card and registration with you?"

"I've got the insurance card in my wallet."

"May we see it?"

As Vincent fumbled around, retrieving his wallet and finding the card, Denise noticed the puzzled looks on the faces of his attorney and Pascoe. What caught Pascoe's eye wasn't the wallet. Vincent pulled out the card from his wallet to show her. The wallet looked like he had had it for a while. It was worn and the color had faded or just rubbed off after years of use.

"Your wallet looks like you've owned it for a while," she said.

"Sarah gave it to me for Christmas when I was in high school."
As Vincent answered his expression became sad, as if he was about to cry. Denise asked, "Do you have any other wallets you use?"

"No, ma'am. I had one before, but when Sarah gave me this one I threw the other one away."

Denise looked at the wallet again and then at Vincent. "Do you know where she got it?"

"I think she said she bought it from the Indian souvenir shop in Arlington. It's the kind the Indians make, stitched with leather trim made from cow skin."

"Thanks, Vincent. That's all we wanted to talk about today."

There was a look of relief on Vincent's face and he seemed to relax his posture.

"Wait a second," Pascoe said, "I have one more question. I see you have a key ring." Everyone focused on Vincent's left hand, holding the ring. That's a lot of keys for one ring. Do you have any more keys, Vincent?"

"N-no, sir. This is all the keys I have."

Reed noticed a slight quiver in his voice. He glanced at Denise, who gave him a look like she noticed it, too. "Vincent," Pascoe continued, "Do you mind telling us what your keys open?"

"Uh, uh, I guess so," he stammered. "This big brass one is the key that opens the door at work. Next to it, another brass key, opens my office door. The small silver key opens my desk drawers."

"Is that desk at work?" Pascoe asked.

"Y-yes, sir."

"How about the rest of the keys?"

"The next key is to my car. The one after that key opens the front door to home." Vincent stopped and stared at the last key.

"Vincent, what about this last silver key?" Pascoe asked.

After fumbling around with the keys Vincent stammered. "I-I-I don't remember what that key is for."

"Aw, come on Vincent," Pascoe said, "You remembered what all the other keys were for. And this key is quite different than the others. It's silver, almost new, and it has numbers stamped on both sides of its round handle."

Again, Vincent stared at it, but didn't respond.

"It kinda looks like a key to a padlock. Do you have a padlock?" Pascoe asked.

Vincent didn't answer. Pascoe asked him again—still no answer from Vincent. After more urging from Pascoe and no response from Vincent, his attorney asked for a moment to confer with his client. They talked in private outside the door to the interrogation room and came back in. The attorney said, "He still doesn't remember, and he's very tired. If that's all you have, we'd like to go home."

"Sure, I understand," Pascoe said. "But, I'd like to resume this interview later this week?"

The attorney looked at Vincent, who wasn't looking back. "Call my office, and I'll arrange it."

After everyone left the interrogation room, Pascoe pulled Denise aside. "I've got to know. What did you find out? I've got no clue what you were after."

"The wallet—it's identical to the description from the gun shop owner who sold the bullets to the killer. You can hear it from the horse's mouth when we talk with him."

"You're getting awfully good at this job," Pascoe said with a smile. "Pretty soon you'll be asking for a promotion."

"Now you tell me about the keys," Denise said.

"That last key looks just like the key I was given by the man that runs the self-storage business on Old Oklahoma Road. I rented a place to put my parent's things when they downsized. I think he's got a locker." Pascoe said. "I made sure he showed both sides of it face up. It's going to be on the video. It won't be difficult to trace."

Denise raised her hand for a high five and Pascoe obliged.

After all the interviews, Pascoe, Smith, Beamon, and the mayor sat in Chief Meadows' office. "What the hell was all that about? To me, it looks like you came up empty," Mayor Coleman said.

Pascoe looked at her with a wry smile. "Yes, ma'am; that's what it was supposed to look like. You'll just have to trust me. It might take a day or two to run down the leads he provided, but my instincts tell me we're about to get all we need for the D.A. to seek an indictment."

The mayor shook her head, and a quizzical look adorned the face of Chief Meadows.

30. RUNNING DOWN THE LEADS

IMMEDIATELY AFTER VINCENT'S INTERVIEW, DENISE CALLED Ike, the owner of Old West Trading gun shop. She made an appointment for him to come by the precinct that morning. In the meantime, they enlisted Judson to run down the keys to see if he could get a match at any of the self-storage facilities in the area. After that, Denise reviewed the follow-up reports on the rest of what the squad had found. Not surprising was a report that Carl Meeker was dead. He was found shot to death in his cousin's trailer the night before. The bullet was identical to the ones that killed Sarah, Blair, Jack Arnold, and almost killed Dr. Edwards. *Our perp has been a busy boy*, Denise thought.

After Pascoe and Smith met with everyone in the homicide unit, they were informed that Chief Meadows was entertaining Lou and Ike from Old West Trading in his office. When they entered Meadow's office, the three men were laughing. "I bet you didn't know I knew these guys," the Chief said. "Before I came to Thomas Glen, I was working out of the Arlington station. I used to shop for my hunting supplies at their store. They said they've never met you."

"That's right," said Denise. "I've talked to them on the phone and we've texted, but until now, I haven't had the pleasure."

"Let me introduce you to Ike Gamble and Lou Furman."

They shook hands and Lieutenant Pascoe said, "I don't want to keep you both any longer than necessary, so let's proceed to the interview room."

"Do you mind if I tag along?" the Chief said.

The first item on the agenda was the viewing of the most recent interrogation of Vincent Thompson. When he pulled out his wallet Lou shouted, "That's him. I thought that was him when you first started playing the video, but the wallet is what confirmed it. That's the guy that bought the bullets."

The Chief was elated. "I'll be damned. You guys just nailed him for us." The Chief looked at Denise. "Good police work. I was wondering about that last line of questions with Vincent. Very impressive."

Judson entered the office with a big smile on his face. "I got a match of Vincent's key with Public Storage on Old Oklahoma. I'll head over there right now with the search warrant if you want me to."

"Hell, yeah," said Meadows. "Let's wrap this mother up right now."

After Lou and Ike departed, Pascoe and Denise sat in Meadows office as he called the D.A., Laura Holmes.

"I think we've got our man for the murders of the grocery store kids," he said. "When do you want to come by and review it with us?"

"First thing after lunch," she answered.

"Perfect," he replied. "And by the way, Detective Judson is on his way to you. He needs a search warrant for Vincent's locker at Public Storage."

"You hit paydirt on the key?"

"Sure did. Can you expedite it so he can get there before Vincent can clean it out?"

"You bet. I'm going to call the judge as soon as we hang up."

***

After Pascoe and Smith walked out of Chief Meadows' office, Pascoe said to Denise. "I'll start reviewing the IT report on Vincent's computer. Do you mind getting the video recording of Vincent's interview on disc so we can assemble the evidence we'll need to get an indictment?"

"They smiled at each other in a familiar way that meant they were excited about their prospects.

Back in his office, Pascoe pulled out the IT report. It opened with the statement he was expecting. It read: *Hard drive scrubbed regularly—no files or data stored on this device. The operator moves data from this device to an alternate daily. Only activity is as a web browser.* The one thing Vincent was unable to do was eliminate the queries made on the internet. Although internet browsing history would never be considered evidence sufficient to convict anyone, it showed what interests Vincent had, and how much detail and depth he sought in matters related to the crimes he might be accused of committing.

A printout followed, listing the websites he visited. It was nine pages long, logging 541 websites. *This is a mountain of information that would be best analyzed by a team of experts,* Pascoe thought to himself. He certainly didn't have the energy or experience to know what inferences could be made by visiting sites that might have a bearing on Vincent's state of mind.

A moment later, Judson walked into his office with Denise. "We've got some photos for you, boss," she said as Miles plugged his IPhone into Pascoe's laptop. At the chime Pascoe's computer made to notify him that an external device had connected to it, Pascoe typed a few key strokes, and the first picture appeared.

"Are those Sarah's diaries?" Pascoe asked excitedly.

"Just wait," Miles said.

Pascoe opened up the next photo image. "Don't tell me." he said. "Is that the murder weapon?" Miles and Denise grinned.

Pascoe clicked on the rest of the photos. One was a hoodie like the one The Verge described. Another was a photo of a Satan mask, and the others were a box of pistol bullets, and a pillow with stuffing coming out of a hole in the middle of the pillow.

"Goddamn! It's all here," Pascoe exclaimed.

Pascoe stood up, raised his hand, and Denise gave him a high five. A moment later Judson joined in for a group high five. They had their killer. Vincent would receive his justice.

The commotion caught the attention of everyone in the precinct house. When Chief Meadows walked in to investigate, Pascoe turned his laptop around so everyone could see the bounty of evidence discovered in Vincent's storage locker.

"This calls for a lunch on the County's tab," Meadows announced. "We'll reconvene at the corner tavern." They all headed out to celebrate.

***

After lunch Pascoe and Denise met with D. A. Laura Holmes. It was a short meeting that consisted of a visit to the Investigation Wall, the video of Vincent's testimony, and the photos from his storage locker. The D.A. smiled and said, "Thank God," I can finally see this nightmare coming to an end. I know you all have worked very hard. Congratulations, I'll call for the grand jury in the morning."

31. THE WAITING GAME

THE D.A. CALLED MEADOWS A LITTLE BEFORE NOON THE next day to advise him of the grand jury's decision to indict Vincent Thompson for four murders and an attempted murder. His arraignment was set for Monday, two days away. Vincent was placed under arrest and jailed, pending his arraignment hearing. The judge confirmed the indictment on Monday, and at the prosecution's motion, he ordered that Vincent be held in jail without bail until his arraignment hearing.

That afternoon, Vincent's lawyer requested a meeting with the D.A. to discuss procedure leading to a trial date. He also wanted to view the evidence the police had up to that time. His request was granted, and the meeting was set for the next morning.

The kind of pre-trial meetings defense attorneys and the D.A. have at the early stages of a capital crime prosecution are important, but they don't usually draw that much interest. Because of the high profile of this case and the rare type of crime for this community, this case was quite different. The public was hungry for details, and the media did everything in its power to help inform them, making the meeting a bona fide media spectacle.

Since such crimes were so rare in this community, everyone in law enforcement wanted to use it as a learning opportunity. Seats at the table in the precinct interrogation room were reserved for the D.A., the defendant and his attorney, leaving three more chairs. Chief Meadows had first dibs and he wanted in. The other two chairs were for Lieutenant Pascoe and Detective Smith, who were there because the D.A. preferred the comfort of their knowledge of the investigation so she could pass notes with them. And there was an unexpected request; Vincent's attorney said his client wanted them in the room.

Chief Meadows asked Pascoe and Smith to come to his office. "The D.A. just called to tell me that you two get to sit at the table in the Vincent Thompson conference. In fact, this Vincent character requested that you two be included."

Detective Smith folded her arms in front of her chest, smiled, and shrugged. "What?" Pascoe exclaimed. "Are you sure?"

"Yeah," said the Chief. "His lawyer brought it up when they arranged it. Is there something you haven't told me?"

Pascoe and Denise shrugged and shook their heads in unison. The Chief waved at them. "Get out of here. Getting anything out of the two of you is impossible."

Once out the door of the Chief's office, Denise asked Pascoe, "How unusual is that?"

"I'll put it this way. I've been a detective for eighteen years, and this is the first time I've been asked to attend a conference by the lawyers on the defense side of the table."

"Got any idea why it's different this time?" Denise asked.

"Nope. But I've got a bad feeling. Is there anything that happened with him when I was laid up?"

Denise paused and squinted her eyes straining to search her

memory for anything that made sense. "Sorry, Reed. I've got nothing. This case…nothing makes sense. Think about it. What's Vincent's motive? I've got to admit, I've had a hunch about him from the beginning. But from everything I've seen, he adored Sarah. Unless…"

"Remember what I said about motive, and we haven't ruled out jealousy," Pascoe said. They're not blood relatives. Maybe he fancied himself ending up with her by his side forever."

"Sure, I get that," Denise remarked. "But why kill her? Why haven't we heard of an argument or at least a scene between them before this?" Why did he put so much effort into hiding his involvement, hacking into our computer system, killing others, trying to kill us or scare us off the case, only to overlook us noticing the storage locker key? Why doesn't he destroy the incriminating evidence instead of making it easy to find it all in one place? Don't you kinda wonder if he's being framed? Maybe that's why he wants us there. Maybe he thinks he knows who did it, and wants us to investigate."

Pascoe smiled at Denise, "This is what I missed about you when I was recovering. Only you could imagine such a scenario. Before anyone goes off on that kind of tangent, we need to hear what Vincent has to say."

***

The morning of the pretrial conference was filled with anticipation. Everyone in the Thomas Glen government was curious, nosey or wanted the opportunity to be seen on television. The media showed up early camping out on the grounds outside the doors leading to the D. A.'s offices.

In the observation room were Mayor Coleman, profiler Ramona Beamon, and State Representative Cummings, a former state prosecutor. After an equipment check, Vincent Thompson, wearing the customary orange jail garb, entered the room with his attorney, Arthur Benator, and sat down. A policeman entered with them and secured the handcuffs Vincent wore to a metal bracket affixed to the wooden table top. The officer also secured his leg irons to a bracket on the floor beneath his chair. A moment later the prosecution team, in suits and ties, entered the room. Detective Smith, who looked very professional in her version of the same, only with a navy-blue skirt, white blouse, no tie with an open collar. The D.A. also wore a blazer, grey with a black skirt and spiked heels. Except for Vincent, a photo of the gathering could easily be mistaken as a corporate board meeting.

This entire time Vincent sat quiet but restless, constantly scribbling on a legal pad that was placed on the table for each participant. Occasionally, his eyes would look up. And when he did, he only looked at Denise, as if he knew she was constantly looking at him, which she was.

The first half hour was dedicated to entirely procedural matters, and those in the observation room were close to nodding off until they discussed his plea. No one acted surprised when his attorney said they would plead–not guilty.

D.A. Laura Holmes, used this opportunity to discuss the evidence. First was the list of potential witnesses. It included the medical examiner, a ballistics expert, Virgil Hempstead, Lou and Ike from Old West Trading, the operator of the self-storage business, the IT expert and the anti-hacking expert. The mood of the meeting changed drastically when the photos of the various crime scenes were displayed. When the photo of the Satan mask appeared, Vincent tried to rise, struggling with his hands in the cuffs and grimacing as if he was in pain. His attorney tried to calm him down, but every time he glanced at the photographs, he winced again. His brow was arched and his eyes were menacing as he focused his wrath on Detective Smith.

His grimacing turned to shouts, "No! Don't show me that trash." After a police officer entered the room and wrapped one arm around Vincent's neck from behind him, he calmed down and sat back in his chair, staring at Denise. "These are not victims. These are defilers and betrayers. You know what they did, Detective Smith," he said to her looking crazed, unlike the nervous, but meek, Vincent she and Pascoe saw at their last interrogation.

Laura Holmes, the D.A., paused, looking at Vincent and then at Denise. By the look on the D.A.'s face, she was confused. Buried under the pile of photographs was a picture of Sarah, alone, lying on the medical examiner's table with dried blood staining her hair. As Vincent noticed the photo of Sarah, his expression changed from agitation to grief. A moment later his eyes welled with tears and he started to whimper.

With a subdued Vincent and a lot of items she needed to address, Holmes continued her display of evidence. Out came the murder weapon, the diaries, Sarah's cell phone, Vincent's key chain, shell casings, and lastly, the pillow with the bullet hole. As she gave the State's version of how she visualized the execution of the crimes, Vincent started mumbling to himself. He was barely audible, and the D.A. was trying her best not to let him distract her.

Listening intently to Vincent was Denise. She heard him say quietly, "He did it. It was Satan, not me. I couldn't kill anyone. I loved Sarah."

The undertone of Vincent talking to Detective Smith while she was talking, became too much for Ms. Holmes. "Can you tell your client not to talk when others are speaking?" she asked Benator.

"Vincent," Arthur Benator said, "Please be quiet while the D.A. is talking."

Vincent didn't look at him or the D.A., but at Denise. "You know I couldn't have done it. It wasn't me. I loved Sarah. She loved me. It was him." Vincent pointed at the photograph of the Satan mask.

A moment later, Ms. Holmes looked at Detective Smith. "Detective, do you have a minute? I'd like to ask you something in private." Laura Holmes stood up, waiting for Denise to walk out. When she did, the D.A. looked at Lieutenant Pascoe. "You too, Lieutenant."

Outside the interrogation room, in the hallway where there were no cameras or witnesses she faced Denise, eye to eye. "What's this undercurrent all about between the two of you?"

"I'm as surprised as you, Laura. We've had no private conversations. He's never acted like this before."

"Come on, Denise. I'm not an idiot. There has to be something," she demanded.

Pascoe interrupted, "I've seen this before. There's something in the way male suspects visualize Detective Smith. She never turns away when they look at her. She's studying them, but they seem to think she's trying to make a connection. Sometimes it's like they're talking to their mother or pastor. I've been there every time we've had contact with Vincent, and it's been nothing more than that. Is that right, Detective?"

"That's right," Denise said. "Wait, maybe not. One night I was attacked while jogging in my neighborhood. I couldn't identify who it was, but my best guess is that it was Vincent. He could have killed me, but a neighbor's dogs attacked him and he ran. He got away. Other than that, I have no idea what's going on with him. It's as if he's another person. We saw a little of this during our last interrogation of him. You've seen that video."

The D.A., paused. "Okay, I do remember the video. Let's go back inside."

They sat back down in the interrogation room. Denise could feel Vincent's eyes on her as the D.A. readied herself. "Sorry for the interruption, Vincent," she said looking at him. "Now tell us about what you were saying to Detective Smith."

That got Arthur Benator's attention, appearing like he wanted to interrupt or object. Instead his expression changed as if he was curious as well.

"Detective Smith has spoken to my parents," Vincent said. "She knows everything about me. She has my computer. If anyone should know I couldn't have done it, it would be her. I don't know why she's doing this to me."

Vincent turned his attention on Denise, "Detective, what have I done to you to deserve this?" Vincent asked pathetically, almost as if he were a child.

Denise looked back at Vincent quizzically. After an extended pause she said, "I think it would be a good idea to take another break in this meeting–only for a few minutes."

Vincent's attorney acquiesced. The D.A., Denise, Pascoe and

Chief Meadows walked outside the interrogation room and into the observation room. "What's going on, Denise?" Pascoe asked.

"Just a hunch. I want to get Ms. Beamon's impression of what she's heard and seen so far." Everyone looked at Beamon, who appeared to be deep in thought.

"I am as surprised as you, Detective," she said. "Half the time, Vincent doesn't fit any of the psychological profiles of a murderer. He's timid, self-conscious, and childlike."

Pascoe interjected, "And half the time he's the guy that got mad and tried to get out of his restraints. It's like he's two different people. Do you think it's an act just to confuse us?"

"It doesn't look like an act to me," Beamon said. "Do you have any reservations that he was acting during your first interview?"

Pascoe and Smith looked at each other and shook their heads.

"If that's the case, then you've got the wrong guy or you have something worse."

"What could be worse?" Denise asked.

"You might have the wrong guy and the right guy," Beamon replied.

"I don't get it," Denise said.

Pascoe slumped against the wall. "Oh, shit. Don't tell me we have a multiple personality?"

"It's a possibility," Beamon said.

"What?" Holmes and Meadows shouted in unison.

"They're very rare. But if it's legit, you'll never get a normal guilty verdict. The mental illness known as Dissociative Identity Disorder is often diagnosed with a finding that the alter ego that committed the crime is insane, which creates an absolute defense as Not Guilty By Reason of Insanity. Until we get an expert to advise us, I recommend you don't proceed any further with Vincent. The only way you'll ever find out if he's got DID is through counseling. The more you scare him, the more his mind will retreat into the depths of the disorder. If that happens, he may never reveal himself."

D. A. Holmes asked, "Has his attorney mentioned this possibility to any of you?" Everyone responded, "No."

"Before we go any further, we need to meet with an expert on DID. Now, let's go back inside and try to finish this as quickly as possible. If the defense hasn't considered such a plea, we don't want to give him any ideas or provide any more indication of what we have discussed here."

Back inside the interrogation room, the D.A. steered the meeting to cover only nuts-and-bolts items that were remaining on the meeting schedule.

After Vincent and his attorney left, everyone in the observation room moved into the interrogation room and began a discussion of the next move. The D.A. said, "We can't proceed until we know more about this D.I.D. possibility and how to deal with it."

Mayor Coleman spoke up. "If I were a betting person, I'd put my money on Vincent. While you were interrogating him, Ramona talked to a colleague at Southern Methodist University. He's one of the best authorities on DID. Tell us all what he told you."

"There's one ray of hope," said Beamon. "Oftentimes a DID pretender will reveal himself if he lets his guard down." There have been several cases where defendants have pleaded DID to get out of a murder rap. Only about half were successful in getting a 'not guilty by reason of insanity' judgment. We'll have to be patient and treat Vincent with kindness."

"Call your expert back to see if he can meet with us," Holmes said.

"I don't need to. I already asked him. He's coming here tomorrow morning at ten."

"Well, then," Laura said. "Those of you who want to hear what he has to say, you're welcome to attend."

***

Denise drove home feeling the best she'd felt since they found Sarah and Blair behind the market. She was looking forward to seeing Zach and the kids. When she opened her garage door, there was no Zach. *You are coming home with the kids, aren't you?*

Denise wrestled with the notion of looking weak if she asked him why he wasn't coming home. *But didn't he say he said he would once the investigation was over?*

Being anxious to be with her family got the best of her and she called him. The one thing she couldn't measure as his phone rang was and how he might react if she didn't handle it right. Her frustration betrayed her. He could hear it in the tone of her voice and the words she chose.

Without much of a greeting when he answered the phone she started in with him. "Did you see the news? We got the killer. I thought you were going to call me once the investigation was over?"

"Hello, Den," he responded sarcastically. "I've been good. How about you?"

She paused for a moment before answering. What did he say? Realizing how she might have sounded, she regrouped.

"I'm sorry, Zach. That's not how I wanted to start. Did you hear we got him? Can we return to being a normal family again?"

"Den, I-I don't know. It's been nice having a predictable life."

"I never promised predictable, Zack. And I don't know if I can."

"I understand. I want to come home, and the kids can't understand what's happening. Let me call you back. I need to think about it."

Denise knew she had to cut off the conversation so she wouldn't say something which could not be unsaid. "I miss the kids, I miss you. But...do what you have to do."

After they said goodbye, Denise began setting up the coffee machine to brew in the morning. She measured only enough for her morning cup. She would wake up, again, alone.

32. INTROSPECTION

AT THE STATION HOUSE, DENISE WALKED INTO PASCOE'S OF-
fice and said, "Who's going to lead the meeting?"

"Good morning, Detective Smith. How are you doing today?"

In an instant, she recognized that Zach said almost the same
thing last night when she greeted him with an attitude. She realized
she was still upset about Zach not coming home. "I'm sorry, Reed.
I had a bad night."

"Let's see if we can't distract you from thinking about it. I expect
D.A. Laura Holmes will run the meeting," he said. "She'll be the
one to prosecute the case, if she thinks there is a case. I don't expect
either of us will play much of a role from here on out. If there is a
trial, we might be called as witnesses."

Pascoe's phone rang. It was Meadows saying everyone was in his
office, and asking him to bring Denise. It was a tight fit, but everyone had a chair. There was D.A. Laura Holmes, profiler Ramona
Beamon and the man they introduced as Dr. Clayton Rayburn,
from Southern Methodist University. Lieutenant Pascoe and Detective Smith sat down to the right of the office door, all facing Chief
Meadows.

Laura Holmes started the meeting. She wanted first to hear

from Dr. Rayburn, who had already studied the videos of Vincent. "I've never been asked to contribute to an ongoing investigation," he said. "In fact, I've never been involved in an investigation before the defendant or his attorney has asserted a Not Guilty by Reason of Insanity or DID defense. It's my understanding that the only reason we're talking about this today is a result of your observation and wondering if you might be dealing with a person suffering from DID?"

Everyone looked around the room and nodded before Ramona Beamon answered. "That's correct. The interrogation was interrupted while we discussed our observations."

"I also understand that there is no video of the original interview of Vincent," Rayburn said. "Is that correct?"

"That is correct," Pascoe responded.

Rayburn paused, considering what to say next. "Since we don't have video of Vincent to observe his alleged different persona or identity, and neither he nor his attorney have mentioned the possibility of this disorder, all you have is speculation. I'm not saying your observations are inaccurate, but they might be premature. I have discussed this potential with the District Attorney, and will remain plugged into your investigation.

Laura Holmes cleared her throat. "It's the position of the Dallas County D.A. that we proceed with this case as we would any other case. I'm asking that the Thomas Creek police turn over the file of Vincent Thompson to my office for the purpose of submitting him for arraignment. Continue to pursue evidence and leads, providing me with updates and reports."

"I'm satisfied we'll have enough evidence, and considering his penchant for killing others, I'm confident the judge will grant our motion that we continue to hold him without bail. If the judge grants our request, I want this office to make sure he will be observed constantly so we can determine if he switches identities."

"How long until we hear what the grand jury determined, and then how long until the arraignment hearing?" Denise asked.

"I'll be visiting with the judge's clerk to schedule it. That won't take more than twenty-four hours. You won't have to call my office to get a report. My assistant will call Chief Meadows within the hour of us getting a decision on both matters."

That ended the meeting, but Denise and Pascoe waited to talk to Dr. Rayburn. "Doctor," Denise said, "what symptoms or behavior should we be looking for once Vincent is in custody?"

"It's Detective Smith, right?" Rayburn asked.

"Yes, sir," she replied.

"You seemed to have sensed it. But it will take interaction with others that will create the opportunities to see if he acts differently, depending on the stimuli. In many DID sufferers, stress is a common agent that instigates or triggers a change in identity or personality. Frustration, grief or if they are angered, are the kinds of stress stimuli that provoke the regular or historical personality to change to an alter ego."

"Thank you, doctor," she said.

"Would you be willing for us to synchronize our video feed to your office computer?" Pascoe asked. "If we observe anything that we think is revealing, I'd like for you to be able to comment or give us advice as quickly as possible."

"I don't see why not," Rayburn said.

"Thanks, doctor. I'll have our IT expert come to your office to help you set it up."

Denise followed Pascoe into his office. "I can't believe we're finally getting somewhere," she said.

"Don't get too excited, Den." We've still got a lot of work to do."

33. THE GRAND JURY

THREE DAYS LATER, PASCOE AND DENISE WERE IN THEIR squad car, waiting for the medical examiner to look at the body of a man discovered floating in a small residential lake.

"Do you think they'll ever try to get Vincent to reveal the alter personality that planned the killings and carried them out?" Denise asked.

"I suspect we'll never know. That's the hardest part of our job. We take sides. It's only natural that we develop favorites for being the perpetrator. Sometimes they go free. We may be certain they're guilty, but sometimes it can't be proven. We cling to the belief that we did all we could to find the bad guys and the evidence that puts them behind bars. Once we do that, we have to let it go, no matter the final adjudication."

"If they don't prosecute him, won't he still be a threat to kill more?" Denise asked.

"Well, then it might be back in our court to find the evidence to put him away. Look, you might be thinking it's over if the D.A. tells us the judge won't try the case until he's assured he's fit for trial. But that might not be the end. He's our killer for the kids and Arnold,

305

and we'll just have to find where he made a mistake faking this DID defense. He can't be infallible."

"So, what you're telling me is that it's not over until it's over—right?"

"Yeah, I guess so. I'm really trying to get you to realize there still might be a lot we can do to nail him. We can't let ourselves get so caught up in the trial crap. I know a lot of detectives. They're all haunted by cases where the bad guy got away. It can happen in this case, but we can't let such thoughts affect how we do our job. If we do, our performance will suffer. It's just that simple."

Denise couldn't resist looking at Reed and thinking, *how did he get so good? He always knows what to say. He tells us all he's oblivious, insensitive, and thick skinned. It's just a cover for what he really is—a pushover. Just like his outfit, he fools you into thinking he's a slick, superficial operator, but underneath, he's thoughtful with a heart of gold.*

The ringing of Pascoe's phone interrupted them. "We got our wish. Vincent's arraignment hearing is set for tomorrow," said the Chief so loudly over the phone that Denise heard every word.

***

The next morning the media met the prosecution team when they arrived at the courthouse. Pascoe and Denise walked past the mob of reporters and cameramen wanting a soundbite, preferring that the D.A. and Chief Meadows get all the notoriety. Once inside the courthouse, void of reporters and those without credentials or tickets, it was not unlike any other day of trials. Sitting on a bench in the far corner of the corridor where the public accessed the court-rooms was Dr. Rayburn with earbuds on, talking to someone on his cell phone.

"I hope we don't have to use him today," Denise commented as she looked his way.

"Yeah," said Pascoe. "If we do, we're fucked." Denise realized Pascoe was referring to the possibility that if the expert witness was questioned, the judge had to have the mindset that he favored giving defendants with mental disorders favorable rulings. She didn't think Judge Minelli was that kind of judge, but that gave her another thing to worry about.

Pascoe opened the door leading into the main courtroom. Sitting at a table on the other side of the gated wooden spindle fence that separated the observers from the participants, was Vincent's attorney, Arthur Benator. Directly behind him in the first row of pews, were Rene and Doug Thompson, both of whom looked to see who entered the courtroom, then turned away. They wore the expressionless face of defendant's family members they had witnessed over the years. It was the face of helplessness.

On the other side of the center aisle were Victoria and David Rogers, about five rows from the front. Sitting next to them was Pastor Dan. "Kind of like a wedding," Denise whispered. The Rogers were engaged in conversation as Pascoe and Denise walked past them and took a seat on the front row on the right side of the aisle. D.A. Laura Holmes was at the table on the right side, just beyond the gate. She was talking to her assistant prosecutor, Kenneth Benson.

Moments later the court reporter entered from doors on the right side of the judge's bench and took as seat at her table. A second or two behind her were the judge's clerk and bailiff. As if this all was coordinated, the courtroom entry door opened and a throng of people entered, led by a security guard. A light above the entry door illuminated, indicating the video equipment was on. A look forward toward the judge's bench, captured the bailiff testing the microphones.

Laura Holmes and her assistant D.A. took a seat at the table in front of Pascoe. They nodded a hello, but there were no smiles. Everyone had on their business face. As usual, Chief Meadows didn't attend the hearing, preferring to sit in his office and receive texted reports.

The clerk asked the D.A. and Arthur Benator if they were ready, and they gave affirmative signals. He nodded to the bailiff, who walked out the door that led to the judge's chambers. A moment later he returned with Vincent, wearing a white, short-sleeved shirt, khakis and a black tie. The look on Vincent's face was what Denise was waiting for. What she saw was, even yet, an expression they had not seen on him before—a look of defiance as he scanned the room while being led to his seat beside Benator.

Vincent didn't look her way until he was seated, and then, as if he knew where she would be sitting, he slowly turned his gaze on her, pausing while his eyes seemed to grow in size as he stared at her, and before turning away she noticed a quick little smirk.

Pascoe turned and looked at Denise. "Did you see that?" she said.

"I did," Pascoe whispered. They looked at each other for a moment, communicating in silence that they both had no idea what to expect from Vincent.

The clerk opened the door on the other side of the judge's bench and disappeared. A moment later he returned and stood in front of the judge's bench.

"All rise," he announced loudly. "The court of Judge Dominic Minelli is now in session. The judge entered the courtroom and took his seat on the bench. He was a tall, husky man with a thick mane of white hair combed from front to back. The only person not rising that Denise could see was Vincent. Instead he sat virtually motionless except for one hand scratching at the skin on his chest between the buttons of his shirt. He was staring at something on the table before him.

"Please be seated," announced the clerk.

There was an eerie, silent pause and the judge scanned some papers. A moment later he looked up and tapped his gavel gently on its base. "Clerk, please announce the case," he said.

The clerk rose and said, "Dockett 14941, The People of the State of Texas, Dallas County verses Vincent Jerome Thompson."

The judge looked at the D.A. and asked, "What are the charges?"

She rose. "District Attorney Laura Holmes, ready for the prosecution your honor. Four counts of murder in the first degree for the death of Blair Rogers, Sarah Thompson and Jack Arnold, Carl Meeker, and one count of attempted murder of Phillip Edwards."

Judge Minelli looked at the defense's table. "What say you?"

Vincent's attorney rose. "Arthur Benator, ready for the defense your honor."

Judge Minelli looked at Vincent and then at his attorney. "Does the defendant choose to rise or remain seated?"

Benator whispered a few words to Vincent. In response Vincent shook his head slowly, still staring at the table. "The defendant chooses to remain seated," Benator replied.

A barely audible, hush of whispers moved around the courtroom creating an eerie and dramatic atmosphere. Every attendee was focused on Vincent, sensing that this defendant wasn't your ordinary accused murderer.

"Mr. Benator," Judge Minelli said, "We're here today for the arraignment of your client and to conduct a preliminary hearing. Unless you have an objection that we proceed, the District Attorney will present the charges in greater detail."

"No objection, your honor."

"Ms. District Attorney, please proceed."

D.A. Laura Holmes walked up to the lectern situated between the tables of the defense and prosecution. "The evidence presented to the grand jury is listed in the State's motion to withhold bail. It includes the murder weapon, shell casings left at the scene, shells purchased by the accused at a local gun shop, and eye witness testimony of an employee of the gun shop identifying the accused as the person who purchased the ammunition used to murder the victims. We have another eye witness who will identify the accused at the murder scene at the time of the killing of Sarah Jane Thompson and Blair Jefferson Rogers, wearing the same mask of Satan found in the accused's possession. The State alleges that the defendant, in a fit of jealous rage, followed the victims, entered their vehicle's back door, and shot them both in the back of the head.

"The State also alleges that the defendant so enjoyed executing unsuspecting victims, that he hacked into the Dallas County Police Records database for the purpose of selecting strangers he would execute that were suspected of felony crimes. His third murder victim, Jack Arnold, was one such stranger he targeted and killed with the same weapon he used to kill seventeen- year-olds Sarah Thompson and Blair Rogers. Not satisfied by these executions, he tried to execute a fourth victim, Dr. Phillip Edwards, allegedly as revenge against him for abusing his sister, Sarah; a crime he discovered when he took possession of her diaries."

"The State considers the accused a psychopath and an assassin, accused of multiple capital murders, bent on satisfying his lust for additional murders. We consider him a flight risk. For these reasons, we move that he be held in the Dallas County Jail without bail until he is tried for these crimes."

"Thank you," Judge Minelli said. "What say you, Mr. Benator?"

"If it pleases the court, your honor, the defense contends that the State's case is purely circumstantial. The defendant does have an alibi and evidence showing he was at work at the time of the crimes."

"Mr. Benator, how does he explain his possession of the murder weapon, the ammunition, and that the bullets for all the crimes were fired from his weapon?"

"The defendant claims that he didn't own any of these items of evidence."

"Looking at the State's motion, they claim this evidence was found in a storage locker rented in his name. Have you discussed a different plea with your client, or suggested a plea bargain."

"Your honor, I have tried to discuss those alternatives and more, but he refuses to talk about it."

"Counsel, do you mind if I ask your client why he has taken this position?" Judge Minelli asked.

"No, your honor, I don't mind," Arthur Benator replied.

There was a pause, and the only sound that could be heard in the courtroom was the whir of the air conditioning system. "Mr.

Thompson," Judge Minelli said, "the charges against you are severe, and if you are found guilty, you could be sentenced to death. It appears you have able and experienced counsel representing you. Do you mind explaining your position to the Court?"

Seconds past, with Vincent still scratching his chest, while the rest of him was stone cold still.

"Mr. Thompson, did you hear me?" He asked again.

Another longer pause, and Vincent's appearance remained unchanged.

"Counselor, please instruct your client to respond," Minelli demanded.

Arthur Benator whispered to Vincent without getting a response and then shouted, "Vincent, you need to answer the judge."

Vincent slowly raised his head, looking at Judge Minelli and said in a loud, menacing tone with a sneer, "I am not Vincent. My name is Lucifer." Vincent stood up, gripped his shirt at the front buttons, and pulled it apart, ripping the buttons from it. And there, carved on his chest, dripping in blood was the word "Lucifer" that he scratched with his fingernails while sitting next to his attorney in silence. The entire court room clamored in horror.

Judge Minelli slammed his gavel several times calling, "Order, Order."

The bailiff raced toward Vincent to subdue him, but before he got there, Vincent was standing on the defense table, facing the gathering. His face was distorted, grotesque. "I am Lucifer," he shouted again. "I am God's emissary, sent here to rid his people of their sins, cleanse their souls and enlist an army of angels that will return his flock to his service."

Victoria Rogers fainted and slumped in her bench seat, unnoticed by her husband whose open mouth gaped with a look of horror. Pastor Dan was grasping the cross hanging from his neck, his eyes closed and his mouth muttering prayers.

When the bailiff tackled Vincent, they both fell onto the chairs at the defense table, everyone in first few rows scattered, except Rene Thompson. She stood there in shock, motionless and horrified.

Several policemen entered the room, helping the bailiff cuff and shackle Vincent. But Vincent did not accede without a struggle that defied belief. He screamed and shouted words in ancient Aramaic as the policemen dragged him out of the courtroom and into the corridor behind the judge's bench.

"Jesus Christ," Pascoe said to Denise. Not only do we have multiple identities, but we might also have a demonic possession."

Denise looked at her partner aghast. "This is incredible! We didn't need a psychiatrist to testify. We needed an exorcist."

34. WTF?

AFTER THE COURTROOM WAS RESTORED TO ORDER WITHOUT
Vincent in it, the judge asked the prosecution, "How do you wish
to proceed?"

"If it pleases the court," the D.A. said in a very polite tone, "in
light of what we've seen today we would like time to reconsider
the charges and meet again with defense counsel before we revisit
arraignment."

"And for the defense, Mr. Benator, what say you?"

"I have no objection to a motion along the lines of a recess as
long as we meet with you before reconvening."

"That suits the court," Judge Minelli said. "And you Ms. Holmes?"

"No objection your honor."

"Good, we are in recess until the court has received a joint motion to resume." With that said, Judge Minelli brought the gavel
down on its block with sufficient force to startle the court reporter.

The bailiff rose and announced, "All rise." Judge Minelli reced-
ed into chambers. The attorneys and officials acted as if in a hurry
to leave, but the throng of onlookers fortunate to get a seat, lingered there, waiting for more; more drama or memories to tell their
friends.

Denise couldn't keep her eyes off Rene, who still appeared to be in shock. Rene's face was a blank slate, her body stiff and measured. Her husband, with his arm around her shoulder, led her out of the courtroom thinking he could protect her from the media. More than likely, Doug was using her to hide behind. Pascoe put on his hat and followed Denise, who was following the Thompsons. They weaved their way through the press and headed for the parking lot where three uniformed policemen were standing as if to block anyone from going beyond them. The police allowed the Thompsons to pass, but held up the trailing media.

Before Rene got in her car she turned around and zeroed in on Denise, who had stopped on the parking lot side of the sidewalk just beyond the uniformed police. The two women connected more than their eye gaze. Denise raised her hand and waved in Rene's direction. It was a slow, sad kind of wave. Her hand barely moved. Rene looked as if she was going to wave back, raising her hand a little, but stopped short, and turned to get into her car.

***

The invitation list for the emergency meeting arranged by the District Attorney's office included Laura Holmes, Chief Meadows, Mayor Coleman, Ramona Beamon, Dr. Clayton Rayburn, Lieutenant Pascoe, Detective Smith, and Prosecutor Kenneth Benson. The only item on the agenda was what to do about the case, The State of Texas v. Vincent Thompson.

Ms. Holmes opened the meeting staring at Dr. Rayburn, their

expert on Dissociative Identity Disorder, slowly shaking her head as if at a loss as to what to do or where to go. Finally she looked around the room, but all of the other faces wore the look of reluctance to offer anything. Back to looking at Rayburn she asked, "Have any suggestions, doctor?"

"I would suggest you contact the two leading authorities on DID, Blackstone and Gross, and ask about the most recent trials involving DID as a defense. I know I've never heard of an alter ego of an actual demon, let alone Lucifer."

"And it seems Vincent's personal version of Lucifer is inconsistent with the Bible. I'm far from an authority, but Lucifer wouldn't be doing God's bidding. It doesn't make sense to me."

"To someone afflicted with DID or similar disorders, accuracy isn't important," Rayburn said. "Their fears and biases take over their thinking, distorting everything to fit their personal agenda. In fact, it would be rare that someone so afflicted could tell the difference."

The D.A. paused and looked at her chief prosecutor, "Ken, after our meeting please get with Dr. Rayburn for contact information on his two DID friends and arrange a conference call as soon as possible."

Turning to Chief Meadows, Ms. Holmes asked, "Do you think you can get your detectives to find out what the medical history is on this Vincent freak. A guy that wacked out has got to have been treated by a shrink, psychologist or even a general practitioner for behavior issues. And get a hold of his employer again. I bet he's had issues on the job."

She looked around the room and everyone was silent. "Get along, folks. We've got work to do."

Meadows, Pascoe and Denise walked out together. When they reached the sidewalk the Chief was about to say something when Pascoe interrupted. "You don't need to say a thing. We got it."

"Denise, do you need to get anything from the office before we head out?" Pascoe asked.

"No, I'm good to go." But I'd like to try to contact Rene. She might be willing to help. I know she's been through so much, but I sense she's pretty resilient. I also have a hunch she's as interested as we are about getting answers to Vincent's behavior and knowing why it all happened. I can trust her, and I think she trusts me."

Pascoe nodded his approval, knowing her powers of perception in such matters.

***

Pascoe and Denise arrived at Zenon Security Consultants unannounced and demanded a meeting with Vincent's boss. This time there was a formal introduction in the manager's office. "We didn't get your name the last time we were here."

"Avery, Avery Bradford," he replied. "What can I do for you today?"

"It's about Vincent."

"I figured that, but isn't he in jail awaiting trial?"

"That's correct, but there seems to be some items we didn't cover the last time we were here," Pascoe said. "You said Vincent hadn't been himself. What did you mean by that?"

"I don't think I said that. I believe I told you that I asked him if he wanted some time off after his sister was killed, and he said he didn't."

"Well, you might have a better memory about it than I do, but he's been acting strange and saying things we don't understand. We were wondering if he's done that in the past. You know, while on the job at Zenon."

"Not really. You do realize that Vincent is a very talented guy? He's high strung and has social issues. Many savants have similar traits. But he's a high functioning case."

"Savant?" Denise asked. "What do you mean?"

"Vincent has special math and computer skills. His focus on problem solving is uncanny. He devises security systems that are at the highest level. His special talent is to custom make each one entirely different from the others. He designs them to fit the customer's needs, physical plant and employees. Very few people in the world can do what he does. I understand you think he murdered his sister and her boyfriend, but that's not the Vincent we know."

"And that's why we're here today," Pascoe said. "Vincent has already been indicted. That investigation is over. What's unsettled is his mental health. Some of us who have witnessed him when he was interviewed or questioned by the police, wonder if he suffers from a multiple personality disorder. His behavior in court today was bizarre."

"I heard about it. But I can't comment on it further. I can only say that we're all pretty torn up about what he must be going through. I care a lot about the guy. He's like family here."

"Can you tell me if he's had any episodes that you're aware of that were bizarre?"

"Not anything like what you've described or how he acted today. Listen, I'm sorry, but that's all I have to say."

"By the way, Mr. Bradford, how did you hear about what transpired in court today?"

"I'm sorry. I can't say."

"You don't remember or you don't want to say?"

"I can't say," Bradford repeated.

"If you change your mind, please give me a call," Pascoe said as he gave him his card.

Back in their police cruiser Denise said, "I wonder how he heard about the scene in court today."

"Yeah. He could have said he heard it on the news or on TV, but he didn't. That usually implies that someone who was there told him about it. I wonder who that might have been. How about him repeating the words, 'I can't say'? Sounds like military jargon for *you don't have the security clearance*, or *that's above your pay grade*; or worse yet, *I've been ordered to give you that answer*."

"You're right," Denise said. "It makes you think that there are more people who are interested in this case than we know about, and they're not civilians."

"Good observation."

As they stopped at a red light, Denise turned and looked at Pascoe. "I'm going to call Rene right now. I know she'll be forthright with me, and besides....I have a feeling she may need to hear a friendly voice right now."

"Sure, give it your best shot."

Denise called Rene and made an appointment to see her.

"Den, I'm not sure how you do it. You were the arresting officer of this woman's son and she somehow finds you a confidante."

"We're just both human—and mother's." Denise said.

Denise smiled and pulled away as the light turned green.

"Why don't you go solo on this? I have a hunch she might open up without me being there."

Denise could always count on Pascoe's hunches. "Yes, sir. I think you might be right about that."

Denise was prepared to conform her visit to whatever seemed best for Rene, while also hoping that she could get the information she needed about Vincent.

***

Rene opened the front door leading Denise to a sunroom off the kitchen, near the porch. The last time she was there it was furnished with patio furniture. Now it was a makeshift art studio, with an artist's easel, and to the left a table with tubes of watercolors, containers of clean and dirty water, and a repurposed soup can holding different sized paint brushes.

"Welcome to my studio." Rene's face was washed out. Denise concluded that she had cried off all her makeup. "This is what has been keeping my sanity."

Denise approached Rene, who in turn, invited her to the easel to view the unfinished piece. "You're very talented." Denise looked up at Rene. "I would never have the patience for such detail work."

"I was an art major in school," Rene stood taller. "When I couldn't make enough money to pay the rent, my parents bargained with me to get an MBA. Which I did. Always, always, though, I was painting watercolors in my head. You know, I'd pass a pretty garden in some office complex, and I'd measure the colors, textures, and hues. Someday, I promised myself, I'd get back to art."

A sharp whistle blew in the kitchen. "Water for a cup of tea. Care to join me?"

"Sounds nice," Denise smiled at her.

Rene walked away from the painting and into the kitchen. Denise tiptoed closer to the canvas for a closer inspection. There were the pale blue yet distinguishable flowers of the bluebonnet, tall and tipped in white, looking soft and innocent. Intermeshed with the blooms were clusters of prickly pear cacti, and to the right one sharply pointed agave plant. In the middle was a large gap, still blank. Denise then glanced to the right, and saw a photograph on a nearby sofa. It was Sarah and Vincent as small children, bending down at the protected state flower. She thought to herself, *at that age they must have known it was against the law to pick a bluebonnet. Vincent had his hand on the stem, while Sarah had hers on top of his. Vincent had his eyes on the bloom. Sarah had a pleading look on her face, looking at her brother as if bargaining with him not to act on impulse.*

"Obviously, I haven't put the children in," Rene interrupted. "I'm having a hard time with that." She handed Denise a cup with a tea bag string hanging down. "You know, my grandmother always said if the children messed up, it was the mother's fault…"

"Rene, don't do that."

"You know, even though I didn't give birth to Vincent, I love him as much as I loved Sarah. Love him in a different way, love him for different reasons. But truly. No favorites." Rene hugged her cup of tea to her chest and walked away from the easel, looking out the window. Denise glanced outside as well. It was afternoon, and the shadows of the trees stole the color and darkened one side of the backyard, while sunlight lit up the other side.

"When Vincent was in high school, he saw a psychiatrist. A Dr. Rubin. He said Vincent was making good progress. Then Vincent turned eighteen. He went to Dr. Rubin for a while, but once he graduated from high school he refused. Dr. Rubin called me, called Vincent, urging him to continue treatment. Said it was critical. Because Vincent was of age, the doctor could no longer tell me anything. Every six months the doctor would call me, see how Vincent was doing. Really, I thought he was fine. Then this summer, as Sarah got closer to Blair, I felt a coldness in Vincent. I tried everything I could to get an appointment with Dr. Rubin."

Denise was still, listening to Rene speak. Rene turned from the window and looked at Denise.

"Goddammit, how I wish I had pushed it harder." Rene, working so hard to be strong, began crying.

Denise resisted the urge to go over and comfort Rene; partly because it would be more professional to remain detached at this point, but mostly she felt a heart as torn apart and broken as Rene's was not ready to receive any consolation—yet.

"How many of us wish we could jump back in time to rewrite history," Denise finally offered. "I believe you did the best you could at the time."

The sound of the air conditioner became louder than Rene's sobs as she calmed down. She took a sip of her tea. "Maybe." Looking over at Denise, Rene said, "I expect you didn't come here for this. Please tell me. What's next?"

"We're assembling a team to evaluate Vincent. As a start, it would help if you gave me Dr. Rubin's contact information. You said you noticed a change in Vincent. How so?"

Rene picked up the photograph on the sofa and sat down. Denise followed suit. "He just began acting…like a zombie. Cold. Distant. If I asked what he had been doing, he'd ignore me. God forbid, if I'd try to give him a hug or kiss him on the cheek. I wasn't sure it was his age, or what. But there was something in the pit of my stomach that told me something was up. Sarah and I talked about it from time to time. It was a lot for her. She had her own life, her own seventeen-year-old stresses. But she was clearly concerned about her brother as well."

"So Sarah agreed something was up?"

"For the most part, but she defended him. Said he had pressures at work. And she was so happy with Blair. He really settled her down. She was looking forward to school—to college…" There was a catch in Rene's throat. Her eyes looked heavy, and her shoulders began to round out over her tea mug. She looked so tired.

"Rene, is Doug around?"

She closed her eyes. "No. Denise, I just don't think he can handle all this stuff. He's at some extended-stay hotel. When I see him, he goes back and forth between anger and hurt. I think he wants to hide, thinking it'll all go away." Opening her eyes, she looked at Denise. "My sister is coming in a day or two. From Denver. I won't be alone. But…I will say, before he left here, he gave me some advice." She paused. "Good advice– if you can believe that. He told me to leave everything to Vincent's attorney."

"That is good advice."

"I just can't believe I've lost both my children in the span of three weeks. I'm never going to have grandchildren." As the last word came out of her mouth, her body shook and tears washed down her cheeks.

"I wanted to come by and tell you we had no idea that we'd see something like we did, or I would have warned you. We were all surprised. Rene, would you mind me calling Vincent's doctor? I don't know if he'd be willing to share anything with us, but we're hoping he can help us find out what might have triggered Vincent's recent behavior.

"You know…" Rene looked into Denise's eyes, "I don't blame you in any way. It's just so surreal. What happened to Vincent? How could he kill Sarah? Where did all this evil come from? How could I not have seen it? I feel I can trust you to find the truth."

Rene pulled out her cell phone, forwarded the doctor's contact to Denise. The women stood up and walked through the kitchen to the front hall. As Rene opened the door, Denise turned around. "Rene, you have my phone number. Please call if you need me."

She hugged Rene before leaving and squeezed her hand as she said goodbye.

***

Back at the stationhouse, Pascoe and Chief Meadows greeted her with good news. Dr. Howard Blackstone, one of the experts on DID, would be in the D.A.'s office that afternoon. Dr. Eugene Gross, the other DID expert would conference in on the telephone as they evaluated Vincent in the jail. Before their visit to the police station they would review the earlier tapes of his interviews and court appearance.

"The county has opened up its purse on this one," Meadows said. "Blackstone is going to stick around a few days after his observation of Vincent in his jail cell. In case you're wondering, Vincent's attorney is visiting him right now. By the way, two other men came with his attorney. Once they leave we'll find out who they are."

Later that day, The Chief walked into Pascoe's office while he and Denise were on the phone trying to convince Vincent's psychiatrist, Dr. Rubin, to meet with them. When they hung up he said, "We've been summoned to the D.A.'s office.

Laura Holmes had the look of someone who had yet to get over what happened in the courtroom that morning. She, Ramona Beamon and the prosecuting attorney, Kenneth Benson, were seated with her in the conference room.

"As if we needed more mystery in this case," Ms. Holmes announced. "The two men who accompanied Vincent Thompson's attorney were lawyers from a Washington, D.C. firm. I looked them up. They're with Kilbride and Jepson, a firm whose clients are predominantly government employees and contractors."

Pascoe and Denise looked at each other, as if they shared a secret about her report. Neither one said a word.

"Dr. Blackstone visited with Vincent in the presence of his attorney and Vincent's doctor," Holmes continued. "Their preliminary opinion is that our defendant has suffered the kind of trauma that can trigger the formation of a dissociative identity disorder. Blackstone won't say until he talks with Dr. Gross. Chief, what have your detectives discovered?"

"I'll let them speak for themselves."

"Detective Smith and I visited with Vincent's boss and his mother." Then Pascoe reported everything except the hunch that Vincent and the men who came with his attorney, all were government contractors. He withheld that nugget until he could be certain. He also related the phone call he and Detective Smith had with Dr. Rubin. The gist of their report was that Rubin refused to tell them anything about Vincent's issues or his treatment. He refused to say anything except that he was barred from breaking the doctor-patient privilege of confidentiality. He requested either a release from Vincent or a court ordered subpoena.

***

Just when everything was coming apart, Harry Richardson was seen on the NBC national news, reporting on what it was calling "The Mysterious Teen Killings Case in Dallas."

"What this investigation has is everything," Harry reported. "A month ago, two attractive teenage lovers were found shot to death, execution style in a trendy, upscale suburb of Dallas, Texas. Now it appears the devil did it, and on top of that, he's a hired contractor for the U.S. National Security Agency."

Harry went on to report that the local police arrested the female victim's brother, who claims he is Lucifer. "That isn't everything crazy about this case," Harry said. "The accused may have killed at least two others, and he tried to kill the lead investigator and attacked his deputy."

Harry continued to report on details, some of which were unknown by the police and matters they thought were hidden from the press and public. Harry Richardson had become the center of attention he dreamed about. He was asked to come in for a meeting, but he declined. The mayor threatened him with a lawsuit over the phone, which he broadcasted on Twitter.

There was now a constant media vigil surrounding the Thompson's home, and some reporters tried to get statements from the parents of Blair Rogers. Both sets of parents were afraid to leave their homes fearing that the paparazzi would follow their every move.

There was a "media shit storm," as Pascoe described it, surrounding the Thomas Glen government offices. The governor called the D.A. and the Texas Bureau of Public Safety was under siege–everyone wanting to know what the hell had happened. Requests poured in from every state, county and local politician wanting face time.

An emergency meeting was held at the District Attorney's office late that day. It included the local investigation team, the chief of police, the mayor, the state attorney general, the TBPS, and local state legislators. The topic of conversation focused on accusations of leaks, either in D.A.'s office or at the police department. Finally, Chief Meadows slammed his fist on the conference table. Everyone stopped what they were saying and listened.

Laura Holmes took command of the crowd, passing around a short agenda and announcing that no leaks originated from her office. "Let's get beyond the fact that a reporter gained access to confidential information. Most of what was in the police arrest file was already in the hands of defense counsel, so that explains some of it. You should also be aware that someone hacked into the Thomas Glen police data base, and got access to all the file material up to six days ago. Since then, they've been storing their records off site. However, that doesn't explain all of it. A separate investigation is now underway to determine if Richardson has a source within the police department, passing him confidential information. There is nothing to report on that because it's only a few hours old."

"What's bothering me the most is his mention of the defendant being a part of our nation's security apparatus, and that he has a security clearance. We never had any information suggesting that."

The meeting continued for over an hour with little accomplished. The fact remained that others had information being withheld from the police and prosecution. The governor's office and the state attorney general said they would contact the Federal Justice Department for a briefing, but until then, there was nothing they could do but wait for a response and endure the circus atmosphere.

***

The next morning the D.A. got the diagnosis on Vincent Thompson from Dr. Blackstone and Gross. They concurred that Vincent suffered from DID, but neither would say that one of his identities was the demon he conjured up. According to the doctors, there have been claims of this, and that a couple of defendants tried to assert such a claim, but the courts refused to charge the jury with that as an alternative verdict, thereby denying *the devil made me do it* defense.

***

The weekend came and went. The D.A. and her prosecutor, spent it poring over the legal precedents on insanity defenses and preparing motions for the judge. Monday mid-morning she invited Chief Meadows, Lieutenant Pascoe and Detective Smith to discuss what she expected to cover in her meeting with Vincent's attorney that afternoon.

Ms. Holmes was going over her expected responses to what she predicted Vincent's attorney would claim when the telephone, positioned in the middle of the conference room table, buzzed and a female voice from the intercom said, "Sorry to interrupt your meeting Ms. Holmes, but I believe you'll want to take this call. It's from the Texas Attorney General. He says it's about the Thompson case."

The D.A. had a puzzled look on her face as she picked up the receiver, considering she recently spoke to him about Harry Richardson. The rest of the meeting attendees had similar expressions, some wondering if the State AG had another interest in the case.

"Hello, this is D.A. Laura Holmes," she said into the phone.

"Hello Ms. Holmes, this is Bennett Frazier, the State Attorney General. I know we talked the other day, so I'd like to dispense with the pleasantries, and get down to the business of my call."

"Yes, sir," she replied.

"I've been discussing the Thompson case with the undersecretary of Homeland Security. Nathan Freeman and Andrew Garlecki, the Deputy Director of NSA. It appears they have a special interest in your case."

"Mr. Frazier, I happen to be in a meeting about the case with a number of interested parties. Do you mind if I take the call in my office?"

"That won't be necessary. Your secretary advised me of the individuals in your meeting, and there is nothing I'm willing to say today that they can't hear."

"Shall I put the call on speakerphone?" Laura asked.

"Please, that might save time."

She reached over to the phone and pressed the speakerphone button. "Okay, Mr. Frazier, we're all listening."

"Hello everyone. I'm Bennett Frazier, the Attorney General for the State of Texas. I got a call today that instigated a conversation with Homeland Security undersecretary Nathan Freeman and Andrew Garlecki, NSA Deputy Director. They told me they are going to intervene in the defense of Vincent Thompson. They claim that he has been a valuable asset in preserving the safety of the U.S. from terrorists and terrorist organizations."

Pascoe and Denise looked at each other with the same knowing look on their faces as if they were expecting it. And then they looked at Chief Meadows, who was staring at the floor and shaking his head in disbelief. The mayor was doing a mirror image of Meadows, but staring at the ceiling.

"They're saying that secrets regarding national security are at stake. There seems to be a lot of worried people in Washington about what he might divulge. You see, the security issues he worked on at Zenon were not local or involved surveillance systems and the like. They won't say anything more, claiming that it's classified.

"They're arranging a conference with the judge and the D.A., Ms. Holmes. That should occur tomorrow. In essence, they're going to ask for a delay so they can evaluate Mr. Thompson — in person and at an undisclosed location. They have also given their word that as soon as they are convinced that it's safe for U.S. interests to resume his trial here, they will return him, allowing the state to resume its prosecution of the charges against him."

"What's your position regarding this development?" she asked. "Do we vigorously resist or acquiesce?"

"I can't advise you either way," Frazier said. "This is a local matter. I'm merely the conduit giving you a heads-up on what's coming down the track. I don't know what you're dealing with down there. I've got a report, but it's not enough to make a call one way or the other. I've got the impression that the defense team may have a certified whacko for a client."

"That's not the half of it," Holmes responded. "There is still doubt that he's crazy. This could all be an act. And now this demonic element…well, we're now just beginning to sort it out."

"I don't understand," Frazier said. "What do you mean by demonic element?"

"It appears he's representing that one of his personas is Lucifer.

"I wasn't told that," the AG said, clearly annoyed. "I wonder if they intentionally failed to mention that part. I had no idea you were dealing with something that messed up. How can I help?"

"Between now and tomorrow, there's not a whole lot that will make a difference," Holmes said. "But, if you've got access to researchers who can find out what all the precedents and rulings are regarding the right of the government to intervene over our objection, that will allow us to focus on the case law, if any, regarding a DID defense that involves a personality that claims they're a character from the bible."

"What's DID?"

"Dissociative Identity Disorder," she said. "It's the same thing we used to call multiple personalities."

"Jesus Christ," Frazier said almost in a whisper. "And this guy knows government secrets. What a FUBAR of a mess that's got to be. Listen, I'll get you help on the intervention issue. I'll have my assistant AG, Paul Steingraeber, get back to you."

When the call was over the D.A. looked at her prosecutor. "Unless you've got something to add to all of this that might make a difference, you may want to get to work on your new assignment–government intervention, and what does FUBAR mean?"

Denise said, "It's an acronym that came out of the military. It stands for *Fucked Up Beyond All Repair*."

The D.A. shook her head and turned to Pascoe. Did you have any idea this Vincent character was working for the security agencies?"

"Not a clue before three days ago," Pascoe said just after glancing at Denise who shook her head. "When Detective Smith and I questioned his employer the other day, the language that he used to tell us he couldn't answer our questions gave us that impression."

Laura Holmes sat in silence for a long awkward pause. She snapped out of her internal conversation with herself and looked at her notes. She looked at Pascoe and said, "This is your last opportunity to tell me something you think I should know. Have you got anything to say?"

"No, Laura, that's all I know."

"How about you, Detective Smith?"

"There's nothing I know that I haven't already said."

35. TEXAS HOLD 'EM

THE TUESDAY MORNING CONFERENCE IN JUDGE MINELLI'S chambers was a lawyer-only affair. Vincent's team of three lawyers appeared in his behalf and D.A. Holmes and Prosecutor Benson represented the State. The D.A. received notice Monday afternoon that the two D.C. attorneys who met with Vincent last week had filed documents with the court that they were added as Mr. Thompson's legal counsel. As they waited outside the judge's chambers, introductions were made.

Benator approached the D.A. "Ms. Holmes, may I introduce you to William Cox and Steven Lieberman. They will be joining me as legal counsel for Mr. Thompson." The two lawyers from D.C. and the prosecutors shook hands and smiled, all very polite and professional.

When they were summoned to enter the judge's chambers, he was standing in front of his desk with his law clerk. No court reporter was present, but the clerk was there to take notes of their meeting.

After they all were seated, Judge Minelli looked at Mr. Benator. "It's been eight days, counselor. I see your client has hired reinforcements. Now, where do you stand?"

"If it pleases, your honor, we have several motions we'll be filing with the court today." Benator retrieved three sets of papers from his briefcase, handing one to the judge, one to his clerk, and one to D.A. Holmes. The first motion asserts that the defendant is currently unfit for trial," Benator began. "We have affidavits from his physician who has treated him for several years, detailing three mental disorders the defendant suffers from, Autism, Asperger's Syndrome, and Dissociative Identity Disorder, the first two of which have plagued him his entire life. The last, commonly called DID, and often described as Multiple Personality Disorder, he began suffering from this disorder a short time before Sarah Thompson and Blair Rogers were murdered. Two additional specialists support these diagnoses, and their affidavits are included."

Holmes and Benson shared glances, indicating they had expected such a defense.

"And what are these motions asking of the court today?" Minelli said.

"The Defense asks the court to suspend the prosecution of defendant Vincent Thompson until after he has received treatment for his conditions and is declared fit for trial by his treating psychiatrist, Dr. Rubin."

"And what is this second motion all about, Mr. Benator?" Minelli asked.

"The second motion asks the court that Mr. Thompson receive his treatment at an undisclosed Defense Department facility beginning immediately, and that the prosecution be barred from intervening until his employer, the U.S. Department of Homeland Security, has debriefed him and has been given the time it takes to remove its operatives out of harm's way that could be impacted by his divulging their identities; and until the information he knows becomes obsolete."

Holmes glared at Benator and demanded, "Under what legal authority or precedence?"

"Your Honor," Benator said, "This is a matter of first impression. We've found no case law or rulings that could provide guidance, but it is a matter of common sense and justice."

Holmes asserted, "What justice? By all accounts the defendant is a cold-blooded psychopath. Courts don't make special allowances for psychopaths. We assume they're messed up, but there's no cure for being one. It would be a horrible precedent to give psychopaths an out such as what the defense is requesting."

"Ms. District Attorney," Judge Minelli said, "I'm inclined to extend such a privilege if national security matters are at risk, thereby only allowing it if the link is inseparable."

Minelli turned from the D.A. and looked at Benator. "Is there a timetable the court can expect the suspension will last?" Minelli asked.

"The removal of the operatives at risk, and revising the products of Mr. Thompson's designs should take less than one year. Treating him to the point where he is fit to stand trial cannot be estimated. It could take six months to never."

"I see," the judge said as he turned to Ms. Holmes. "What does the prosecution assert?"

"Your honor, if it pleases the court, I would like to begin by responding to the second motion first."

"Proceed," said the judge.

"The prosecution contends that there is no precedence for the government to intervene for the purpose of debriefing a defendant—no case law, nothing. He is not in the military. He is a private citizen, and I see nothing in the motion that alleges he's a spy. Additionally, there is no precedence that a defendant, during trial can be removed from the jurisdiction to be housed or treated at a facility outside of the State's police powers and correctional facilities. We ask the court to deny this motion accordingly. They might have had that opportunity before he was charged, but they lost it when he entered the State's penal system," D. A. Holmes argued.

"As to the motion that asserts the defendant is unfit to stand trial due to his mental health, the law is quite clear. The court, after a competency hearing not open to the public, can rule on his competency, however, there is no case law or any other precedence that allows him to be removed from the custody of the State once he enters the State's penal system. The prosecution for the State of Texas demands that the defendant remain it its custody from this day until a jury, after a trial, finds him not guilty of the crimes he is accused of, or until he has been found guilty and has served out his sentence."

Judge Minelli paused for quite a long time. He didn't look at the motions or the briefs in support of the motions; he simply stared as if in a trance. "Let me ask you, Mr. Benator, what is your client's job? I want to hear what he does for the Department of Homeland Security."

"If it pleases your honor, I'd like to refer that question to Mr. Cox."

"Okay. Mr. Cox, let's hear it."

"Without going into the details, Vincent Thompson is gifted with special talents that are very useful to the intelligence community. A person so gifted is considered to have a savant syndrome.

He has neurological disorders that allow him to block out all other mental functions and concentrate on things such as math, counting and memory. This talent allows him to devise programs for security systems that are practically impenetrable. What makes this talent so valuable to Homeland Security is that each program and system he creates is unique, unrecognizable by hackers–no patterns, no sequences are ever the same, and their complexity is such that search engines haven't been devised to ask all the right kind of questions necessary to break the codes he invents. You see, resources like Vincent Thompson have to remain secret, invisible to everyone, and not in any agency directory. They have to remain contractors, separated from any direct line of communication. The court cannot even disclose the nature of his defense. If it did, it would be disclosing classified information."

"I see," said the judge. "So that's why you filed this third motion. I see it requests that all parties, including the court, shall be under a gag order, preventing any information about the proceedings to be distributed to any person not in this room."

Ms. Holmes stood up and objected. "I don't have that motion. I haven't seen it."

"Please sit down, Laura," Judge Minelli said apologetically. "You don't have it because it's asking that the court keep it secret "in camera", reviewable and considered only by the trial judge for the special purpose of protecting its confidentiality, and the secrets of the nation's defense departments." After a short pause, he continued. "I rule that you all are under a temporary gag order until such time I say it is lifted. I will consider these motions and make a ruling by the close of court on Friday."

"What?" the D. A. said in amazement. "This is incredible, your honor. I've never heard of such a thing. Do I get to appeal your ruling?"

"Ms. Holmes, you can't appeal the gag order, but you may appeal my ruling on the motions, but your appeal will have to be under seal and held in complete confidence with the court. And there will be no fuzzy line on the gag order. Nobody says anything to anybody who is not in this room right now. If it is violated, I assure you, the penalty will be severe. Believe me Ms. Holmes, with what I've seen about the media circus out there, you're going to be thankful for the gag order."

The D.A. was about to say something, when Judge Minelli stepped close to her, nose to nose. "Uh-uh, Ms. Holmes. This conference is over. I'm sorry, but this is the way it has to be. I'll call the Texas attorney general and advise him of the gag order. That should give you some comfort your silence will be understood."

She stopped herself in stunned disbelief. She was disappointed, but she walked out of the judge's chambers and into the corridor leading to the side entrance of the courthouse with an odd smile on her face.

"What's so funny, Laura?" asked Benson. "We just got steamrolled."

"It's finally started to sink in. This is a once-in-a-lifetime case. Could you ever imagine you'd get the opportunity to try one case with all these absurdities? They make movies about stories like this one."

She looked down the corridor through the windows on the exit door. Outside, waiting on the sidewalk, was the press, perhaps a multitude of twenty to thirty, waiting for the lawyers to come out and provide a sound bite. She laughed out loud. "It's a comedy,

Ken. Don't you get it? We're going to walk out of here and over to our office surrounded by the media, who are dying for our comments. And we can't say a peep–nada."

The video of the D.A. walking from the courthouse were on all the news channels. Every couple of steps she would break the eerie smile on her face to say, "No comment." News people reporting the event were mystified by her appearance, speculating that she was pleased with the outcome of the conference.

Everyone in the local justice system wanted to hear her explanation. They got nothing from her, and she made sure they got nothing from Prosecutor Kenneth Benson by threatening to fire him and label him as the source of any leak that found its way to the media.

***

Speculation was rampant in Thomas Glen regarding the status of the Teen Killing case. Chief Meadows and everyone in the police department were upset and complaining to everyone in the D.A.'s office. David Rogers, father of one of the victims, was on the warpath and trying to get a meeting or a phone call with Judge Minelli. The media hounded Rene Thompson until she left town to visit with her sister. The one person who started the reason for the gag order, Harry Richardson, was suddenly out of information to report. His source in the police department had nothing she could leak to him, and what was worse, the TBPS was investigating his informant, Patrolwoman Worthy, as well as him.

The judge's gag order did the intended job, and it allowed the prosecution and defense teams to prepare their briefs and oral arguments in peace. The problem for the prosecution was the dearth of case law or precedent to deny the motions. The identical situation had never been reported in the records in any jurisdiction. Without any previous decisions on the issues D.A. Holmes was facing a matter of first impression. That meant that whatever ruling Judge Minelli ordered, it was going to be appealed by one or both sides, and that was going to take a long time.

***

When all the parties appeared in court on Friday, it was a mystery to everyone what the judge might rule. He wasted no time, ruling in favor of the defense on every motion. In essence, there would be no trial until Vincent's physicians ruled he regained his mental health and was fit for trial.

David Rogers bellowed, "No. No, you can't do this. We deserve a trial."

Minelli owed no explanation, but gave one. "In this matter, I had to weigh what's at stake with both sides. The prosecution is losing nothing but time—the delay in the proceedings. On the other hand, the defense has two urgent issues, the need to get treatment for the defendant's illness, and the government's interest in safeguarding its secrets and the protection of the nation."

"I wish there was case law to guide us, but there was nothing on all fours. As a result, I'm issuing an order that the defendant shall be transferred to the custody of the U.S. Attorney General until such time as he determines that the defendant is no longer a risk to divulge government secrets. And that a team of three psychiatrists, one chosen by the defendant, one chosen by the prosecution and one agreed upon by the two previously chosen psychiatrists to be the third, whereby the majority vote of the psychiatrists shall determine that the defendant is fit for trial.

The judge banged the gavel down with vigor, stood and left the courtroom in silence. Moments later everyone filed out, most by the main doors, but the parents of the victims and the lawyers were given the opportunity to leave via the door that led to the corridor behind the courtroom and out the side entrance. The attorneys exited via the main entrance, allowing themselves to be questioned by the majority of the press. Denise Smith and Reed Pascoe exited with the Thompson and Rogers families. The press waiting outside that door, presumably there for the human-interest comments, ignored the detectives and surrounded the two sets of parents.

"What did the judge mean when he said there was no case law on all fours?" Denise asked her partner.

"I asked the same question some years ago. Picture a table with four legs," he said. "If one of the legs is missing, it won't stand up. It'll fall apart. It infers that there are no previous rulings or decisions that resemble all the issues in this case. So, the judge can't point to a previous case as precedence to follow because those cases are missing essential elements, or legs, that appear in this case. The previous case won't support the current one.

Denise looked at her partner in awe. "What the.... Don't tell me you were a lawyer in a previous life?"

"No, but I studied to be one in college. I never stood for the bar exam. Too dry. Not enough excitement for my appetite."

Pascoe's answer struck a nerve in her. That was the same reason she joined the police.

***

Back at the police station, the government's lawyers arrived within fifteen minutes after the proceedings were adjourned. Along with them were officers from the Justice Department wearing their badges on the pocket of their dark suits. They handcuffed Vincent and led him out the back door and up to the rear doors of a black van without windows.

Denise watched it all, wanting to secure the memory of it, all the details. Unlike Rene, Vincent did look around to see who might be watching. He spotted Denise standing at the rear door of the police station just before he stepped inside the van. He paused and winked. Nothing surprised her at this point, but the eerie grin he displayed caused shivers to run down her spine.

***

As she approached home that evening, Denise saw Zach's truck was in the driveway. She wondered if that grey cloud that found its way into her psyche was breaking up. He greeted her as she entered. "We need to talk," he said with a smile. Denise didn't care if he came home because the case had ended, he was tired of fighting with her about the demands of her job, or he missed her. Drake and Zoe were in the kitchen, and she basked in the comfort of normal family conversation, miles away from all the law enforcement issues of the past month. It was comforting to be normal and boring, if just for a short while.

EPILOGUE

One Year Later

Waiting for her friend, Detective Denise Smith sat in the outdoor patio of a trendy Asian restaurant in Dallas. It was a beautiful, cool, late September day with the promise of autumn in the air. She was seated at a front row table, looking out at the square noting all the activity; mothers playing with their children, couples holding hands, shoppers scurrying back and forth, and several young professionals chatting as they sauntered to their working lunches. Denise sat back, closed her eyes and breathed in. She was looking forward to seeing Rene as well as bringing her up to speed on developments in Vincent's case.

The vibration of her phone brought her back to the present. She peeked at it and saw a fresh text message. Rene would be there shortly. Although they talked a few times on the phone, it had been six months since the spring when they last met, and Rene had been optimistic about a romance, happy with her job in a real estate attorney's office.

The last time they met, Denise could tell that Rene had not gotten over the loss of her daughter Sarah. Back then, Rene told her that Sarah would want her to remain optimistic, in her honor.

"So sorry I'm late," Rene floated in, breathless. "I got a phone call just as I was leaving my office, and I had to take it. You know real estate deals. Everyone always waits until the last minute." Denise took a moment to inspect her friend, who was tanned, slender, with a new hair style that made her look ten years longer.

"You look fabulous!" Denise got up and hugged Rene. Then stepped back. "You're glowing!"

Rene smiled. "Thanks. I feel good. For the first time in months, I'm feeling more myself than ever." "What about you? How are things with you?"

"Fine," Denise was succinct. "Drake is doing well at Tech. Wants to rebuild bridges and make the infrastructure of the world better and safer. Zoe's just entered high school." Denise responded honestly before realizing her friend could not reciprocate with any positive updates on her children. The waiter came, gave them their menu's, and took their drink orders.

Denise turned her eyes down. "Rene. I'm sorry. That was insensitive of me."

"Stop it. This is my life now," Rene's voice was low, nearly a whisper. "I'm learning to live with it, and I'm not going to deny it. I wish we had met under different circumstances where I could tell you the wonderful things Sarah was doing. But please. Never stop sharing your life with me or treat me with kid gloves. Not you of all people, Denise. That's what I couldn't stand." Rene sat up. "So, now that we have that out of the way, what about you? I know last time you were...," she paused. "You were in negotiations with Zach. He didn't want you to take the promotion to lieutenant."

Denise reset, clearing her head and refocusing on Rene. "No, he didn't. But I took it. I told him I wouldn't be complete without working as hard as I could....Looking back, I've been pretty lucky. I told Zach I am who I am. Rene, I've never changed. I've always been this hyper-focused, intense person. Trying to be less, then I wouldn't be me."

"So, how'd Zach take it?"

"Well, we're still married. I think he gets I gotta do what I gotta do. He's understanding that he fell in love with me for a reason, and to deny who I am, would make me..."

"Not Denise?"

"That's why I love you, Rene. You get me!" She paused. "What's going on with your dentist friend who you talked about last time?"

"Friend? Let's just say we remain friends, but have moved past that milestone."

"Rene, tell me!"

"I think last time we talked I told you I had this feeling that there was something growing between us. I wanted to see if I was right, but I didn't want to wait for my next appointment. Instead, I gave him one of my paintings as a gift for being so kind to me when he heard what I was going through." Rene looked up from her menu. "A few weeks later he called me with a proposition."

"Oh? "Denise smiled.

"Yah, only it wasn't like that. Robert had hung up the picture in the lobby. A customer liked it and wanted to buy it. He called to see if I could paint another one and sell it to his customer. Then he told me to paint whatever I wanted, put price tags on them, hang them up, and see if they sold."

"And did they?" Denise asked.

Rene laughed, "I can't keep enough canvases on their walls. They keep selling."

The waiter came and they both ordered salads with their unsweet tea.

"Long story short, we see each other at least twice a week. I never thought I could feel like this again. We know everything about each other, the good, bad and ugly, and it's all good. No secrets. No hidden agendas."

Robert had been Rene's family dentist since the children were small. He had nursed his wife, who had cancer that lingered for years. For some reason, they connected on more than a doctor and patient relationship. When the media was hounding her, Robert did more than listen; he was there for her when Doug walked out of her life. And when his wife was ill and he was exhausted, Rene had a compassionate ear. Both losing loved ones, they supported each other, counseled each other.

Denise squeezed Rene's hand. "I'm so happy for you."

"You know, losing my daughter, my son being arrested, my husband filing for divorce—I thought being dead would be easier." She paused, wrinkling her brow and looking seriously at Denise. "But now…. I'm so happy…. Sometimes I feel guilty."

"Stop it!" Denise said, "Rene, you deserve to be happy."

Rene smiled, inhaled deeply, and looked at her friend, "Thank you." There was a respectful silence. "But you know, Vincent never gravitated back to me after his arrest," Rene said. "Doug visits him every now and then. He keeps me posted." She sounded sad, then looked up at Denise. "Even though I email often, I haven't seen Vincent since December, and only heard from him on my birthday last month. We talked, but it was very short. It wasn't what I'd call a conversation. I'm not sure what's going on other than what Doug says, and he claims therapy is going well. I don't know how Doug does it, helping Vincent through all this. I'm glad he can forgive him. Honestly, I do. He's a sick young man. But I'll never understand why Doug can't forgive me."

"The reasons and the logic don't matter anymore. I guess some things are meant to be. Doug must have felt he had to leave, and Vincent is where he belongs, Rene."

"I know that," Rene studied the napkin in her lap. "And to think he's an asset to the government? How crazy is that? It's surreal."

Rene paused and looked at Denise, eye to eye. "At times it feels so strange not being a real mother to them anymore. Vincent was my son, too. Just doesn't feel like it now. Like this all happened to someone else, and I have no children."

Denise didn't want to dwell on that. "How's it been between you and Doug since the divorce?"

"I can only say it's civil. Can you tell me anything about what's going on with Vincent? Is the state ever going to prosecute him?"

"I don't know," said Denise. "I saw the latest report from the court-appointed psychiatrists. They're convinced that Vincent suffered his identity crisis the moment he pulled the trigger on the gun that killed Sarah. In one of his personas, he's remorseful, and the psychiatrist believes this identity is closest to the Vincent you knew. In that persona, he says he never went to the store with the idea of harming anyone.

"He claims everything came crashing down on him when he found Sarah's diaries and read them. Supposedly, it was then that he became afraid she didn't care about him anymore. That was two weeks before the store incident. And according to his psychiatrist, during that period, his mood had been alternating from fear of losing her to anger at Blair for alienating her from him. That was the beginning of the dissociative disorder – having two separate perso-nas, the sad one and mad one, beginning as moods."

Rene gasped, "And that's when I noticed something, begged Vincent to see Dr. Rubin. God. If only…" Rene's voiced trailed off as she looked absent mindedly at the water fountain in the mall's courtyard.

Denise waited a moment then continued. "Supposedly, what contributed to his moodiness was a fundamental inability to under-stand that unrequited affection wasn't a life or death situation. He interpreted every one of her romances as betrayals."

"The photo album I showed you - I knew there was something wrong with it," Rene said.

"He consistently claims he just wanted to confront them, and tell them how he felt," Denise continued. "The gun–he says he brought it just in case Blair misunderstood and tried to hurt him. That's what was going on while the three of them drove around for almost two hours. And when they returned to the store, Vincent said Blair became angry. That was the trigger. He said Blair became abusive. Not connecting that he might die, he shot him so he would stop yelling at him.

"According to the report, He said Sarah lunged toward Blair, re-acting to try to protect him. Vincent claims that her sudden move-ment startled him and the gun fired again, unintentionally, sending a bullet to her brain.

Tears were welling up in Rene's eyes. She was reacting as if she was there, watching it. "This is where the shrinks lose me," Denise said, looking closely at Rene and trying to tell if she wanted to hear the rest. She decided to continue.

"They say that his unintentional killing of Sarah triggered the identity crisis we see as multiple personalities. One identity is Lucifer, the evil influence that sent him to the grocery and pulled the trigger of the pistol. It's also the identity that appears whenever he becomes so lonely for Sarah he breaks down. His remorse and guilt becomes too much to bear and he needs to escape who he is. That's when the demon takes over. In that persona he killed the rapist, tried to kill Dr. Edwards, poisoned my partner–inducing a stroke, and tried to hurt me. According to the psychiatrist, that's the persona we saw in the courtroom."

"What you're saying makes sense to me," Rene said. She took a deep breath and paused. "I've had a long time to think about it....I can live with that. I'm praying they dont prosecute him. I don't blame Vincent anymore. He was sick, and we failed to appreciate to what degree."

"I'm really sorry Rene. You were always a good mother."

"I keep wondering...what I could have done differently. Given Vincent more attention? Did we favor Sarah too much?" Rene shook her head.

Denise rested her hand on top of her friend's. "Rene, you're doing so well; you've worked so hard," Denise wasn't just saying things to make her friend feel better, she genuinely believed it.

Rene smiled and whispered, "You know, I'm lucky to have met you." She looked at her friend in genuine appreciation. "Thomas Glen is lucky to have you."

***

Not long after the funeral of their son, Pastor Dan had warned David and Victoria Rogers of the high mortality rate of marriages after the death of a child. They agreed to do whatever it took not only to remain together, but to be unified as husband and wife as they worked to try to rebuild their shattered life.

The pastor began weekly counseling sessions in the Roger's home. Pastor Dan surprised the couple with an observation when in the middle of one of the early sessions, David mumbled as few words in Hebrew. "Through the years, I've seen people leave the churches of their parents, come to my parish, only to return to the tradition of their childhood. Tradition is comforting. And that I shepherd my flock in such a way they long for that comfort of childhood always reaffirms my leadership."

"What are you saying, Pastor?" David needed him to be direct with him.

"I'm suggesting, Vicki, that you consider the solace David has gotten from his Jewish roots. Remember both Jews and Christian worship the same God of Abraham."

"I agree," Vicki was quick to respond as she stared hard at her husband. "David, I have seen it, too. Pastor Dan is right. It's the same God; just some differences on our perceptions. I must admit I'm a little jealous of the beautiful rituals. I've stolen a few glances at you, and read about the traditions. I'd like to understand more of what they mean."

"You're not saying you want to become Jewish?" David looked puzzled.

"No. I love the practices of my childhood, too. But it doesn't mean I can't begin to understand your customs. Why they bring you comfort. David, like it or not, it's you. You were born Jewish. I

love you enough to leave you to be who you are. I'd just like a part
of that, too."

This invitation at first was too much for David to comprehend.
He wasn't even sure if he believed in God. But he did know the prayers
of his ancestors gave him some peace in an impossible situation.

Although they had agreed to always worship together when they
first married, they amended it. That wise suggestion from a Baptist
pastor added a strength and bond to their wounded marriage. They
agreed to attend the high holy days of both faiths, Christmas and
Easter for Vicki, Yom Kippur and Passover for David.

What they found is these new family traditions helped heal the
entire Rogers family. With each Jewish service, there were often live-
ly discussions as to the reasons of the rituals, how they were alike
and different from the services they were used to. In these conversations Blair was often brought up. "Blair would have liked that,
huh, Dad?" one of their surviving children once said. And they all
agreed; indeed, Blair would have approved.

They also talked about how much they missed Blair, the huge
void he left behind. Although it had been twelve months since they
lost Blair, the hurt still lingered.

Together this day, approaching the Jewish New Year, Rosh
Hashanah, they finished the Mourner's Kaddish, vowing to pray
every year at Yom Kipper to keep the memory of Blair fresh in their
lives. David put on Kippah on his head and picked up the Shofar,
the ram's horn.

In their living room, David led them as they responded a great
amen:

May abundant peace from heaven, and life, come to us and to
all Israel. AMEN.

May the One who brings harmony on high bring harmony to us and to all Israel and to all who dwell on Earth. AMEN.

And finally, they had to practice forgiveness. They understood that the person who took their son from them was sick and deranged. There was no one to blame–not anymore–they were done with that. With forgiveness there has to be acceptance. Accepting the reality that we all are imperfect, and some of those grow worse without a cause or reason. In their case, their son was in the path of an imperfect soul, gone haywire.

David raised the shofar to his lips. And he blew–long, hard and loud. He blew for the years he wouldn't have with Blair, the memories which would never be made and the unborn grandchildren who would never come. Tears rolled down his face. Still David Rogers wailed his breath into the horn.

As the shofar sounded, he knew each year for the rest of his life, each Rosh Hashanah he would blow with equal intensity. Blair would not be forgotten.

***

I've been told that I have returned to singularity or oneness in being. Nevertheless, I am in a desolate place. There is nowhere to hide or escape. That's what I had been doing. Perhaps to some extent, I've been doing it my entire life. But on that day in August I escaped to a different dimension. It was wrong all right. I was wrong...again.

I still feel the hurt of rejection. I've felt it before...many times. But on that day it felt so permanent, so deep. I hated myself. I hated want-

ing what I couldn't have. Now I see that I chose to want things that were not right for me. Sarah was my sister. Not my blood related sister, but still...my sister.

I now understand there are many kinds of love. When she said she loved me, it wasn't fairy tale love. It was brother-sister love, not her and me together forever love. I was blind not to see it that way. I've been told that I was blind to things I wanted that didn't want me back. I couldn't see that it was something I had been imagining ever since Sarah told me she didn't love me the way she loved Blair.

I've been told that I convinced myself that those were my failures... that I had become a failure. I've been told that I convinced myself that I couldn't live with another failure. I had to prevent it. I've been told that's when I escaped into some sort of imaginary cocoon and transformed myself into someone who could reinvent himself. What emerged was someone who thought he could make what he wanted come true by scheming and deception.

I convinced myself that it was Blair's fault. If he wouldn't go away, my new version of me would make him go away. It was all wrong. I tried to convince him that August night, but he wouldn't listen. I thought I could change that with the gun. He still didn't get it. I lost my patience. That reinvention of me was also ruthless. I pulled the trigger.

In all my scheming, I never imagined that Sarah would try to stop it from happening. When she did...somehow I pulled the trigger again. It ended her life. I couldn't bear it. I've been told that I tried to escape again, but when I did, another version of me emerged. In that version I convinced myself that I was pure evil...a demon.

I'm alone with myself now...the way it used to be, but without Sarah to talk to. I wish I could have become a better version of me. One that could see things the way that was real. But that didn't happen. I wish by accepting my punishment, it could bring her back. It can't. What I did was terribly wrong. I know it now. My last hope, if they decide I should not be put to death, is that I can find a way to atone for my sins.

***

Before Denise got in her squad car to return to the stationhouse from her lunch with Rene, the familiar ring tone of Reed Pascoe wafted in her ears. "Hey, Reed, what's up?"

"Cathleen and I are celebrating our twentieth wedding anniversary on Saturday, and we're inviting our closest friends over to help us do it in style. Bring the entire Smith clan. Oh, by the way, I've been meaning to ask you something for a long time. Remember when the D.A. pulled us out of the interview with Vincent and his lawyer; I told her that male suspects often felt they made a connection with you because of the way you looked at them. I was trying to explain it to a female detective in this office. She said it was a sexual attraction thing. What do you think it is?"

"Really, of all things, that's been bugging you? Of course it's a sexual thing. Every male I've ever known except one thinks your interest in him is sexual. My rule – if that's what works for me – use it."

Reed paused for a moment. "Who was the exception?"

"Oh my God....You really have to ask that. Think about it, and if you can't figure it out, call me sometime." There was a pregnant pause, and they changed the subject.

Mr. Oblivious and Denise talked for a while longer, catching up on their lives. Pascoe, now that he was the Homicide Chief for the entire county, Denise was promoted to his old position at Thomas Glen. Even though they didn't work together as a team anymore, their relationship was important to both of them. They shared lunches together and dinners with their families. Without fail, the one topic that always came up was the Teen Killings. They wondered if Vincent would ever be prosecuted for full justice to be realized. They don't say it aloud, but there is no doubt that the case had a profound effect on their lives.

It opened their hidden wounds, their deepest fears and insecurities. The fact remained, everyone connected to the victims or the investigation suffered mightily. It was a testament to its profound senselessness.

The impact of the tragedy and the empty sadness of a loved one that was caught up in the madness of the perpetrator, changed the entire community.

The almost perfect small town of Thomas Glen still gave the impression to the casual visitor that nothing bad could ever happen there.

ABOUT THE AUTHORS

Jeremy Logan

I PARLAYED MY EXPERIENCE with the individuals I came across in my legal career to create the characters in my novels. Some were real life heroes; a serial killer, a contract mercenary working for the CIA, a schizophrenic who threatened to kill the US president, a person with Dissociative Identity Disorder (multiple personalities), and a lot of incredibly brilliant people who did a lot to shape the world we live in today (inventors, corporate giants, medical giants, and the list goes on). My corporate specialty, disaster responder/investigator in the energy industry.

I was always in love with creative writing, and I'm happiest when I'm working on my next novel. My talent lies in creating suspense and drama in a plot that keeps the reader so involved he/she doesn't expect the ending.

Brenda Sevcik

FICTION DISPLAYING BEAUTI-
ful language in tandem with illu-
minating the strength of the human character and growth of the
individual, have always called to
me. In my work, I attempt to offer insight, light and hope to my
readers.

It has been a pleasure collab-
orating on *The Trigger Effect* with
Jeremy Logan.   He has kindly
showed me the process of writing
a novel and uncovered a few mysteries for me. May you enjoy our
combined efforts, as you unfold the many layers of intrigue in our
novel.